# KARA LENNOX

—

## For the Right Reasons

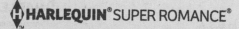

**HARLEQUIN**® SUPER ROMANCE®

Recycling programs
for this product may
not exist in your area.

ISBN-13: 978-0-373-60840-9

FOR THE RIGHT REASONS

Printed in U.S.A.

# "Very good work, MacKenzie. I think I might have something here...."

Bree dug into her purse. "I do. Would you like a glitter heart or a gold star?"

"Heart, heart, heart, heart!"

Eric was touched. Had Bree put those stickers in her purse just for MacKenzie? Or... "You must have kids."

A stark sadness flashed across Bree's face before she masked it. "No, no kids. But I keep a few things on hand for children who come through the emergency room."

"So emergency medicine is your specialty?"

"Yes. I work at the county hospital."

He wondered how many men faked serious illness in the hopes that lovely Bree would minister to them. Images flashed through his mind of Bree's soft, pale hands touching him—in the most innocent, doctorly ways, of course.

God, what was he doing? He clenched his eyes shut until the images dissipated. He couldn't afford to think of her like that. He needed to get her and her misguided agenda out of his life.

Dear Reader,

Ask any parent what they would be willing to do to save their child's life, and most will answer without hesitation, "Whatever it takes." The bond between parent and child is said to be the strongest of any human attachments. Otherwise timid, gentle people will turn into superheroes when their offspring are threatened.

That's the situation Eric Riggs faces in this story. (If you read *In This Together,*—Harlequin Superromance, October 2013—the previous book in this series, you might remember Eric as the brother Travis Riggs risks everything to free from prison.) Eric will do what it takes to keep his fragile little girl safe, even if it puts his newfound love for Bree in jeopardy—even if it means he might go back to prison.

It's been a long time since I wrote a book in which a child was a major character, but I became so attached to Eric's daughter, MacKenzie, that she threatened to take over the book! I hope you enjoy watching Eric and Bree pick their way through a minefield of choices and challenges as they try to forge those all-important familial bonds, but I especially hope you enjoy MacKenzie's role. Maybe someday I'll give her her own book, when she's grown up.

All my best,

Kara Lennox

# ABOUT THE AUTHOR

Kara Lennox has earned her living at various times as an art director, typesetter, textbook editor and reporter. She's worked in a boutique, a health club and an ad agency. She's been an antiques dealer, an artist and even a blackjack dealer. But no work has ever made her happier than writing romance novels. To date, she has written more than sixty books. Kara is a recent transplant to Southern California. When not writing, she indulges in an ever-changing array of hobbies. Her latest passions are bird-watching, long-distance bicycling, vintage jewelry and, by necessity, do-it-yourself home renovation. She loves to hear from readers. You can find her at www.karalennox.com.

## Books by Kara Lennox

### HARLEQUIN SUPERROMANCE

### HARLEQUIN AMERICAN ROMANCE

#Project Justice
*Blond Justice
**Firehouse 59
***Second Sons

Other titles by this author available in ebook format.

For my husband, Rob Preece, without whom I never would have made it to the end of this book! Thank you for keeping me sane and refilling my coffee cup.

# CHAPTER ONE

"I THINK MOST of you know Eric Riggs." Daniel Logan, the billionaire CEO and founder of Project Justice, spoke from an enormous video screen positioned at the head of a gleaming mahogany table, making it appear as if he were actually in the conference room, presiding over the staff meeting.

Eric nodded in acknowledgment and tried not to look as nervous as he felt. This conference room was not so different from countless others he'd visited as an attorney. But it had been three years since he'd worn a suit. Three years since he'd focused on anything except proving his innocence and getting out of prison.

He'd accomplished that goal, with the help of his brother and this very organization.

Eric had always thought that once he was free, he would simply start living again—albeit without his wife, the woman he'd thought was his true love. But nothing about his life was simple. Prison had changed him.

His old firm hadn't wanted him back. They were a stodgy lot, and they wanted nothing to do with what they referred to as Eric's "unsavory notoriety." But Daniel Logan had generously offered him a temporary job here, just until Eric got his bearings. His specialty was real estate, not criminal law, but Daniel had assured him he wouldn't be required to do that much—maybe file a few pleadings, oversee contracts with clients and act as a consultant.

He was still nervous as a kid facing a dentist with a drill. He surreptitiously wiped his palms on his pants.

Today's gathering was a routine weekly staff meeting. Lead investigators gave updates on cases they were working, and everyone brainstormed through any roadblocks and used each other as a sounding board. The creativity and passion gathered in this one room was mind-boggling. But his new colleagues went out of their way to make Eric feel at home. He even made a couple of contributions, discovering that he could recall his criminal-law classes. No one laughed or rolled their eyes. Maybe he'd do okay here.

He had to do more than survive. He had to keep this job until he found something else. MacKenzie needed him—not just his emotional support but his financial sustenance. She was seeing the best child psychologist in Houston on a weekly basis, and the therapy didn't come cheap. Then there was the private school, the karate lessons. None of these would make up for the fact that she'd witnessed her mother's bloody murder. But he was determined to give her the best of everything.

The last few minutes of the meeting were devoted to going over new cases, which Daniel assigned to his senior people based on interest, expertise and availability.

"The last case I want to talk about is an interesting one," Daniel said. "This man was convicted seven years ago of rape and attempted murder. The crime was believed to be connected to a string of murders. The victim, Philomene Switzer, was the only one to survive.

"The man was convicted based solely on the victim's testimony. There was no DNA, no fingerprints, just one very credible and sympathetic witness. However, that witness recently recanted."

"Sounds like a slam dunk," said Ford Hyatt, a former cop who had been with Project Justice since the beginning.

"Not so fast," Daniel replied. "The victim confided in a friend, but she refuses to go on the record. So whoever takes this case has some work ahead of them. Who among you is feeling persuasive? Oh, here's our man, by the way. His name is Kelly Ralston."

Eric's head snapped up. *My God.* A prison ID photo of a man scowled at them from the video screen. It was him. Ralston. Eric brought a reflexive hand to his chest and rubbed it over his dress shirt.

"You think that man's *innocent?*" Eric blurted out.

Everyone in the room turned their heads in unison to stare at him.

"Everyone looks bad in their prison ID photo," said Jillian Baxter-Blake, the foundation's newest investigator, a young, stylish blonde with a deceptively innocent look and a sharp intellect. "I'm sure yours didn't make you look like a movie star."

"Jillian!" Daniel glared at her.

"No, it's okay," Eric said quickly. "No offense taken. I didn't mean to imply Ralston must be guilty because he *looks* like a bad guy. The truth is, I know him. We were housed in the same cellblock at Huntsville. And there's no way that guy should be let loose on an unsuspecting public. He's…he's a monster."

"A monster?" Daniel sounded dubious.

Eric realized this group of seasoned professionals, obviously very good at what they did, weren't simply going to take his word for it. He was the outsider here. They didn't know him and had no reason to trust him. They were going to take some convincing.

"He tried to kill me. He cut me."

Silence. Then Daniel broke the quiet. "Eric, as I'm sure you know, prison doesn't bring out the best in anyone. People do things when they're locked up that they would never do as free citizens. Here at Project Justice, we concern ourselves solely with the crime for which the client was convicted."

"That's just it. Ralston isn't innocent." Though the room was cool, Eric's forehead broke out in a sweat. "He raped that woman and tried to kill her. He killed other women, too. He used to brag about his crimes in the most bloodcurdling detail. He cut them up, right? Lots of stab wounds? That was the part that turned him on." He paused, forcing himself to slow his breathing and lower the timbre of his voice, then looking at first one, then another of his coworkers. "Do you want me to go on?"

"Obviously this changes things," Daniel said. "If you're sure he's guilty—"

"I'm positive." Except that he wasn't. In truth, he'd never heard Kelly Ralston say word one about the crimes he'd committed. Eric had just told the biggest lie of his life.

"Then I guess we'll deep-six this one. Unfortunately, I told our applicant that we were taking on her case. Someone has to tell her we're not going to help get her boyfriend out of prison."

Kelly Ralston had a girlfriend? That was hard to picture.

"I think the best man for that job is you, Eric."

"Me?" He'd thought his job was all about filing papers with the court. No one said anything about meeting with the deluded girlfriends of scumbag serial rapist-murderers. He was still reeling from just the sight of Ralston's face on a screen. How was he supposed to now greet that man's girlfriend with any sort of professionalism?

"Frankly, I don't think this woman would believe me if I repeated your words," Daniel said. "I think she needs to hear it from you. And she'll be in the lobby in about ten minutes."

Eric was stunned to numbness. He couldn't believe

what he'd just done. He'd lied, straight-faced, to the man partly responsible for giving him his life back. Kelly Ralston was going to stay buried in Huntsville, and Eric was responsible for that, too.

*Prison is where Ralston belongs.* The man was a dangerous psychopath. Kelly Ralston had said that if he ever got free, he would find Eric and slit his throat. Even worse, he'd threatened MacKenzie, a six-year-old girl who was the picture of innocence.

MacKenzie had been the victim of enough crime in her young life. She might never recover from the trauma of losing her mother in such a violent manner; she still had nightmares about blood. Eric would do whatever it took to protect her.

Even lying.

After reminding everyone that the building would be fumigated on Thursday and everyone should plan to take the day off, Daniel disconnected.

Eric dragged his feet on the way down to the lobby, opting for the stairs because he didn't want to talk to anyone about his outburst. *Helluva way to start the second day of a new job.*

The marble-floored reception area was deserted except for Celeste Boggs, the foundation's office manager, receptionist and self-proclaimed head of security. As far as Eric knew, her actual job responsibilities had nothing to do with security, other than keeping undesirable visitors from gaining access to the rest of the building from the lobby.

But she was pretty scary. In her seventies, she was the antithesis of a sweet little old lady.

"Mr. Riggs," she greeted him without the hint of a smile on her blood-red lips. "Leaving so soon? You haven't even had time to warm up your office chair or fill out forms for the personnel office."

"Actually, I'm looking for someone. A woman named Brianna Johnson has an appointment—"

"At ten, yes, I know. She's not here yet. I can call you when she arrives."

"Okay. I'll just…be in my office." He could start setting up a filing system or…count paper clips or maybe prepare a resignation letter. So far breaking the bad news to Ralston's girlfriend was the only thing anyone had asked him to do.

He turned and had almost made it through the frosted-glass wall that separated the lobby from the rest of the building when he heard the front door open. He turned—and froze. The woman who walked through that door was mind-bogglingly beautiful. She had creamy white skin, black hair and deep blue eyes—he could see the color even from a distance. She reminded him of a young Elizabeth Taylor, except in a more petite package.

She dressed like a River Oaks debutante—a brown suede jacket over a creamy silk blouse and black wool trousers, along with black leather high-heeled boots. And she walked with the grace of a ballet dancer. This couldn't possibly be the girlfriend of a rough character like Kelly Ralston. No possible way.

The woman smiled uncertainly at Celeste, who didn't return the favor. "Hi, I'm Brianna Johnson. I have an appointment with—"

"Sign here. And I need some ID." Celeste thrust a clipboard at her.

As the woman signed her name in three quick strokes and accepted a clip-on visitor badge from Celeste, Eric continued to study her. She had pretty hands, but the blunt, unpolished nails didn't really match up with the rest of her.

Celeste glanced over at Eric, waiting for him to say something.

"Ms. Johnson?" He closed the distance between them and extended his hand. "I'm Eric Riggs."

"Oh, hello. You can call me Bree." She shook his hand firmly, decisively. This was a woman of confidence and power. She had either money or a prestigious job. Or both. Again he had to wonder why someone like that would associate with a vicious, violent man like Kelly Ralston.

Bree treated him to a steady, measuring gaze but without a hint of recognition. A month ago Eric had achieved minor celebrity status when the governor had pardoned him, and his conviction for murder had been overturned. Eric's brother, with Project Justice's help, had found the real killer, who had damn near taken another victim before being subdued. But a few splashy headlines later, it appeared Eric's fifteen minutes of fame had run its course. Or maybe Brianna didn't watch the news or read the papers.

"So are you going to handle Kelly's case?" Bree asked.

Oh, boy. This wasn't going to be easy.

"Why don't we…" He started to say they should go to his office. But it was still a mess. No diplomas on the walls, boxes sitting around unpacked, and there was only one guest chair. He'd rather go somewhere more comfortable.

"Yes?" She looked at him with bright, inquisitive eyes.

"Why don't we go to the break room. I need a coffee." Or a shot of bourbon.

"Okay."

He led her down a long hallway toward the kitchen, which was always stocked with all kinds of healthy snacks as well as the ubiquitous office vending machines and a huge bowl of candy. Daniel insisted his people eat well and take care of themselves. The foundation had a workout room, too.

"You can't imagine how excited I was when I got the news that Project Justice was taking up Kelly's cause. For seven years I've been trying to get someone to listen to me, to believe that he couldn't have committed a violent crime. Finally, someone is willing not only to listen but to *do* something."

This was getting worse by the minute.

"Coffee?"

"Okay, sure. Black, please."

The sitting area adjacent to the kitchen was deserted. It was furnished with a couple of comfy sofas, coffee tables and a selection of recent magazines. Occasionally it was used as a waiting area for guests, since the lobby was intentionally without any chairs.

Bree settled with her coffee in a wingback chair—the highest chair in the room. The power seat. He sat on the sofa opposite her, his stomach feeling as though a nest of vipers had taken up residence.

Without delay she placed her briefcase on the coffee table and opened it.

"Daniel said to bring all of the materials I have relating to Kelly's arrest, conviction, appeals—"

"Bree, wait." He couldn't let this go on any longer. It was awful to have to be the one to crush her hope, but better now than later. He would hate to make her cry. "I know Daniel told you we were taking on your, um, boyfriend's case, but circumstances have changed and, unfortunately, it's not going to be possible."

Bree stared at him, her mouth open for a few brief seconds before she clamped it closed.

"I'm sorry—"

"What circumstances? I only talked to Mr. Logan yesterday."

"Sometimes priorities can change rapidly, and our first responsibility is always to the cases we're already working—"

"That's a load of crap! Something happened. Someone got to you. Was it Needles?"

"Who?"

"Sam Needles, the Becker County prosecutor

who tried Kelly's case. That bastard would stoop to just about anything to prevent this conviction from getting overturned. Frankly, I can't imagine Daniel Logan bowing to pressure, and I don't even know how Needles would have found out—"

"It's nothing like that. No one applied any pressure."

"Then what happened? Specifically? Mr. Logan said he would assign the case to an investigator this morning. Was that person you? Are you refusing the case for some reason?"

"Actually, I'm an attorney for    "

"Oh, I get it. You're the cover-your-legal-ass guy. You want to make sure I can't sue Project Justice for breach of contract or something."

"That's not it at all." This wasn't going as smoothly as he'd envisioned. And Bree Johnson had lost any resemblance to an angel. But was Eric a sick puppy for feeling even more attracted to her now that she was angry?

Those blue eyes of hers practically shot sparks, and her cheeks were pink with passion.

"Then what is it? You owe me an honest answer."

Eric had hoped to duck out of taking personal responsibility for causing Daniel to make this unpopular decision, but apparently Bree wasn't going to let him off the hook.

"We're not taking on Ralston's case because he's guilty."

"What? Wait a minute. Yesterday Mr. Logan

said my evidence was compelling. Why this sudden change of heart? You can't possibly know he's guilty, because he isn't. As I've told anyone who would listen for the past seven years, Kelly is not a violent man."

"I happen to know he is."

For a few moments they locked gazes. He'd seldom seen a woman look so furious.

"Look, Bree, it's often hard for an inmate's loved one to see the person as they really are. There's a blind spot. No woman wants to believe she fell in love with a bad person." Lord knew it had taken Eric a very long time to believe his beloved Tammy had cheated on him. "Criminals often compartmentalize different parts of their lives. You see it all the time. The devoted wife and father turns out to be a child molester. The quiet neighbor is suddenly arrested as a serial killer. I'm sure Kelly has a good side. He may truly love you. But your boyfriend—"

"He's not my boyfriend."

"Oh. I thought he was."

"Did you even read my application?"

"Well, no. I only learned about your case this morning. But Daniel did."

"Then he didn't read it closely enough. Kelly and I dated in high school. It didn't work out...." A fleeting sadness crossed her features, but she quickly masked it. "But we've remained friends. We've known each other since preschool. I've become his champion because there's no one else and because he deserves to have a voice. He's not violent."

Eric was going to have to tell her all of it. Otherwise, she wasn't going to give up and go away. A woman like her—intelligent, well-spoken—could cause trouble for Project Justice just by telling some reporter that Daniel had gone back on his word. He owed it to the foundation to make sure she didn't do that.

And he owed it to her. He couldn't let her go on deluding herself, wasting her time, energy and money on someone who wasn't worth it.

"I know more of Kelly Ralston than you think. I know him personally, in fact."

"Wait. What?" She searched his face as if trying to find something familiar about him. "You aren't on his defense team. I know all of those lawyers."

"I know him in a different capacity. Actually...I served time with him."

She looked horrified. "You're an ex-con?"

"My conviction was overturned. But that's immaterial. What matters is that I know Kelly Ralston. Rather well. And I can vouch for the fact that he is, indeed, violent."

"What, because he got into fights in the prison yard? As I understand it, that's pretty much a given. If you don't defend yourself, you— Well, I'm sure you know what happens to the guys at the bottom of the food chain."

She was right about that, and unfortunately, he did

know. Prisoners went for the weak ones, like lions picking out the weak impala in a herd. He'd had to toughen up fast.

"Do you know what a shiv is, Bree?"

"Yes, of course. It's a homemade knife."

"I witnessed Kelly Ralston attack someone with a shiv."

"I don't believe it."

He hadn't wanted to go this far, but she'd forced his hand. He shrugged out of his suit jacket and loosened his tie.

"What are you doing?" Her voice was laced with suspicion.

"Just bear with me." He pulled the tie off, then began unbuttoning his shirt.

Her eyes widened in alarm. "Stop it."

"Don't worry, Bree, your virtue is safe. But I need to show you something, because clearly the only way you're going to believe me is if you see the evidence with your own eyes."

Her whole body tensed as he yanked off his shirt, then pulled his undershirt over his head.

"Oh." All the wind went out of her sails as she stared at the ugly scar that ran nearly fifteen inches in a diagonal path from his left shoulder to the right side of his abdomen.

"Yeah, oh." He hadn't shown the scar to anyone other than the doctor who'd treated him in prison. "Kelly Ralston did that to me. And no, before you ask, it wasn't in self-defense. I was stupid enough to try to *prevent* a fight, and this is what happened to me. I got a staph infection from it, too. I almost died. So when I say Ralston almost killed me, I'm not exaggerating."

# CHAPTER TWO

BREE COULDN'T SEEM to do anything but stare at Eric Riggs's bare chest. The first coherent thought that came into her mind was, *Damn, this guy has one hot bod,* quickly followed by the realization that her observation was inappropriate.

*Then* she saw the scar. "You're saying Kelly Ralston—*my* Kelly Ralston—did that to you?"

"Yes, ma'am."

Someone chose that moment to walk into the small lounge, a woman about Bree's age dressed in an off-the-shoulder sweater, hot-pink jeans and platform shoes. Her blond hair was in one of those chic bobs that moved with her, then fell right back into place.

The woman skidded to a stop, took in Eric's state of undress and backed out of the room with her eyes closed. "Don't mind me. I was never here."

"Great," Eric muttered as he quickly pulled his undershirt back on and shoved his arms into the sleeves of his shirt. "Wonder how long it'll take Jillian to spread this all over the office grapevine."

"Well, don't blame me," Bree groused. "You're the one who chose to perform a striptease."

"Only because you refused to believe me without proof."

"Who says I believe you? You could have gotten that scar some other way."

"Why would I make up something like this?"

"I don't know." That was the problem. She didn't know. If Project Justice didn't want to take on Kelly's case, they could have just rejected her application. They could pick and choose which cases they wanted to devote their energies to. Sadly, there was no shortage of innocent people behind bars.

Eric finished dressing, knotting his shimmery blue tie just so. "I don't know what else to tell you."

"Okay, fine. For the sake of argument, let's assume Kelly really did attack you in prison, unprovoked. That doesn't mean he committed the crime he was convicted for."

"He did, though." Eric took a deep breath, almost as if trying to draw strength. "He confessed to his crime, to anyone who would listen, in excruciating detail. And he bragged of the murders he'd committed for which he was never arrested. Multiple women. Brutal attacks."

That stopped Bree. She couldn't immediately come up with a handy reason why Kelly would do such a thing. He had always adamantly professed his innocence. "You're lying."

Eric shrugged. "Believe what you will."

Bree quickly returned to safer territory—the argument she had rehearsed. "If you would just review the facts—if you would just talk to Philomene—you would have no choice but to believe Kelly is innocent."

"Lay it out for me," he said with obvious reluctance.

"They picked up Kelly because he was walking in Philomene's neighborhood with no obvious destination in mind right after she called 911. He never admitted guilt—"

"Not to you."

"He never admitted to knowing Philomene. They put him in a lineup, and Philomene identified him. There was no physical evidence linking Kelly to the case. And, in fact, his DNA does not match the sample collected from one of the other murders thought to be part of the serial killer's pattern. But when that result came in, the police decided to separate that one case out from the others and claimed it must be unrelated, even though the M.O. was exactly the same.

"They took Kelly to court, and Philomene again identified him as her attacker and even added a couple of details she claimed to have remembered, like his tattoo. It was an easy victory for the prosecution."

"Sounds like it. A credible witness is very hard to overlook. She had no motive for lying about it, especially since she didn't even know him."

"So flash forward to a couple of months ago," Bree continued. "I'm working in the emergency room at the county hospital when Philomene comes in—"

"Working at the E.R. in what capacity?"

"Physician."

"Oh. I didn't realize…"

"Yes, you've already demonstrated that you're remarkably badly briefed on this case. Anyway, this woman comes in having an acute asthma attack. I treated her, and then I recognized her, though it was several years since I'd seen her. She remembered me, too. I was a character witness for Kelly during his sentencing. I couldn't resist bringing it up, even though I know it's cruel to remind a woman of the most traumatic time in her life. But she seemed to want to talk about it. She jumped at the chance. She said she needed to get something off her chest. And that was when she told me that she didn't really recognize Kelly in the lineup. The prosecutor was with her in the room, she was nervous, he was putting all kinds of pressure on her to identify her attacker.

"She said they gave her hints about which man she was supposed to pick out, and she did it. And the more times she said it, the more sure she became in her head that he was the one. But later, after all the pressure was off, she knew she'd made a terrible mistake, that she'd sent an innocent man to prison. But she was afraid to change her statement. She was afraid she'd get into trouble—her record isn't exactly sterling and she has reason to be afraid of the police."

"What makes you think she's telling the truth now?"

"She wasn't lying. She had no reason to."

"Maybe she's starting to feel guilty about sending a man to prison for life, even if he is guilty. Maybe she's downplayed the severity of his crime in her mind over the years. Maybe a friend or relative went to prison for sexual assault, and now she sees the crime from a different point of view. Hell, for all you know, Kelly has been writing letters to her from prison, and they've fallen in love. Weirder things have happened."

"You wouldn't say that if you met her. She was telling the truth. I know it."

"Bree. Kelly Ralston is where he belongs."

"You wouldn't say *that* if you knew him the way I know him. He's kind. And gentle." She rushed ahead before he could bring up his scar again. "If he cut you, he had a reason. But he wasn't really trying to kill you."

Eric looked away, only for a moment, but long enough that she knew she'd hit home.

"It's not even my decision to make," Eric tried again. "Daniel has the last say."

"He changed his mind because you convinced him to. And you can unconvince him. Just talk to Philomene. She promised she would speak with someone from Project Justice so long as her statement didn't go on the record. She's committed to finding the real culprit, who's out there somewhere, and she's willing to undergo hypnosis or answer any questions. She just doesn't want to talk to the police. Please, talk to her. Ten minutes. If you aren't convinced after that, I'll drop it."

"And if I don't agree to meet with her?"

She smiled, letting him see her teeth. "I won't give up. I'll be your worst nightmare."

Eric sighed. "All right, I'll meet with her."

Bree grabbed a pad and pen from her purse and scribbled down an address. "This is the local diner, called the Home Cookin' Café. Best meat loaf in the world. Might as well have dinner while you're there." She ripped off the page and handed it to him.

"Tonight? You want to do this tonight?"

"Sooner the better."

"You'll be there, too, right?"

"Of course. Philomene is very fragile. I wouldn't send her to meet a strange man alone."

"Then I'll see you…" He looked at the paper again. "Tuckerville?" He'd heard of it but had no idea where it was.

"Only a couple of hours away."

"A couple of hours? I have a little girl at home. Evenings are the only time we have together."

Bree found herself smiling. "Really? How old?"

"Six."

"I love that age. I'll keep her entertained while you and Philomene chat. Heck, bring your wife, too. Make it a family outing. Tuckerville is a charming little town."

His features hardened. "I don't have a wife. Look, I'll be there. I said I would. But don't get your hopes up."

"Fair enough." She stood and gathered her things.

She'd sold jewelry to help pay her living expenses in college, and she knew that when she'd made the sale, it was time to leave—before she ruined it. She was frankly surprised that Eric had agreed to meet Philomene at all. "I'll see myself out."

"I'll walk you to the door. If I don't, Celeste will eat me for lunch."

"Let me guess. The lady at the front desk?"

"That would be the one. The first thing they told me when I walked through the door yesterday morning was to do what she says, or else."

They retraced their steps to the lobby. Now that she was less on edge, Bree was able to take in her surroundings more. The hallway was floored in a beautiful parquet pattern, and original oil paintings lined the walls. The light fixtures were real chandeliers.

They parted ways at the front desk. Bree shook Eric's hand again. "See you tonight."

Just as she hit the door, she heard Celeste say in a loud stage whisper, "You work fast."

Then came Eric's rapid denial. "It's not a date."

Of course it wasn't a date, Bree thought as she tried to remember where she'd left her car. She didn't spend much time in the city and wasn't used to having to park blocks away from her destination. But her heart felt lighter knowing she'd once again pulled Kelly's case out of the ashes of destruction and blown the embers to life. And maybe because tonight she'd be seeing a certain dashing single-dad lawyer again and would find out why he was making up lies about Kelly.

Then she was going to make sure he knew the meaning of the word *justice*.

"DADDY!" THE MOMENT Eric hit the front door of his brother's house in Timbergrove, MacKenzie launched herself at him like a cat on a very large mouse. He scooped her up into his arms and reveled in the sweet little-girl smell of strawberry shampoo and crayons. She clung to him like a burr.

"Hello, angel-cakes. How's my big girl?"

"I'm good now that you're home."

Judging from the chatter going on in the kitchen, and the smell of garlic and tomatoes, his brother, Travis, was already home from work and making dinner with his wife, Elena. Between the two of them, Travis was the better cook, but Elena could whip up a few Cuban dishes from her homeland.

He hoped they weren't going to too much trouble, given that he was going to miss dinner.

"Uncle Trav is making spaghetti," MacKenzie said as Eric slid her down to the floor. She didn't seem to want to let go of him. Once upon a time, MacKenzie had been a bright, inquisitive, fearless child. But ever since a lowlife named John Stover taught her that there *were* things to fear in the world, MacKenzie had been a different person—shy, timid, withdrawn. During those few times she'd been allowed to visit Eric in prison, she'd barely said a word.

She was starting to come out of her shell now that she had her father back, but she had a long way to go. For one thing, she was excessively clingy and wanted to know where Eric was every minute. He'd warned her that he wouldn't be home until after five o'clock, that he'd started a new job, but she'd still had a meltdown when she'd arrived home from school and found him gone. Elena, who was watching MacKenzie after school, had called Eric, and he'd been the only one who could calm her down and reassure her that he wasn't back in prison and that he would be home soon.

It almost killed him that he had to leave again—and all because he'd been suckered by a pair of eyes as deep as the ocean. Philomene Switzer could say whatever she wanted, but Eric wasn't going to change his mind.

He told himself he'd agreed to Bree's proposition because it was the only way to get her out of his hair. She'd promised to back off if he did this one thing, and he was going to do it. He couldn't afford for Daniel to devote any more time, attention and effort to the Ralston case. Because if he looked into it very deep, he'd find out Eric was lying. Daniel's investigator could talk to other prisoners, cell mates, friends and relatives on the outside, and he'd discover that Kelly had never confessed his crimes to anyone. In fact, tough and mean as he was, he'd always vehemently proclaimed his innocence.

Eric still believed he'd done the right thing. And

the proof was this little girl, clutching his hand with complete trust. Ralston had said he could get to her even from prison—that if Eric ratted him out, he could count on never seeing his daughter again, one way or another.

Eric hadn't said a word to the warden. He hadn't even sought medical treatment for the cut, not until the infection got so bad that a guard found him unconscious in his cell. Still, when questioned, he'd refused to name Kelly Ralston.

Somehow, though, the warden had found out, and Ralston had gone into solitary for a week, pretty much guaranteeing that his upcoming parole hearing wouldn't go well.

So far Ralston hadn't made good on his threat. But if he were free, taking his revenge against Eric and his family would be child's play.

MacKenzie dragged Eric into the kitchen. "Daddy's home," she said proudly, as if she had personally caused him to appear. In a way, she had. If not for her, he probably would have just headed for Tuckerville right after work.

Travis grinned. "Hey, how was your first staff meeting? Did Daniel kick your— Um, did he give you any trouble?"

Travis and Daniel Logan had a rocky past, but they'd come to terms.

"I only saw him on a video screen. How much damage could he do?"

"Plenty," Elena answered. She had been Daniel's

personal assistant until recently. "I've seen him reduce a grown man to tears over video conferencing. But he wouldn't have any reason to be on your case."

Oh, wouldn't he? How about if he knew Eric had told a big fat lie?

"Dinner will be ready in about twenty minutes," Travis said. "You want a beer?"

"Maybe later. Unfortunately, I have to leave again."

"What?" MacKenzie shrieked.

"I have to go out. It's important, or I wouldn't."

"But you just got home! I haven't showed you the picture I colored or my homework papers I got an A on." MacKenzie was in a near panic.

"You can show me later, okay?"

"When?"

"I should be home about nine-thirty."

"I have to go to bed at eight-thirty. No, Daddy, don't leave." She was about to have a full-blown tantrum. Already little tears were squeezing out of her eyes, and she was holding on to him with the grip of a lumberjack on his ax.

"Where are you going?" Travis asked. "I mean, not that it's my business—"

"It's work-related," Eric said.

"Daniel's making you work late your second day?" Elena was incensed. Then she whispered, "He knows MacKenzie needs you."

"You can go out later," MacKenzie wheedled, "after I go to bed. Don't leave, Daddy."

When she looked up at him with those big blue eyes, it was impossible to deny her. But he'd given his word to Bree that he would meet Philomene. She'd said he could bring MacKenzie with him....

"MacKenzie, how would you like to go for a drive with me?"

"What?" Travis and Elena said at the same time.

But MacKenzie clapped her hands together gleefully. "Are we going to get ice cream?"

"You can have ice cream if you want when we get there." He couldn't imagine any diner that didn't serve ice cream. "But it's a long drive. About two hours. We'll have to take a snack with us."

"Where are you going?" Travis asked again.

"To talk to a reluctant witness."

"You think it's okay to bring a child to—"

"I have a babysitter lined up."

Travis looked as if he wanted to say more, but he resisted.

"I'll make her a peanut-butter sandwich," Elena said.

"Great. I'll go change clothes."

Ten minutes later Eric was in the car with MacKenzie snug in her car seat with a sandwich and his iPhone, where she was watching cartoons. She was quiet for a long time, leaving Eric far too alone with his thoughts.

He couldn't stomach even the thought of anyone hurting his little girl. Though Ralston's threat had been issued years ago, when Eric was a green convict, Eric recalled every word as if it were an hour ago.

*You better not rat me out, Riggs, or your life won't be worth the ink on your fancy law degree. You may leave here. You may think you're safe. But vengeance will come when you least expect it.*

At that point everything about prison had scared Eric. He still didn't know where he'd come up with the courage to try to stop a fight. But when Ralston and the other man had squared off, each of them brandishing a homemade weapon, Eric had been naive enough to try to calm them down.

Stepping between them just as the second man struck hadn't been his sharpest move. Ralston's vicious countermove had cut Eric stem to stern.

Reflexively, he rubbed his chest again. The scar still throbbed when he was nervous.

*I don't care what happens to me.* That was what Eric had retorted, because at the time, he'd thought death might be preferable to the hell of prison.

*No? What about that cute little girl of yours? What's her name? MacKenzie? When I get done with her, there won't be enough left to identify at the morgue.*

Eric's gut twisted as he recalled Ralston's threat. He'd wanted to tell Ralston to back off, that if he touched one hair on his daughter's head, Eric would kill him. Painfully.

But the words hadn't come. It had been all he could do not to puke.

Ruthlessly, Eric shoved the memory aside and focused on the upcoming meeting. This shouldn't be a big deal. He would listen to Philomene's story, then politely tell Bree that he was sorry, but his decision stood. Then he'd buy MacKenzie an ice cream and come back home. MacKenzie would probably go to sleep during the drive home. She loved riding in the car.

"Daddy, when are we gonna get there?"

"We're more than halfway there. Are you tired of your cartoons?"

"Uh-huh."

"You can look out the window. We're going to a new place you've never been before. Tuckerville." What a name. He could only imagine what kind of backwater wasteland Tuckerville was. Why a woman of Bree's obvious intelligence and sophistication chose to live there was a mystery. He couldn't imagine wanting to live so far from any big city, so far from shopping and fine restaurants and…good haircuts. That was one thing he'd really missed in prison—getting a decent haircut. Sometimes it was the small things.

"It's dark out there," MacKenzie said. "I can't see anything."

"Look off to the right. There's a radio tower. See those red lights?" They were driving through farm and ranch land. Not much to see at night. "When we listen to the radio, that's where the sound comes from."

"Oh."

At least MacKenzie was talking again. When he'd first gotten out of prison, he could barely get two words out of her. But more than two months later, she was starting to open up a little. The foster home she'd lived in during his incarceration had been a pretty bad place, though no one knew how bad until Travis had realized the foster parents were selling MacKenzie's clothes and toys on eBay.

"Now look up at the sky."

He heard MacKenzie give a little gasp of surprise, and he smiled. It was a clear winter night, and they were far enough away from the city now that the sky was blanketed with stars. When Eric was a kid, he'd loved the stars, even though he hadn't been able to see all that many in the city. He'd checked out book after book on astronomy and had even thought he might make that his life's work. He remembered dragging Travis up onto the roof of their apartment building and pointing out the constellations—the Big Dipper, Orion's Belt, Cassiopeia's Chair.

"There's so many stars," MacKenzie said softly, almost to herself, a tinge of awe in her voice.

"Some weekend we'll go camping, and we'll get a telescope and look at the stars and the moon and the planets. Would you like that?"

"Uh-huh," she said almost absently, her head leaning against the window as she took in the blanket of diamonds overhead. She remained quiet for the next thirty minutes, just looking at the night sky. It warmed his heart to think maybe she'd inherited his love for studying the heavens.

"Are we almost there?"

"Almost. Suzy says ten more minutes." Suzy was the name they'd given the female voice on his car's GPS.

MacKenzie sighed.

"What flavor ice cream do you want?"

"Pineapple," she said decisively.

"They might not have pineapple ice cream. We'll just have to see. Did you finish your sandwich?"

She held up what was left of the half sandwich Elena had made for her. She'd eaten a few bites, at least. At her foster home, MacKenzie had developed the unfortunate habit of hoarding food. She seldom ate very much, choosing instead to save her food for later. No matter how many times Eric reassured her that she could eat as much as she wanted, she obviously was still fearful about going hungry.

"I'm going to have dinner at the diner before my ice cream," he said. "How about you?"

"Do they have grilled cheese?"

"I imagine so. Maybe soup, too." She loved soup, and it wasn't something she could hoard.

The momentous decision of what to choose for dinner occupied her until they crossed the city limits of the great metropolis of Tuckerville.

It was a little bigger than he'd expected, with a quaint main street boasting old-fashioned streetlights, a theater showing last year's movies, an antiques mall and a quilt shop. Most everything except the theater was closed, the sidewalks deserted. Then he spotted the Home Cookin' Café, right where Bree had said it would be, at the corner of Main and Maple.

The café was like something out of an old movie, all chrome and rounded corners and an Art Deco neon sign advertising Shakes, Malts and Sodas. He wondered if it was the real thing or someone's retro fantasy.

He pulled into the small parking lot, which was nearly full. Clearly the place was doing a brisk business.

MacKenzie was more than ready to be released from the confines of her child seat.

"What is this place?" MacKenzie asked.

"It's a diner. Or a café. Have you ever been to one?"

"Is it like McDonald's?"

"Sort of. But they serve the food on real dishes and they bring it to your table."

"Oh, like Little Italy?" Little Italy was a neighborhood restaurant that Travis and Elena had introduced them to. It hadn't been open when Eric had lived in the neighborhood, before Tammy's death. Funny, that was how he thought of his life now, in three distinct segments: Before Tammy's Murder, Prison and After Prison.

"You'll see what it's like."

She grabbed on to Eric's hand. New situations and

new people made her nervous. No, more than nervous. Really stressed.

"Will there be people there?"

"Yes. We're going to meet a nice lady named Bree. You'll like her."

"No, I won't," she said decisively.

Eric didn't challenge her. He couldn't make her like people and she certainly knew that not all adults were worthy of her esteem. Eric himself wasn't sure he liked Bree—although he was looking forward to seeing her again. She wasn't exactly all sweetness and light, and clearly she had a sharp tongue when she had a mind to use it. But he admired her passion. Passion was attractive, even if it was for a cause he didn't agree with.

Eric and MacKenzie entered the diner and stood next to a please-wait-to-be-seated sign. The place was busy, but there were still a few tables and booths available.

A hostess with a mile-high beehive greeted them, fitting right in with the retro theme. "Two for dinner?" she asked brightly.

"Actually, I'm meeting someone here. Her name is Bree. About so high, black hair, blue eyes you can't miss—"

The hostess was nodding. "That's Dr. Bree."

"And a friend of hers, too. They're not here yet, are they?" He scanned the whole seating area and didn't see Bree, and she wasn't the sort of woman easily overlooked.

"No, haven't seen her, but I'll keep an eye out. Come right this way."

Eric started to follow the hostess, whose name tag identified her as Molly, but MacKenzie suddenly dug in her heels and wouldn't move.

"No, Daddy, let's go home."

"What? We just got here."

"I don't want to meet the lady! I want to go home!"

# CHAPTER THREE

ERIC PRAYED MACKENZIE wasn't about to throw one of her fits. "Why don't you want to stay here?"

"I just don't."

"Well, we came a long way, and I'm hungry, and we're not leaving until I get some dinner. Don't you want your grilled cheese? And ice cream?" He knew bribing a child with food wasn't the recommended way to get her to cooperate, but he didn't want to risk a tantrum, not now.

"I'm not hungry. I want to go home."

"I'm sorry, MacKenzie, we can't go home right now. Daddy promised to be here, and I have to keep my word."

"You want a coloring book, precious?" Molly asked. "I have Goofy and Cinderella."

MacKenzie pressed her lips together in a mutinous frown.

"Go with Cinderella," Eric said to the hostess. Then he scooped up MacKenzie and carried her to their designated booth. He would lie down and die any day of the week for this child. But the psychologist had emphasized that he had to be firm, too, and not let her walk all over him. Just because she was troubled didn't mean she couldn't also learn to be manipulative.

Once they were seated, he tried to get MacKenzie interested in the menu. She was a good enough reader that she could make out a lot of the words by herself.

"It says this diner has been here for more than sixty years," Eric read, pointing to the words. That answered his question about whether it was authentic.

MacKenzie didn't seem interested. She kept looking over her shoulder, as if she expected the bogeyman to be after her.

"MacKenzie, what's wrong? What are you afraid of?"

"I don't want a shot!" she said, bursting into tears.

"A shot? What makes you think… Oh." *Dr. Bree.* "She's not going to give you a shot. She's just a nice lady." A nice lady who was late. If he'd driven all this way for nothing, he was going to be more than irritated.

"No shots?"

"No. Just dinner. It says here they have a soup-and-sandwich special. How about a grilled cheese and tomato soup?"

After thinking about it, MacKenzie nodded.

A couple of minutes later Bree bustled through the door, looking a bit harried. Molly smiled at her and pointed toward their booth, and Bree hurried their way, waving as she caught Eric's eye.

The sight of her had a stronger effect than he'd anticipated. She had her hair pulled back in a ponytail now, and several unruly strands had escaped to frame her face. She'd changed clothes since this morning, opting for a simple white blouse and gray pants. Again, he could tell at a glance that the clothes were high quality. Could a woman even buy clothes like that in Tuckerville?

Didn't matter. The sight of her made his mouth go dry. He couldn't recall reacting that strongly to a woman since…well, since Tammy. Tammy, the supposed love of his life, who'd turned out to be aggressively unfaithful.

*You can't trust a sweet smile.* Bree had already proved she had a sharp side. During their very first meeting, no less.

"I'm so sorry I'm late," she said as she slid into the booth opposite them. "I got held up at work. I hope you haven't been waiting too long."

"Just a couple of minutes."

Then Bree's attention focused on MacKenzie, and her face was transformed with a look of such sweet maternal softness that Eric found himself struggling to breathe.

"And who have we here?" Bree asked.

MacKenzie ignored her.

"This is my daughter, MacKenzie," Eric said. "MacKenzie, this is Dr. Johnson."

"Hi, MacKenzie. You can call me Bree." Her voice was soft, nonprovoking. "Nice to meet you."

MacKenzie kept her eyes on her coloring book, where she was filling in Cinderella's dress with a brown crayon.

"Is that Cinderella?" Bree asked.

"Mmm-hmm," MacKenzie replied.

"You're good at coloring. You really know how to stay inside the lines. Me, when I color, I'm really messy. I bet you get gold stars in your art class."

"I get all As," MacKenzie said matter-of-factly.

"Where's Philomene?" Eric asked. "I'd like to move this along so I don't keep MacKenzie out too late."

"Of course." Bree looked around. "I'll go ask if she's here. If the waitress comes, order me a meat loaf special and a coffee."

"Caffeine doesn't bother you this late at night?"

"Unfortunately, no. If it did, maybe I wouldn't drink so much of the stuff." She slid out of the booth and headed for Molly. Eric studied her retreating form at leisure, especially those gently swaying hips.

MacKenzie was staring, too.

"See, she's not so scary," Eric said.

MacKenzie shrugged and turned her attention to the menu. "I don't see ice cream on here."

Eric flipped the pages until he found desserts. "Right here. Chocolate, vanilla and strawberry."

She put her finger on the menu where Eric had pointed and attempted to sound out the words. The waitress stopped back, and Eric dutifully ordered Bree's meat loaf special. "I'll have the same thing," he added. "And a grilled cheese and tomato soup for the little one."

"You want a soda with that?" the perky waitress asked.

MacKenzie nodded, but Eric shook his head. "Milk." Bree might not be bothered by caffeine, but it made MacKenzie spin like a top.

As soon as the waitress left, Bree returned, a worried frown on her face. "Philomene's not here. She should have gotten off work at six."

"Maybe she got held up."

"Maybe. But wouldn't she call?"

"You're asking me? I've never met this woman."

"She should have called," Bree said decisively.

Eric stifled a groan. He should have known this was a fool's errand. "Sounds like maybe she had a change of heart."

"When I talked to her yesterday, she sounded really eager to unburden herself. The guilt has been eating her alive."

"You said she was nervous about changing her story. She probably just got cold feet."

"I hope that's all it is." Bree already had her phone in her hand. "I'll call her and see what's what."

The waitress brought MacKenzie's milk and Bree's coffee. Bree took a healthy gulp of the stuff, black, while waiting for Philomene to pick up.

"Hi, Philomene, it's me, Bree," she said after a few moments. "I'm at the diner with Eric Riggs from Project Justice. Please call me when you get a chance." She was still frowning as she hung up.

"Look, Daddy, I finished." MacKenzie displayed her coloring work. Although the colors were a little drab, she'd kept within the lines in her usual meticulous fashion.

"Very nice, sweetheart."

Cautiously, she turned the page around and slid it toward Bree.

Bree smiled, and again her face was transformed. *She ought to smile more often,* Eric thought.

"Very good work, MacKenzie. I think I might have something here…" She dug into her purse. "I do. Would you like a glitter heart or a gold star?"

"Heart, heart heart heart!"

Eric was touched. Had Bree put those stickers in her purse just for MacKenzie? Or… "You must have kids."

A stark sadness flashed across Bree's face before she masked it. "No, no kids. But I keep a few things on hand for children who come through the E.R."

"So emergency medicine is your specialty?" She'd said earlier today that she'd met Philomene in the E.R., but he wanted to keep her talking about herself.

"Yes. I work at the county hospital."

He wondered how many men faked serious illness in the hopes that lovely Bree would minister to them. Images flashed through his mind of Bree's soft, pale hands touching him—in the most innocent, doctorly ways, of course.

God, what was he doing? He clenched his eyes shut until the images dissipated. He couldn't afford to think of her like that. He needed to get her and her misguided agenda out of his life.

"Oh, no," Bree said under her breath, her gaze fixed on the door.

Eric turned to look. A big, beefy guy with dark close-cropped hair in a well-tailored dress shirt and pants had just entered, accompanied by a shorter, more slender man with thinning curly hair and thick glasses. The shorter one's clothes were rumpled, and as Molly showed them to a table, he walked with a slightly lurching gait, as if he had an issue with his hip or knee.

"Darn it, they're headed this way." Bree lowered her head and took another sip of coffee, playing with a strand of her hair to shield her face.

"Well, if it isn't the crusading lady doctor." The larger of the two men, clearly the alpha in this pack of two, had paused by their booth, proving Bree's attempt to be inconspicuous hadn't worked.

"Hello, Mr. Needles," she said wearily, offering him a tight, almost hostile smile.

"Aren't you going to introduce us?"

"Eric, this is District Attorney Sam Needles, the man who put Kelly in prison. Sam, this is Eric Riggs. He's an attorney with Project Justice," she said meaningfully.

Sam Needles didn't take the hand Eric extended. Instead, he laughed. "Surely you're kidding. You actually think Project Justice can get your no-good boyfriend out of prison? You ought to know that dog won't hunt."

Eric withdrew his hand, which had clenched into a fist. He didn't know Bree very well, and he even agreed with Needles's assessment of Ralston. But Needles had no call to be out-and-out rude.

"Sam," the other man said to his friend, "leave her be."

"Eric, this is Ted Gentry," Bree said in a friendlier tone of voice. "He's our county coroner. Normally a perfectly nice man, though he could keep better company."

Gentry grinned. "Sam's okay if you catch him on a good day. And he said he'd pay for dinner."

"Least I could do, after you let me keep all the fish we caught," Needles said with a hearty laugh.

"We did some fishing last night out at Willowbrook," Gentry explained. "Sheriff's got a place there. I like to catch 'em, not eat 'em."

Sam Needles sobered. "Don't drag me back to court, Bree. It's a waste of everyone's time." He sauntered off.

Gentry shrugged apologetically. "You know how it is. If he says a man's guilty, he doesn't like being proved wrong."

"A common trait among prosecutors," Eric said amiably, though he was far less accepting of Sam Needles's behavior than he let on. The fact was, the prosecutor's attitude got Eric's back up. He felt this tremendous urge to say, "Hell, yeah, Project Justice is taking on this case and you're gonna eat your words."

Even if Eric did agree with the guy.

But he kept still. He didn't want any arguing, particularly not in front of MacKenzie, although she seemed engrossed in her coloring book and looked as if she'd tuned out the adult conversation.

"If you need anything from me, just let me know," Gentry said. "I don't like being proved wrong, either. But as I recall, I wasn't able to contribute a whole heck of a lot to that case."

"Thanks, Ted." Bree gave his hand a quick squeeze.

A jolt of some uncomfortable emotion shocked Eric's system; it took a moment before he realized he was jealous.

The coroner left to join his friend at a table thankfully far away from theirs. Bree watched them for a few moments. "Of course. They're sitting down with Sheriff DeVille. Birds of a feather," she grumbled, then turned to look at Eric. "See what I'm up against? Good-ol'-boy network can't stand the thought that they might be proved wrong, by a woman, no less. 'Crusading lady doctor,' my foot."

"It's an attitude I'm familiar with. The coroner seemed a nice enough guy, at least."

"He's okay. We go way back, actually. We were in med school together. He's kind of weird, but you'd have to be kind of weird to, um, do what he does all day."

The waitress arrived with their food, and for a few

minutes they made small talk. Under any other circumstances, Eric would have found Bree delightful. If this had been a first date, he would have wanted a second.

But he didn't date. Even if he had been ready to trust another woman with his heart—and he wasn't—there was no way he would make MacKenzie negotiate the minefield of Daddy's girlfriends. She'd had to endure so many changes so quickly, not the least of which was discovering the foster father who'd cared for her the past three years had killed her mother. That was *after* losing her mother to murder, then having everyone tell her her own father had done it.

While MacKenzie was working on her scoop of vanilla ice cream, Bree tried to call Philomene again but still got no answer.

"I'm worried about her."

"Philomene sounds like a woman who can take care of herself. I read up on the case, you know." He hadn't exactly had a ton of work to do so far at the foundation. "She came across as gutsy, standing up to her attacker, testifying in court against him—"

"Against the wrong guy. If you met her, you'd know she's not very tough at all."

BREE SEEMED INDECISIVE as she pulled out a credit card to pay for their meal.

"Wait, you don't have to pay for dinner." Eric was already reaching for his own wallet.

"Of course I do. You drove all this way, for nothing, as it turns out. I'm so sorry she didn't show."

"Crime victims don't always behave rationally. If I'd been through what she has, I'd be scared, too." Come to think of it, he *was* scared.

"But this was our one chance to get someone at Project Justice to listen. She understood that!"

Eric wished he knew what to say to make Bree feel better.

"I'm going to swing by her apartment and see if she's home," Bree said. "I don't suppose you want to come with me—in case she's there? Maybe I can still get her to talk to you."

Eric was torn. He wanted to be done with this matter. At the same time, he didn't want to say goodbye to Bree forever. She was a bright and interesting aspect of his life all of a sudden, even if she did bring trouble. He honestly hadn't thought he would ever be interested in another woman after Tammy. But this one—she caused something to stir inside him, something he'd thought dead and buried right along with his duplicitous wife.

"If it'll save me another trip out here…" He tried to make it seem as if he were merely being practical.

She quickly paid the bill, deftly refusing Eric's attempt to do so himself, and soon they were all headed out to the parking lot, though not without a brief tussle with MacKenzie, who wanted to take her ice cream with her.

"Do you want to ride with me?" Eric asked Bree.

"It's not far, is it?" How far could one drive in Tuckerville and not go beyond the city limits? "I'll drop you off here when we're done."

"Okay, if you don't mind."

By the time he got MacKenzie settled in her car seat, Bree was already ensconced in the front of his Nissan, looking right at home. She brought with her not only a healthy dose of femininity but a light, clean scent that reminded him of an alpine meadow—like Colorado in the spring. He was on the verge of asking her what the perfume was, then realized that would sound much too flirtatious for this situation. But the feminine scent produced a ridiculous surge of pleasure.

As he fastened his seat belt and started the car, Bree took a small bottle out of her purse and squirted something into her hand. It was an antibacterial gel, he realized. The alpine scent grew stronger, and he felt like an idiot. No chance she'd gussied up for him.

"Habit," she said as she tossed the bottle back into her purse. "Hospitals have so many germs that I put this stuff on every five minutes."

"When MacKenzie was a baby, we were so paranoid about germs we went through a bottle of Lysol about every day. Our hands were always chapped from washing."

"She must be your first, then."

"First and only. I don't see how people do it, the ones who have half a dozen, I mean. I worry about her all the time."

"I guess you figure it out as you go along." She sounded wistful.

He knew it was harder for women, doing the whole husband-and-kids thing when you had a high-pressure career. He'd heard enough of his female attorney colleagues say so, anyway. Tammy'd had a career as a bookkeeper before MacKenzie. After the baby came, she'd insisted there was no way she could work and be a proper wife and mother, and Eric had never pushed her to. They'd done okay on his income. If he'd known she was putting MacKenzie in day care so she could carry on with the guy from her coupon club—

No, he couldn't think about that.

"Turn left at this next stop sign," Bree said. "It's the second house on the right. She lives in the apartment over the garage."

It seemed a cheerful enough neighborhood, with lots of pecan trees and picket fences. Eric pulled his car to the curb and stopped.

"Where are we going, Daddy?" MacKenzie asked. He'd thought maybe after her dinner and ice cream, she'd go right to sleep.

"Just a quick stop. Then we'll head home."

"Who lives here?" she asked as Eric helped her out of the car seat.

"A friend of Bree's."

The three of them walked up a set of wooden stairs lined with clay pots overflowing with pansies. A light was on inside, but that didn't necessarily mean

Philomene was home. People often left their lights on to foil burglars.

Bree knocked sharply on the door. "Philomene? It's Bree. I'm just checking to see if you're okay. Did you forget our meeting?"

No one answered. But Eric heard someone moving inside.

"Did you hear that?" Bree asked in a low voice.

"Clearly she doesn't want visitors."

Of course, Bree was too persistent to just give up. She tried the latch, which wasn't locked. She opened the door a crack. "Philomene? I'm coming in, okay? I just want to make sure you're all right." She turned to Eric and whispered, "I mean, what if she's sick or hurt or something?"

*Unlikely, unless cold feet could be considered an injury.*

Bree knocked one more time. "I don't think she would normally leave her door unlocked at night. I'm going in." She pushed her way inside.

It was a tiny apartment—just a combined living/dining room and a galley kitchen separated by a half wall. A single door probably led to the bedroom.

"This looks a lot like the place I lived in college," Eric said. "With two other guys."

Bree wasn't up for chitchat. "I know I heard someone in here." She crossed the living room toward the kitchen and peeked behind the half wall. Eric was right behind her, gripping MacKenzie's hand. He suddenly had a bad feeling they shouldn't be here.

Just because the door was unlocked didn't mean they had the right to barge in.

"We should leave," he said just as someone burst out of the bedroom and streaked past them, straight out the front door.

"Hey!" Eric yelled, a purely reflexive outburst. The last thing he really wanted was for the guy to stop, not when Eric had his six-year-old daughter with him.

MacKenzie squeaked in surprise and Bree whirled around. "Who was that? Was it Philomene?"

"Definitely not, unless Philomene resembles a large male wearing overalls."

Bree shook her head and walked to the door to look out. The guy's footsteps had long since faded; he'd beat it out of there pretty damn fast.

"Does Philomene have a roommate or boyfriend?" Eric asked.

"No roommate. I don't know about boyfriends. But whoever that guy was, he wouldn't have run like that if he was supposed to be here."

Bree walked over to the bedroom door and stuck her head in, then checked the bathroom. "She's not here. Eric, did you get a good look at the intruder?"

"No. Just his general size and coloring, but he rushed past so fast. Look, Bree, I must have been insane to come here with my little girl. We have to go—now."

"But Philomene might be in trouble."

"That sounds like a matter for the police." Eric

was already heading for the door. He needed to get MacKenzie home, tucked in safe and far, far away from anything that smacked of "trouble."

"The police. That's a joke," Bree muttered as she followed Eric out. "Tuckerville doesn't even have its own police force. We rely on the Becker County Sheriff's Department. They wouldn't stir themselves to look for a missing woman."

"Most law enforcement won't search for a missing adult unless there's clear evidence of foul play. Because ninety-nine percent of missing adults are missing because they want to be."

"What about that one percent?"

"I'm sure she'll turn up." Was he? They'd interrupted a possible crime, and Eric's bad feeling hadn't gone away. But his job wasn't to investigate missing persons.

They rode in silence back to the café's parking lot. Finally, when Eric stopped to let Bree out, she spoke. "I'm sorry you came all this way for nothing."

"Not nothing. That was awfully good meat loaf."

"I don't suppose you'd come back if I set up another meeting.... No, I can see it in your eyes. You've already been more than reasonable, and... Never mind. It's not your problem. Have a safe drive home. MacKenzie?" Bree's demeanor changed dramatically when she addressed his daughter. "I enjoyed meeting you."

MacKenzie actually smiled. Then she said in a tiny voice, "I hope you find your friend."

"Me, too, kiddo."

Eric was touched. He'd thought MacKenzie would tune them out the way kids did when they weren't interested in adult conversation, which they usually weren't. But apparently she'd been paying attention, and she'd overcome her initial shyness to express compassion for someone else. She was an amazing kid.

With more empathy than her father, apparently. He felt guilty for not showing more concern for Philomene. He felt a sudden urge to reverse himself and tell Bree he would do whatever it took to locate Philomene and make sure she was safe, that he would listen, that he would look into Kelly Ralston's case and see that justice was being served.

But Bree was already gone.

## CHAPTER FOUR

BREE HAD NEVER thought of herself as a stalker. But she'd tried calling Eric Riggs three times and hadn't been able to get through. She was not going to give up easily, however. Not when a woman's life was at stake. So here she was, lurking outside the Project Justice offices, waiting for someone to exit.

She had known better than to actually go inside and face the Dragon Lady, Celeste. Celeste was the one who had repeatedly foiled Bree's efforts to speak with Eric.

When someone finally did exit the building, it was the young blonde woman she'd seen on her first visit, the one who had interrupted what she must have thought was some kind of romantic tryst.

"Excuse me, Jillian?"

The woman whirled around. "Yes?" Then she smiled with recognition. "Oh, you're Eric's girl-friend."

Bree let Jillian believe what she wanted. "I've been trying to reach him. But there seems to be some trouble with the phone, and he's not answering his cell."

"He's probably in the courtroom," Jillian said.

"You get in big trouble with the judge if your cell phone goes off during some proceeding." Jillian looked slightly guilty, as if she might know this from experience. "He was supposed to appear this morning for some reason or other. You can probably still catch him down there if you hurry. You know where it is?"

"Oh, sure," Bree said breezily. "Thanks."

"No problem. I'm just glad to see Eric has someone in his life. I don't know him very well, but he seems like a really nice guy, and he deserves someone nice."

As she hurried back to her car, Bree felt slightly guilty for having perpetrated the white lie on unsuspecting Jillian. But extreme circumstances called for extreme measures.

Ten minutes later she was lurking on the courthouse steps like a lovesick teenager or an ambitious paparazzo, ready to pounce if she saw any sign of her target. It wasn't as if he would be hard to spot, with those wide shoulders and the glint of gold in his hair. Although he'd cut it ruthlessly short, she bet it would turn beach-boy blond if he let it grow and spent a little time in the sun. Might get rid of that prison pallor, too.

Yeah, she'd done some research on him. It wasn't hard—he'd been convicted of stabbing his pretty socialite wife to death, and his trial had been reported and analyzed ad nauseam in dozens of newspapers across the state. It had even been on TruTV. He had indeed been pardoned and then his conviction over-turned when the real killer had tried to kidnap Eric's future sister-in-law.

Bree hadn't known anything about the original crime, because she'd been in her medical residency then, oblivious to anything but her patients and the few hours of sleep she could grab. Plus, crime news had never been something that interested her. She'd had her fill of it during Kelly's arrest and trial.

It was a wonder she'd survived that period of her life, fighting for Kelly's freedom *and* getting through med school.

"Bree?"

She whirled around, nearly tripping and falling down the stairs. Eric grabbed her elbow to steady her, then quickly released it, as if touching her had burned him.

"How did you get past me?" She tamped down the ridiculous pleasure she felt at seeing him again. Something about him was so reassuring. Maybe that was a glamour he'd developed to deal with skittish clients. "I've been watching that door for the past twenty minutes."

"I came out a side door. I just happened to glance this way on the way to my car…. Bree, what are you doing here?"

"I needed to talk to you."

"A phone call wouldn't have worked? Not that I'm not happy to see you," he quickly added. "A man would have to be crazy to… Never mind."

He was flirting with her, though she was pretty sure he hadn't meant to. And why did she care? She'd come here for a reason, and it wasn't to set her hormones all aflutter. "I tried calling, but your overzealous watchdog refused to put me through."

"Overzealous… Celeste?"

"She said once an application had been rejected, there was nothing I could do to change Daniel's mind, and policy was to not put calls through from people like me."

"That's Celeste. She doesn't bend the rules for anyone. How did you know to find me here?"

"I saw that woman, Jillian, coming out the front door and she steered me here. I'm sorry, I know I'm acting like a stalker, but I really needed to talk to you."

"What is it? What's wrong?"

"It's Philomene. She really *is* missing. When I didn't hear from her by the next day, I called her at work. Her boss said she hadn't shown up for work in two days."

Eric's brow furrowed. "That doesn't sound good."

"No, it really doesn't."

"Did you call the police?"

"For all the good it did me." Bree's legs were suddenly tired. She sank back down to sit on one of the steps. "They said I had to wait seventy-two hours. And even then, unless there's some evidence of foul play, they won't look for her."

"As I said before—"

"I know. It's a common-sense policy employed by most law enforcement agencies—I get that. But they were so... They just dismissed me! They already think I'm a kook, I'm afraid. I didn't exactly make a lot of friends at the sheriff's office when Kelly was arrested. Now they think I'm overreacting. But I'm not. Something doesn't feel right. I think Philomene's in trouble. We have to find her before it's too late!"

"We?"

"I don't know who else to turn to."

"I'm not a cop. I'm not an investigator of any kind. I'm just a lawyer—a real-estate lawyer, if truth be told. This job with Project Justice is a temporary deal, filling in for an attorney on maternity leave."

She slumped and rested her elbows on her knees. "I'm sorry to have bothered you." Oh, God. She hoped she wouldn't humiliate herself further by crying.

Bree fully expected Eric to walk away. But instead he sat down beside her, heedless of getting his expensive suit dirty. "Bree. What is it you think I can do? I'd like to find your friend. How is it you think I can help?"

"I figured you knew people. Given your job...."

"This is my first week. I've met some of the people who work at Project Justice, but truthfully, I don't know any of them very well. But *I* could try to help. Maybe if I talked to the sheriff."

"You'd do that?"

"I have tomorrow off. They're fumigating the

building. Sometimes just seeing a new face could shake someone out of complacence. And the fact that I'm a lawyer won't hurt. People are afraid of lawsuits."

"I'd be really appreciative. I'll pay you—"

"That's not necessary. But have you considered hiring a private detective?"

"I thought I would talk to you first. Do you know any good private detectives?"

"No. But I could find you one. Project Justice uses them from time to time for surveillance and such. But let me check a few things first." He took his phone out of his jacket pocket and opened the notepad. "Do you know Philomene's full name?"

"Philomene Switzer, that's all I know."

"What's her approximate age?"

"Late twenties, I'd say."

"With that and her address, our data analyst can probably find out a lot. But it's not exactly kosher to ask him to work on something that's not foundation business."

"It would *be* foundation business if you'd taken on Kelly's case." Her muscles tensed as she remembered the casual way Eric had dismissed her. The way he was so sure Kelly was guilty, when he couldn't be.

"But we didn't. And the foundation isn't in the business of randomly looking for people."

"Philomene's disappearance is connected, though. Think about it. On the very day she's about to unburden herself to someone who might be able to get

Kelly out of jail and prove the real criminal is still at large, she inexplicably goes missing. I feel the wrongness of that in my bones, Eric."

"Then why don't you come with me to talk to Mitch. Maybe he'll work on the problem on his own time."

"Of course I'll come. Can we do it now?"

Eric stood and offered his hand. "Let's go."

His hand felt incredibly warm and reassuring. Bree had been alone for so long, the solitary crusader on Kelly's behalf. No one had stood by her—not Kelly's family, certainly not her family. They'd hated Kelly since he and Bree were teenagers, and his arrest and conviction had delighted them because they could say "I told you so."

And now, after all these years, Bree had Eric.

Granted, his support was grudging. And could be withdrawn at any point. But even though he had his own reasons for disliking Kelly, Eric saw something in what Bree had told him. She'd gotten through his bias, or she'd at least opened a small crack. Now she was going to stick her foot in that crack and make sure he couldn't close it back up. *For Kelly,* she told herself. *All this is for Kelly.*

She waited until they were in Eric's car and on the road before she made a confession. "You should probably know—I sort of gave Jillian the idea that I'm your, um, girlfriend."

Eric slammed on the brakes. *"What?"*

"Sorry, it was just the most expedient way to…

You're getting honked at." He'd stopped in the middle of a busy road.

Eric pulled over to the curb. "I can't believe you did that. Do you know how long and hard I worked to convince Jillian that you and I weren't..." He seesawed his hands back and forth. "The whole office thought we were having sex in the break room. On my second day of employment."

"Well, *I'm* not the one who ripped my shirt off." She wasn't going to take all the blame.

"Now everyone is going to think I'm a liar as well as a sexual deviant. Why did you do that?"

"She assumed, and I thought it would take too long to explain, and I needed to find you." He seemed far more distressed at the thought of her being his girlfriend than he ought to be. "I'll explain it to her. I didn't mean to cause you so much grief, really."

"I'm sure you didn't," he muttered, putting the car in gear and slowly easing into traffic.

"If it makes you feel any better, Jillian didn't seem at all judgmental. She thinks you're really nice and that you deserve to be with someone. Nice." Not that she qualified. Other than buying Eric a meat loaf dinner, she'd done nothing but cause a giant pain in his butt since the moment they met.

"Whatever."

Now Bree felt bad. She really hadn't meant to diminish Eric in his coworkers' eyes. But she wouldn't like it if her coworkers thought she was boffing her boyfriend in an empty exam room. Her professional reputation mattered to her, and it appeared Eric's did to him. She'd do what she could to fix things.

By the time they'd parked Eric's car in the Project Justice garage, Eric seemed to have shaken off his pique. She caught him smiling when she stopped to pet a small dog on a leash held by someone exiting the building.

"They let people bring their pets to work here?" Bree asked as Eric used his security card and a PIN number to gain entrance to the building. She was glad they were coming through the back rather than having to face the grim Celeste.

"You can pretty much do anything you want here so long as you get your work done and you don't impede anybody else's ability to work. I actually never met that woman with the dog, so I'm not sure she works here. She might be a client or someone's personal trainer. You just never know."

"Wow. I can't imagine working under such... friendly conditions. I'm used to being abused at my job—long hours, dinner breaks too short to do anything but grab a candy bar from the vending machine, not even a comfortable chair to be found."

"Yeah, but you get compensated well, I'm sure."

"At County? Not as well as you might think. And I have student loans to pay off."

"What would you do if you were out of debt?" he asked.

She thought about it for a moment. "Probably keep doing what I'm doing," she confessed. "I hate the bureaucracy of the place, hate my boss, but I love my work. I can't think of any other job where you can have such an immediate and dramatic impact on someone's life. They come in dying or thinking they're dying or wishing they would die, and by the time I'm done with them, they're better. I ease the pain, I sew up the cuts, set the bones, reassure them. It's…gratifying."

"What about when they die?"

"Well, there is that. I try not to dwell on those losses. They're inevitable in most branches of medicine. Except maybe dermatology."

He smiled again, though he tried not to let her see it.

The first place they went was a large room at the end of a hallway that housed a number of desks and file cabinets arranged in a rather haphazard fashion. The place was buzzing with activity. Men and women, mostly in their twenties and thirties, talked on the phone, tapped away on computers or spoke with each other in voices that were subdued but full of energy. Their clothing ranged from formal business attire to jeans and T-shirts.

"This is the bull pen," Eric explained.

"Like at a police department?"

"A lot of the people who work here are former police officers. This arrangement seems to make them feel comfortable. Though the dress code here is pretty lax."

"Apparently so."

Eric led her to a far corner, where a man with long-ish curly blond hair and big black-framed glasses sat at an impressive array of computers. Three monitors, two laptops, a tower and a couple of cell phones sat on his desk. Around it were various peripheral gadgets she couldn't come close to recognizing.

"Mitch," Eric said. "Do you have a minute?"

The man named Mitch quickly blanked his screen and swiveled his chair, simultaneously whipping off his glasses, revealing a pair of hazel eyes. He was quite good-looking in a wild and lawless way. She wasn't too surprised to see a crash helmet tucked under his desk.

"Sure," he said. "What's up?" He eyed Bree up and down, not in a sexual way but with idle curiosity, before inviting them to pull up chairs.

"This is Bree," Eric said.

"I'm not his girlfriend," Bree blurted out. "I told Jillian I was, but it's not true. We barely know each other."

As Eric stared at her as if willing her to shut her mouth, Mitch quirked one eyebrow at her. "Ooookay."

"I don't know what you've heard," Bree went on, wanting Mitch to understand, "but he only took off his shirt to show me a…"

Eric was shaking his head, looking alarmed.

"Well, never mind," Bree finished lamely.

"Hey, makes me no never mind whatchall been up to," Mitch said in a lazy drawl that could only have come from Cajun country. "What can I do you for?"

"A friend of Bree's is missing," Eric said. "The police won't look into it because… Well, you know how the police are about missing persons."

"I take it you think something bad happened to your friend?"

Bree explained as briefly as she could, without mentioning specifics, that Philomene was connected to a crime, and that she was in a position to identify a possible serial murderer, and that they'd come across some kind of intruder in her apartment. She gave Mitch everything she knew about Philomene, which admittedly wasn't much.

"Her name can't be that common," Mitch said. "I'll find her. Give me a few minutes, okay?"

"Yeah, sure." Eric looked at Bree. "You want lunch?"

"I'm not hungry," she said automatically. She ought to pay more attention to her diet and stop living on coffee and jelly beans, but she couldn't imagine putting food into her knotted stomach right now. "I'll just sit here and wait."

"Oh, Bree, I see you found him!" Jillian entered the bull pen with a flourish. Bree suspected it was hard for the woman to appear inconspicuous.

"Yeah, about that…" Bree began guiltily, but Eric jumped in.

"Jillian, do you have a few minutes? We just want to pick your brain. It's not official foundation business," he added.

"Of course." She perched on the edge of an empty

desk and crossed her legs, revealing an impressive length of thigh and mile-high shiny black platform boots.

"I'm not really his girlfriend," Bree blurted out. "I lied. But I was in a hurry and I just wanted to find him. So I let you believe what you wanted."

"Oh." Jillian seemed disappointed.

"I'm sorry. I'm usually a very honest person. I shouldn't have lied. I put Eric in an awkward position, and I didn't mean to."

"So if you're not his girlfriend, why was he stripping off his clothes?"

"It wasn't sexual," Eric said. "I don't want people thinking I had a liaison at the office my second day of work."

Jillian shrugged. "Okay. But honestly, no one cares. If you had any idea the amount of sex that's gone on in this office between people who should know better, you'd understand. So what do you guys want with me?"

Eric held a chair out for Bree, then rolled another over for himself. "Bree needs some help finding someone."

"I just want to know that she's okay," Bree added. "But I'm worried something happened to her."

"Oh, that's easy. Talk to Mitch."

"We did that," Eric said.

"Then he'll find out soon enough whether she's used her phone, bought gas, bought an airline ticket, left the country…"

"Really?" Bree was astonished. "He can do all that? Is that legal?"

Jillian and Eric shared deer-in-headlights looks.

"Ah," Jillian said. "Since you're not a client, you haven't signed a nondisclosure agreement. So we can't say any more about how we do things."

"She's right," Eric said.

"I'm not going to tattle," Bree said. "If you want me to sign something, I will. But you don't have to tell me any more. All I want to do is find Philomene."

"Okay." Jillian got down to business. "In all likelihood, Mitch will tell you where and when she's used her phone and credit cards and provide a list of people she knows—family, friends, coworkers, neighbors. Your job will be to chase down those people and see if any of them can tell you where she is or if they've seen or heard from her. I assume you've tried calling her?"

"She doesn't answer," Bree said. "She doesn't call back. It's possible she just doesn't want to hear from me."

"Call her from a number she won't recognize. Have someone whose voice she doesn't know leave a message like they want to send her a check, a gas company deposit from years ago, something like that. People *always* respond if they think you are going to pay them."

Jillian outlined some other offbeat ways she'd heard of for finding missing persons. She seemed to enjoy sharing her expertise.

"People can try to hide," she said, "but their personalities are the same. So your friend might seek out the same kind of job. If you can pinpoint a city, you can check businesses similar to where she worked. If she gets her hair done professionally, she'll seek that out. If she wears acrylic nails, same thing. Sometimes Mitch can get hold of gas station security video near where you think she lives. That's tedious, going over days and days of video. But people have to buy gas."

Bree was truly impressed. No wonder Project Justice was so good at solving crimes the police had bungled.

"Well, I didn't think up any of this stuff," Jillian said modestly. "I've been taught by some of the best investigators on the planet. So let's see, what else? You can—"

"Hey, got something," Mitch said. "Philomene bought gas in San Antonio. She also used her cell phone there. She called another mobile number in the same area, but that one is a throwaway. We'll never find who it belongs to."

"Someone could have stolen her phone along with her credit card," Bree pointed out.

"Okay, here's one more call," Mitch said. "Ah, we're in luck. To a landline this time. Registered to a Mildred W. Hayes. Also in San Antonio."

"Do you think Philomene might have had friends or family in San Antone?" Eric asked Bree.

Bree shrugged. "I didn't really know her all that well. But we can call this Mildred Hayes, right? Ask her if she knows Philomene?"

"It would be better to go there in person," Mitch said. "If Philomene is hiding, her friends might lie for her. It's harder to lie face-to-face. You could also see if Philomene's car is parked near Mildred's place."

"Can you get any info on this Mildred Hayes?"

"Workin' on it." Mitch tapped for what seemed like an eternity, but probably it was less than a minute. "Okay, here we go. Mildred is sixty-two years old. African-American." He tapped some more. "On SNAP and disability. Doesn't own a car. And... doesn't live in the greatest neighborhood."

"Can you give me her address and phone?" Bree asked. "I'll go talk to her."

"Not alone, you won't." Eric peered at the Google Earth image on Mitch's monitor. "That does not look like the kind of place a woman should wander by herself."

"Yeah, well, it's unlikely I'll get a police escort."

"I'll go with you. I told you I'd help you out tomorrow. Now how about lunch? You might not be hungry, but I am."

"I'll keep working on this while you eat." Mitch pulled a sandwich and an apple out of his desk. "I usually work through lunch any— Okay, that's weird."

"What?" Bree stepped closer to peer over Mitch's shoulder. But the lines and lines of type on the monitor swam before her eyes.

"Another purchase on the credit card just popped up. From the Gap. She just bought...a leather jacket."

"That does not sound like Philomene," Bree said. "Eric, you saw her place. She lives modestly. She drives a ten-year-old Toyota."

"Maybe she forgot to bring a coat. A front is supposed to be moving through tonight."

"That doesn't make sense. There's something wrong here. Because if Philomene met with foul play, it means I was right. Someone wanted to keep her quiet. Someone doesn't want the truth to come out. Which means someone besides Kelly raped Philomene and killed all those girls. You just don't want to admit it."

Eric was about to retort when his phone rang. He pulled it out of his pocket and walked a few steps away, but spoke only briefly before returning.

"Sorry, Bree, but I have to get back to work."

"Of course."

"I'll meet you tomorrow morning at the Home Cookin' Café. Nine o'clock. We'll find Philomene. Ernie?" He addressed a young man at a nearby desk. "Please show Dr. Johnson out. She's parked in the garage." Eric did an abrupt about-face and left the room—as if he couldn't wait to get away from her.

## CHAPTER FIVE

As HE STIRRED half-and-half into his coffee, Eric could have slapped his own face for putting himself in this position. Having Philomene disappear was a stroke of good luck. Without Philomene, Bree had no case. No case, no chance Kelly Ralston would ever see daylight.

Finding Philomene was the last thing he wanted. Yet he was helpless to walk away. What if she really had met with foul play? He couldn't just ignore the fact that a woman was missing, and no one gave a damn. No one but one passionate, determined doctor who made his knees go wobbly.

He didn't think Philomene was in any real trouble. She probably just had cold feet about recanting her story, as he'd thought all along. Perjury was a serious crime. She'd unburdened herself to Bree on impulse, and Bree had grabbed on to the possibility of helping Kelly and refused to let go. Now Philomene had second thoughts. She probably had friends or relatives in San Antonio, where she could hang for a while and hope that Bree would forget about her.

Bree wouldn't forget. Unfortunately. And Eric was caught in the middle.

If he didn't help Bree, he reasoned, she would find someone else to help. She would find Philomene on her own. At least if he remained involved, he could keep a close eye on things and try to turn the circumstances his way. Because if Kelly Ralston got out of prison, Eric would be the one disappearing. He would take MacKenzie and go to Canada. Or maybe South America, where people could get good and truly lost.

*Vengeance will come when you least expect it.*

"Sorry I'm late." Bree slid into the booth across from Eric. He'd been so engrossed in his dismal thoughts he hadn't seen her arrive. "I worked the graveyard last night so I could have today off, and I *had* to shower and change before I came here. A patient threw up on me last night."

"Oh, God."

"I should know by now to jump out of the way faster. People are always barfing in the E.R. Whether they're drunk or have a head injury or severe stomach virus, or they're just terrified."

Was it him, or did she seem entirely too cheerful given the subject matter?

"You really love your job," he observed.

"Yeah, I do. I think most young girls want to grow up and get a job that 'helps people,' but few are lucky enough to find a vocation where you can provide such immediate aid. I go home at the end of a shift knowing I've made a difference. Maybe a small difference—stitching up a cut or just telling someone their injury isn't serious and they aren't going to die still has an impact. Have you had breakfast? I thought maybe we could get coffee and something to go—in the interest of time."

"Sure, sounds good." They flagged down a waitress and ordered a couple of breakfast burritos. The paper cups of coffee arrived first, and Bree gulped down half the cup without taking a breath.

"Need caffeine much?" Not that Eric didn't drink an impressive amount of coffee himself, but she'd drunk it scalding hot.

"I was too busy to drink any at home. I need the caffeine, trust me."

"Doesn't it bother you, being a doctor and all, having an addiction, even if it's only coffee?"

"It was a necessity in med school and during residency. Now that my schedule is a little less hectic, I *could* wean myself off. But then I have a day like today. I haven't slept in twenty-four hours and it's not likely I will for another twelve."

"I guess there are worse vices."

"Sorry if I'm a little hyper," she said in a voice that sounded deliberately slower and softer. "I delivered a baby this morning."

"Really? In the E.R.?"

"By the time they wheeled her in from the ambulance, the baby was crowning. It happened so fast. Basically all I did was catch the kid as he came out. But still… It certainly doesn't get old."

"Did you ever think about becoming an obstetrician?"

"Oh, sure. Most med students do. I mean, babies and all those excited parents, seeing the start of a new life. But the other side of the coin...I don't think I could handle that."

"You mean when things go wrong."

"Yeah." She grew still, and for a moment she was very far away.

He stirred his coffee and took a sip. He had no idea what to say.

She snapped out of her reverie, smiling brightly. "Did you watch MacKenzie being born?"

Eric really didn't feel like sharing anything about those days. He'd lived in a different world back then—perfect job, perfect wife, perfect kid. He'd known poverty and loss, and he'd convinced himself that those days were over. He didn't like being reminded of how fragile life was, how everything could change in one heartbeat. One minute he was driving home, looking forward to a nice dinner with his family. The next, he was staring at his wife's brutalized body on the kitchen floor and trying to calm his screaming daughter while dialing the police.

"I'm sorry," Bree said when he didn't answer. "I'm babbling like a crazy person, prying into things that are none of my business. Blame it on sleep deprivation."

"It's okay. Bree, you've never asked me why I went to prison."

"You said your conviction was overturned."

"They thought I murdered my wife. Turned out her lover did it. So you can understand why I don't really want to talk about the tender moments with her."

"Oh. I'm so sorry. I wasn't thinking."

"You didn't do anything wrong. I'll pay for breakfast—no arguments." His macho pride still stung a little from letting her buy him dinner Tuesday night. The waitress motioned for them to pick up their breakfasts at the counter.

Eric drove to San Antonio while Bree fidgeted in the front seat. He sipped his coffee and ate his burrito while Suzy the GPS led them unerringly to the run-down home of Mildred Hayes. It didn't take as long as he'd feared, only about ninety minutes from Tuckerville.

Eric was glad he drove a modest car. Back when he was a hotshot real-estate lawyer, he'd driven a BMW. Those chrome rims wouldn't have lasted long in this neighborhood.

He found a parking spot along the edge of the curbless street, having strong reservations about bringing Bree to a place like this. But before he could voice his doubts, she was out of the car and charging toward the apartment building where Mildred Hayes lived. He grabbed a folder from the backseat and hurried to catch up to her.

The interview with Ms. Hayes was a waste of time. The friendly silver-haired woman could tell them only that the call had come from her hoodlum grandson, Jerome Taylor Hayes, who had probably called her from a "borrowed" phone. She didn't know how to locate him, as he'd never given her a permanent address. She thought he was in a gang, and probably a drug dealer.

"So some hood has Philomene's phone? This isn't good. Not at all."

"I agree. So maybe the sheriff's department will listen now."

"I doubt it. They'll just say this Jerome person must be a friend of hers."

"If the sheriff's department won't do anything, maybe the San Antonio police will."

"Or maybe it's up to us. How can we find this Jerome character?"

"Whoa. Bree, we aren't cops. We can't go around interrogating people like we are. Jerome's not the kind of person we want to tangle with."

"If you won't help me, then I'll just do it myself."

"Get in the car, okay?" Great. Now Bree knew just how to push his buttons. She knew he was just protective enough of her that he wouldn't want her poking and prodding at lowlife drug dealers by herself. "I'll go with you to talk to the sheriff. And if he doesn't take it seriously, I'll drop Daniel's name. Sometimes that's all it takes to light a fire under someone."

For the next few minutes, Eric focused on getting them out of the hood. He breathed easier once they'd found the freeway.

"You know Daniel Logan pretty well?" Bree asked.

"Some. He's hard to get to know. My brother doesn't get along with him—Daniel threatened to kill Travis at one time. But despite that, Daniel offered me a job when I got out of prison. He knew I'd be a mess, and he gave me a safe place to land. That was pretty generous of him." If Eric did drop Daniel's name, he'd have to be careful not to come out and say his interest in Philomene was official Project Justice business. The work he and Mitch were doing was completely unofficial, and Daniel would blow a gasket if he thought Eric was invoking his foundation's name where it wasn't legitimate.

But no harm in letting the sheriff—and maybe that obnoxious D.A.—know that Eric *knew* Daniel Logan.

"He seemed really nice when I talked to him. I thought if anyone even read the application I sent in, it would be some intern or something. I was shocked when the head guy himself called me."

"Most of the time Daniel doesn't get personally involved in cases. But occasionally he sees something that intrigues him."

"I really thought he was going to help me."

Eric felt that twinge of guilt, which was becoming way too familiar. "You were right—it was my fault the case got dropped. But I felt like I didn't have any choice."

"You did, though," she said quietly. "You shouldn't have let a personal vendetta get in the way of justice."

Oh, hell, he shouldn't have brought this up. They were just going to end up yelling at each other again.

But Bree didn't yell. "Maybe you could talk to him."

"Talk to who?"

"Kelly. Maybe if you guys talked about what happened—"

"Are you insane? There is no way I would ever go face-to-face with that guy again. Not ever." Eric fervently hoped that Kelly had forgotten about him. What a horrible mistake it would be to jog the convict's memory. "It was a long, hard battle getting myself out of that hellhole. No way would I ever set foot in Huntsville again."

Bree was silent for a while, then said, "Now imagine if you didn't have people on the outside who loved you and wanted you to be free. Imagine if you'd been stuck in that disgusting place the rest of your life. I am the only one standing between Kelly and that fate. He doesn't deserve what he got. He doesn't deserve what you got."

Ah, hell, she was crying. Before, she'd shown him only anger. That he could deal with. But the tears?

"I'm sorry, Bree. I know it has to be hell for you. But I did what I believe is the right thing." *Except, perhaps, for telling Daniel that huge lie*. Daniel was not a man to be lightly crossed. If he ever found out, the results wouldn't be pretty. But Eric would face the consequences if he really believed Kelly was harmless. Unfortunately, that just wasn't the case.

Bree said nothing, just dabbed at her eyes with a tissue. Eric couldn't think of one thing to say that might comfort her. For a guy known for his facility with words—one of the reasons he'd joined the legal profession—he was remarkably unskilled at saying the right thing when he was with Bree.

"NOT THIS AGAIN." Becker County sheriff Bobby DeVille was a caricature of a bumbling but corrupt local cop. In fact, he had more than a passing resemblance to Jackie Gleason as he'd appeared in *Smokey and the Bandit*. So far he'd been barely civil to Bree, and he'd shaken Eric's hand only with obvious reluctance. "How many times am I going to have to listen to this story?"

"I have new information," Bree said in a calm, neutral voice. Eric admired her control. "Philomene's phone was stolen. It turned up in the possession of a drug dealer."

"And how did you come across this information?" the sheriff asked.

"The drug dealer's mother found the phone and started calling the recently called numbers to find out whose it was." This was the story Bree and Eric had agreed on, rather than implicating Mitch in what had obviously been some kind of illegal access to phone records. "It's sounding more like Philomene met with foul play, right?"

"Do you know how many cell phones get stolen in a day?"

"Sheriff DeVille," Eric began, "I know you don't have the resources to chase down every person who leaves town without telling someone where they're going. But a number of factors grouped together like this—"

"Save me your big-word lawyer speech," the sheriff said tiredly. "Find me some blood. Or find her car abandoned someplace. Then I might think about suspecting foul play. But Philomene Switzer isn't some innocent kid. She has a checkered past—been arrested a time or two."

"Not for a long time," Bree objected. "She's worked so hard to straighten out her life. She had a good job, an apartment—"

"And a boyfriend who'd run up her credit cards." The sheriff raised one eyebrow. "I see I've surprised you. I'm not as ill-informed as you seem to think. It's entirely possible she disappeared to avoid paying her debts."

"You're right," Bree said, sounding just short of defeated. "I didn't know that."

"What does this boyfriend look like?" Eric asked. "Maybe he's the one we saw at her apartment Wednesday night."

"I got a picture of him. He's not exactly a stranger here." The sheriff disappeared but returned shortly with an old-fashioned mug book. God, was the sheriff's department not even computerized? How could any modern law enforcement agency survive without access to the NCIC database? Or AFIS, to run fingerprints through?

DeVille flipped a couple of pages in the book until he found what he wanted. "There. Jerrod Crowley."

Bree and Eric both bent their heads over the book. They were so close that Eric felt her hair brush against his ear as it fell across her cheek. He could smell her. A certain part of his anatomy stirred and he jumped. The sensation was both familiar and alien—alien because it had been so long since he'd let a woman do this to him.

Why her? Why now?

"Is that the guy?" Bree asked.

Eric forced himself to concentrate on the mug shot of Jerrod Crowley. Large build, straggly medium-length brown hair, fair skin. "It could be him. I'm not a hundred percent sure—he ran by really fast."

"Was he wearing overalls?" the sheriff asked.

"Yeah. How did you know that?"

"'Cause that's all Jerrod Crowley ever wears. Musta been him, then. Came over for a booty call, found the place deserted and decided to see what he could steal."

"Or he did something to her." Bree's hard-fought-for calm had deserted her. "Aren't you even going to question him?"

"Please. Crowley doesn't have the brains or the drive to commit a murder and then conceal it. He tried to steal a car once." The sheriff burst out laughing. "What an effing joke that was."

"But he might know something," Bree insisted. "He might have seen something."

"If I run across him, I'll have a chat," the sheriff said mildly. "Anything else?"

Bree and Eric exchanged a look. She wanted him to play the Daniel card, but he honestly couldn't figure out a way to work it into the conversation.

"Well, maybe Daniel Logan will talk to him," Bree said. "Eric works for him, you know. Mr. Logan is very interested in the Kelly Ralston case and everything associated with it, including Philomene."

Eric took a sharp breath. What was Bree doing?

"Am I supposed to know who this Logan fella is?" the sheriff asked.

"Daniel Logan. The oil billionaire, runs Logan Energy?"

The sheriff shrugged one of his massive shoulders. "Means nothing to me."

"He's a very powerful man," Bree said. "He's personal friends with the governor."

"Well, if he comes here throwing his weight around, I'll tell him the same thing I told you. No sign of foul play, no investigation. He's welcome to look into it all he wants."

"Sheriff DeVille—Philomene wanted to recant her testimony about Kelly. She said she felt pressured to identify him in the lineup. What if the real murderer—"

"I don't want to hear this crap!" the sheriff exploded.

"Now, wait a minute," Eric objected. "You can't talk to your constituents that way."

"Oh, really? In my office, I can talk any way I damn well please. Now get out, both of you. Before I find something to charge you with."

"Fine," Bree said tightly. "But when she turns up dead, it'll be on you."

Eric held his tongue until they were outside. "Bree! I thought we agreed we weren't going to lie about Daniel's involvement."

"I didn't. Well, not exactly. Daniel *was* very interested in Kelly's case. Until you ruined that."

"I'll only warn you once more. Daniel will not take kindly to anyone using his name without permission. He'll come after you."

"So you never intended to play the Daniel card at all?"

"If I had, I'd do it without crossing the line. Which you left far behind in your rearview mirror."

She challenged him with her blue-eyed laser stare, but he didn't back down. He was right about this, and she needed to understand about Daniel, for her own good.

Finally she looked away. "Okay. Maybe I got a little carried away. Didn't matter anyway. DeVille was completely immune to the threat of Daniel's involvement."

"A possible sign that despite his rudeness, he's not corrupt. Or derelict in his duties, at least not to his mind. He didn't show a lick of fear."

"No, he didn't. So what now?"

"I don't suppose you'd consider giving up? No," he said quickly when she shot him a venomous look.

"We're gonna talk to Jerrod Crowley."

"I was afraid of that."

# CHAPTER SIX

BREE KNEW SHE wasn't playing fair. She'd found Eric's Achilles' heel—he had a chivalrous streak a mile wide—and she was exploiting it. She wasn't normally a manipulative person. But too much was at stake for her to play nice. First Kelly's freedom and now Philomene's life. No matter how the evidence stacked up, Bree was convinced the woman had not left Tuckerville of her own free will.

"You're sure you want to talk to this guy?" Eric asked. They'd found Crowley's address easily enough. All they'd had to do was stop at the gas station on Main Street, where a bunch of guys had been hanging out, smoking and drinking not very well-disguised beer. They'd looked like the kind of lowlifes who would associate with someone like Crowley, and sure enough, they were. Turned out he'd lived with his brother and sister-in-law in a spare bedroom since his parents had kicked him out. The gas station lowlifes hadn't even hesitated to bad-mouth their supposed friend.

"How did Philomene hook up with a jerk like Jerrod?" Eric asked as they let his GPS lead them to Crowley's address.

"A lot of people said the same thing about me when Kelly and I were dating," Bree said a bit huffily. "'What's the mayor's daughter doing with a guy whose father is a drunk and whose mother works at the counter of a doughnut shop?'"

"I've wondered that myself," Eric said. "Though I didn't know you were the mayor's daughter."

"Kelly was a sweet guy. Yeah, he'd been in a few scrapes, but nothing serious. Shoplifting. Probably because he was hungry, or he wanted something for his mom. I remember once, on Mother's Day, he didn't have enough money to buy her a present, so he stole a potted daylily off someone's front porch." She laughed.

"I'm sure his mother was proud," Eric said, tongue firmly in cheek.

"She was thrilled. And she didn't ask how he got the money, though she probably knew he hadn't bought the plant at the local nursery. Anyway, Jerrod Crowley must have some redeeming qualities. Maybe Philomene saw something about him that no one else did. Maybe he was just nice to her, and that was all it took. Philomene is..." Bree shrugged.

"Damaged from the rape? Low self-esteem?"

"Yeah. She didn't grow up with a good home situation. I don't remember her when she was younger, but I'm guessing she was the kind who always tried a little too hard, wore too much makeup and let any boy have his way if she thought he had feelings for her. Girls like that are so easy to victimize. And I don't think that rape was the first time she was a victim, either. I mean, I don't know her that well. Not well at all. But I can read between the lines."

"That's sad. I really hope I can raise MacKenzie to think more of herself than that. I mean, she's already a victim, indirectly. In all likelihood she witnessed her mother's murder. It's certainly had an effect on her."

"Oh, God. I didn't know that."

"We don't know for sure, because she doesn't remember that day. Or at least, she won't talk about it if she does. But she hasn't been the same since it happened."

"She seems bright. And sweet."

"She is. I just hope she's not *too* sweet."

"Arriving at destination," Suzy the GPS said, "on right."

"The brown brick house," Bree said.

They were in a 1950s subdivision of cookie-cutter houses.

"Nice trees," Bree remarked. The houses might be cheap and a little shabby, but mature live oak trees elevated the neighborhood's appeal.

A pleasant-looking woman in her thirties with a toddler on her hip answered the door wearing a look of caution. "Yes?"

"Does Jerrod Crowley live here?" Bree asked. Eric was content to let her do the talking; she was less intimidating and people were more likely to drop their guards.

If anything, the woman at the door looked even more wary. "Jesus. What's he done this time?"

"Nothing that we know of," Bree said. "We're trying to find his girlfriend."

"Oh. Well, Jerrod's not here. He's supposedly out looking for a job now that he's got a car. That'll be the day."

"Do you know when he'll be back?"

"God only knows. He comes home when he runs out of money to buy beer." The woman's sturdy body blocked the door. There was zero chance she'd invite them in to wait.

"So he has money now?" Eric asked.

"He comes up with a little cash every once in a while—mows a lawn or details someone's car. That's what he used to do when he had a job. What's up with Phil? Is she in trouble? I don't know her that well, but she seems like one of the nicer girls he's gone with."

"We can't find her, that's all," Bree said. "Has Jerrod said anything about her disappearing?"

The woman frowned. "No. God, I hope…"

"You hope what?" Eric prodded.

"Nothing. Oh, hey, you're in luck. That's him now."

A blue Toyota Corolla was coming down the street way too fast. It whipped into the driveway with a screech of brakes.

"Oh, my God," Bree said under her breath.

Exactly what Eric had been about to say. Jerrod was driving Philomene's car.

RATHER THAN WAITING for Jerrod to exit the car, Eric was across the postage-stamp lawn in three long strides. He wasn't going to give this jerk a chance to flee as he had the other night. The second the driver's door opened, Eric had the man by his elbow and was dragging him out of the car.

"Hey!" Jerrod screamed as Eric shoved him up against the car. "What the—"

"Jerrod Crowley. Want to tell me what you're doing with that car?"

"I didn't steal it, if that's what you're thinking. Get the hell away from me before I break your nose!"

Eric wasn't worried. This guy was soft and doughy, and the fear in his eyes gave him away. He was the type to run rather than fight. Eric could take him any day of the week.

"How did you get this car?"

"It's my girlfriend's."

"And where is Philomene?"

"Look, I don't know. She vanished couple of days ago, no warning. Then she texted me, said she was leaving town for a while. Check my phone. The text is still there."

Eric loosened his grip on Jerrod, just enough that the man could reach in his back pocket and pull out his phone.

Jerrod scrolled through his texts for a few seconds, then handed the phone to Eric. "Right there. See?"

The text was dated Tuesday, the same day Philomene had stood them up at the Home Cookin'

Café. The message had originated from Philomene's phone—Eric recognized the number by now.

HAD TO LEAVE FOR A WHILE. PICK UP MY CAR AT CURRY ROAD & 238. KEYS UNDER MAT. LOVE YOU.

"He could have texted that message to himself," Bree said.

Eric jumped. He hadn't realized she'd come up behind him. "So he could explain why he has her car."

"Are you guys cops?" Jerrod asked dubiously.

It was tempting to say yes. The second Jerrod knew they were civilians with no authority over him, he would cease to cooperate. But impersonating a cop came with some pretty severe penalties. Eric wasn't above allowing someone to believe something that wasn't true, but he wasn't going to lie about it. He'd done enough lying this week to last him awhile.

"We're not cops," Eric said.

"Then get your friggin' hands off me." Jerrod shook off Eric's grip.

"We're worried about Philomene," Bree said. "And if you care anything about her, you should be worried, too."

"She took off. What's the big deal? People do it all the time."

"Then why did she abandon her car at some intersection in the middle of nowhere?" Bree countered.

"I figured she met some guy there. Phil wasn't too

happy with me lately—it was only a matter of time before she moved on. I was kinda surprised she left her car with me. She never loaned it to me, not after I put a big scratch in the side. But then I thought maybe that was her way of saying sorry. You know. For dumping me."

Jerrod's story was plausible...barely. At any rate, Eric wasn't willing to threaten the guy with any more violence. Already Eric could be charged with assault. He took a step back, giving the other man some breathing room.

"Sorry, dude," he said. "I'm just worried about Philomene. I went a little crazy there."

"Why do *you* care about her?" Jerrod asked suspiciously. "She sleeping with you, too?"

"No, nothing like that."

"We're her friends, that's all." Bree placed her hand on Eric's arm. "Come on, this is getting us nowhere. Let's go look somewhere else."

Eric would have preferred to stay here and pound some more answers out of Jerrod. If they really were cops, they would ask the same questions over and over in different ways, trying to get Jerrod to change his story. But Bree was uncomfortable.

"If you find her," Jerrod said, "tell her to call me. She's still got some DVDs of mine, and if we're through, I want 'em back."

"You don't sound that broken up about getting dumped," Eric observed.

Jerrod shrugged. "Like I said, it didn't come as a big surprise."

Bree said nothing until they were back in the car. "Wow. Here I thought you were some mild-mannered lawyer, and you go all Rambo on that poor guy."

"'That poor guy' is our best suspect. Why would Philomene abandon her car if she was leaving town? And why would she give it to a guy like that?"

"Yeah, but *someone* texted Jerrod. If he did it himself, why didn't he cook up a better story?"

"Because he's not too bright?"

"Yeah, well, bright or not, he could have you arrested for the way you manhandled him."

Since Eric had been thinking the same thing, he didn't argue. He didn't quite understand the urge to physically intimidate Jerrod—he wasn't a naturally violent person. He'd just taken an instant dislike to Crowley.

"Do you normally solve conflicts with your fists?"

"No."

"Did you get into fights in prison?"

"You know about at least one."

"Yeah, but according to you, that was an accident. You were trying to *stop* a fight. Were there other times?"

"Sometimes it's unavoidable. If you don't defend yourself, you become your cellblock's favorite punching bag." Or worse. He'd had no choice but to learn to fight.

"Before you went to prison, would you have pushed Jerrod Crowley around?"

He had to think about that for a few moments. She seemed genuinely interested, so he tried to give her an honest answer. "I'm not the same person I was before Tammy's murder. It's hard for me to even remember what it felt like to be that 'mild-mannered lawyer' you mentioned. But, yeah, before prison, I hadn't raised my fists since high school."

"So prison can change a man."

"I would argue it's impossible to spend *any* time in prison and not be fundamentally changed."

"So isn't it conceivable that the Kelly Ralston you knew wasn't violent when he went into prison? That the environment changed him into the person who knifed you?"

Damn it. She'd tricked him. He was supposed to be the one with the logical arguments, yet he'd stumbled right into that one.

"I don't deny it's possible. But I don't believe it."

"You're just being bullheaded."

"What's he like with you? I mean, do you visit him?"

"Sure. Not all that often. Every month or two. And he's...the same guy my teenage self fell in love with all those years ago. A little sadder, maybe. He never used to be depressed like he is now. He used to be so full of plans, a man of big ideas. But he's still kind and gentle and loving—loving in an I-still-care-about-you-even-though-we-broke-up way."

"So the way he behaved with you is completely contrary to how he acted with the other inmates. We're talking about two months ago, three months ago. Therefore, isn't it possible he showed you a different side of himself even back when he committed the crime? That he showed you a kind and gentle side, and when you weren't around, he was violent?"

"I would have seen some sign of that in him," Bree said stubbornly. "I knew him better than anyone."

Eric let it ride. He would never convince her that her old flame was a monster. "So where is this intersection where Jerrod picked up Philomene's car?" Eric asked.

"You think we should go there? It's an intersection a couple of miles out of town. No houses or businesses around, so there aren't any potential witnesses to interview."

"I just want to have a look around." He didn't know precisely what he would look for. Tire tracks? Footprints? Blood?

Hell, it was only a couple of miles. He felt as if he needed to gather as much information as possible.

Once they left the Tuckerville city limits, they found themselves in the middle of nowhere. Farmland spread out on either side of them—crop fields, grazing land, an old windmill that still turned lazily in the breeze.

They were on Highway 238, which was nothing but a rough two-lane farm-to-market road.

"Curry Road is that next stop sign," Bree said after a couple of minutes.

Eric pulled his car over before they reached the stop sign. If there were any tire tracks or footprints, he didn't want to obliterate them. He unfastened his seat belt and got out.

Bree followed suit. "Do you really think you'll learn anything?"

"No." He walked slowly toward the intersection, looking around, listening. All he heard was the wind in the tall grass, a few bird chirps, the occasional moo of a cow.

"Is the land around here all privately owned?"

"I think so."

"Is there any water nearby?"

"Just watering tanks for the cattle."

"No private lakes?"

"Oh, God. You think whoever left Philomene's car here might have—" Bree shuddered "—disposed of the body here?"

"I don't really think that," Eric said quickly. He didn't want to upset Bree more than necessary. She'd no doubt dealt with violent death before—car accidents and the like. But she probably hadn't known anyone who'd been murdered. She might even be feeling guilty because she was the one who pushed Philomene to talk about her false identification of Kelly. "This scenario might also fit the theory that she fled. She could have met her ride out of town here just to be sure no one saw who she left with."

"The only reason she would do that is if she felt threatened. Which begs the question, who threatened her?"

"Maybe no one, directly."

"I'm sorry, but a case of cold feet wouldn't cause her to go to such extreme measures. She could have simply told me she'd changed her mind. And if she did leave town, why give up her car? Doesn't add up."

Eric was beginning to agree with Bree.

They walked through the intersection to the other side, and Eric found something interesting. The ground had been wet two nights ago after a recent rain. He could see the impression of two tires, the treads clearly defined and hardened, now that the ground had dried out.

As Eric contemplated the tire tracks, which looked to be those of a passenger car, not a large truck or ATV, Bree crouched down to examine something else.

"Whatcha got?" Eric asked.

"Maybe a footprint. Like someone was standing behind the car."

*Pulling something out of the trunk?* Eric refrained from speculating out loud, but he probably didn't have to. Bree could speculate very well all on her own.

"There's not very much detail, but we could at least determine the shoe size," she said.

Obviously, they didn't have any way to take a cast of the impressions left in the mud. But Eric did have his phone, which had a good camera. Now all he needed was something to indicate scale. Crime scene photographers always had some kind of ruler with them. Eric would have to improvise. He pulled his phone out of his jacket pocket. "Do you have anything that's a standard size? Or just something we can measure later?"

"Oh, clever." She reached into the back pocket of her jeans. "I have a packet of tissues."

"That'll do."

Bree placed the tissue pack alongside the clearest of the tire impressions, and Eric snapped a few shots. They repeated the process for the footprint. Then Eric measured the distance between the two tires by walking between them toe to heel.

"What are you going to do with these pictures?" Bree asked.

"I figure we'll tell the sheriff what we learned about Philomene's car, then send him copies of the photos."

"Oh." She sounded disappointed. "He probably *still* won't do anything. He'll argue the same thing Jerrod did—she must have met a boyfriend out here and left with him. The tire prints probably came from her car. And he'll say the text message proves she was okay. Lazy SOB," she muttered.

As they returned to his car, Eric pondered the problem. He could show the photos to Beth at Project Justice. She ran the small but well-equipped lab at the foundation, and with Mitch's help she could get her hands on just about any database—including tire and shoe patterns—to identify who and what had stopped by this roadside.

But he'd only been working there for a few days. It wasn't as if he'd racked up any favors he could call in. And asking his coworkers to work on a case that wasn't foundation business, on their own time, was a pretty big favor.

"If DeVille still won't investigate, maybe we could talk to the Texas Rangers," Eric suggested.

"Oh, man, the sheriff wouldn't like that at all. He doesn't like anyone interfering in his business."

"Yeah, but he's told us loud and clear that he doesn't consider Philomene's disappearance his business."

"Ooh, good point. Still, I can't imagine the Rangers would listen to me. They probably have more important stuff to do than look for someone who might not really be missing. Even if I'm sure she is."

But Daniel had friends at the Texas Rangers. If Project Justice had taken on Kelly's case, Eric would have been free to ask anyone for anything, and no one would have blinked. Daniel would have been on the phone to someone at the Rangers in seconds flat.

Eric didn't voice any of these thoughts aloud. He didn't want to give Bree any more reason to try to persuade him to change his mind about Kelly. And that was all it would take. If Eric went to Daniel and said he had second thoughts about Kelly's guilt,

Daniel would reverse his decision and put Kelly's case in the queue.

*No way.* He wasn't going to do *anything* that might result in that animal being let loose on society.

On him and his family.

"Let's wait and see what DeVille says. Then you can decide whether to talk to the Rangers. Maybe there's some other way to light a fire under the sheriff. Maybe threaten to lodge some kind of complaint against him. Or tell him you'll go to the press. That's usually a pretty effective gesture."

"Doubt it would work with DeVille. He's buddies with every judge in Becker County and a few on the state level, as well."

"What about the newspaper? Or a local TV station? Get some enterprising investigative journalist interested in this, and we won't have to investigate anything. He or she will take over, and they might be better at it than we are."

"Actually, I think we've done pretty well so far. We found Philomene's car, and we figured out who has or had her phone, and we have a suspect."

He didn't want to burst Bree's bubble, but they'd probably gone about as far as they could go on their own.

Obviously sensing his ambivalence, she persisted. "Oh, come on, you don't think we make a pretty good team?"

So tempting to agree with her. Under any other circumstances… He tried not to visibly grimace as he ruthlessly suppressed the attraction he felt toward her. Perhaps they would make a good team if they both had the same goal. He contemplated the slight pout she wore on her face—not a manipulative expression, he was sure, but a genuine reflection of her disappointment in him.

"We've accomplished more than I thought we would," he finally conceded.

"Well of course we did, since you didn't think there was anything *to* investigate."

"I'm still not sure there is." But the argument was knee-jerk at this point. He hoped Philomene would turn up. As uninterested as he was in having her dredge up Kelly Ralston's crimes and call his guilt into question, he would feel awful if anything happened to her.

They stopped by the sheriff's office, but DeVille wasn't around. Nor could dispatch locate him.

"He probably forgot to turn on his phone again," said Joan, the longtime dispatch operator, who seemed far more interested in watching the video streaming on her own phone than being of service. She probably didn't have a lot to do in this tiny rural county, which had a distinctly Mayberry vibe. And she probably liked it that way. "You want to leave a message?"

"Yes." Bree pulled a notebook and pen from her purse and spent a couple of minutes writing out a note for the sheriff. Eric couldn't see exactly what she wrote, but he noticed her underlining several words and phrases, sometimes three or four times.

Joan took it from her without comment and set it on her messy desk. Eric suspected the note wouldn't be Joan's first priority when the sheriff returned.

Once they were outside again, Bree sighed. "Sometimes I hate living in a small town. I mean, I love knowing almost everyone, and the slower pace is nice. And the lower crime rate. And the lower cost of living."

"It's cleaner here, too. I was amazed how many stars I could see."

"Yeah, I guess. But it's backward here, too. Lots of outdated attitudes. People here are suspicious of anyone or anything that's different. Just convincing women here that they need to get mammograms is a huge battle, and the hospital has had the machine for twenty years!"

"Small towns have no monopoly on inflexible people, trust me." He checked his phone for the time, surprised and oddly disappointed that the day had gone by so quickly. Despite not finding Philomene, he couldn't deny a certain degree of…stimulation spending time with Bree. He'd caught himself more than once watching her when she wasn't looking, pondering what motivated her, what made her so determined to free her ex-boyfriend and now just as determined to locate a woman who was only an acquaintance. Most people would have washed their hands of this situation by now, but not Bree.

He wondered what she was like at work. Not that he wanted to become a patient at the E.R. to find out, but he bet it was a sight to see. She would fight like a wildcat to give her patients the best care, and she would take it hard—perhaps even personally— if they died.

"The traffic is going to get bad if you don't head back pretty soon," she said.

"I don't have to rush off. If there's anything else you think we should do—"

"Come on, I saw you checking your phone. If I don't abuse your goodwill, maybe you'll come back sometime."

It surprised him how much he would like that. What was going on here? He had no business think- ing about Bree on any terms except professionally. "If there's anything I can help with, I'm willing. I started out helping you under protest, but the mys- tery of Philomene's whereabouts has gotten under my skin." He was way more invested in that than in prov- ing Ralston's innocence, even though the two might turn out to be connected. "Maybe this weekend?"

*God, let her say no.*

"I don't want to drag you away from your little girl," Bree said. "But you could bring her with you."

The last time he'd brought MacKenzie to Tucker- ville, he'd regretted it. The memory of interrupting Jerrod during his break-in still turned his stomach. "I don't think I should involve her."

"Oh, right. Of course I wouldn't want to expose

her to dangerous neighborhoods or sketchy people. But maybe…" Bree shook her head with a rueful smile. "Never mind."

"What were you going to say?"

"Nothing. Let's get going so you can get on the road."

"Trying to get rid of me?"

"Trying to stop making unreasonable demands on you. You've helped a lot, really."

"I'm not done yet. I'll get back to you about the tire prints and footprints."

"Okay."

She looked sad. Did she not have anyone else to lean on, anyone who could shoulder this burden of worry with her? "Bree, I've never asked this, but maybe I should have. Do you have family here? A husband, boyfriend, parents, siblings?"

"Parents. My dad's a county judge now. They live on a little hobby farm—a few cows and chickens."

"What do they have to say about your quest to free Kelly?"

"I don't speak to them about it."

So she was a lone crusader. He couldn't help but wonder if that was significant—that she'd never enlisted anyone else to help her. No one but him, anyway.

Was the woman crazy? Was he thinking with his gonads? She seemed reasonable, but maybe he was fooled by the fact she was a doctor and so well-spoken. Educated people with good vocabularies always sounded reasonable, even when what they said was crackers.

"What time is it, anyway?" She dug through her purse for her own phone and wasn't coming up with it.

"It's a little after three."

"Oh, jeez, I'm gonna be late for work. Would you mind dropping me off at the hospital on your way? I can get a ride to my car later. It's a little out of your way—"

"It's no problem."

"Thanks." Her smile was warm. Little by little, Bree Johnson had been dropping her guard around him. He hadn't missed the fact that the harder and longer he worked toward finding Philomene, the warmer she got.

Now he had to question not only his own judgment for getting involved in this mess but his ethics, too. Was he helping her because he genuinely believed Philomene was in trouble? Or did he want something else?

The familiar guilt settled around his heart as he opened his car door for Bree, letting his gaze linger on the smooth skin above the collar of her shirt, the gentle swell of the tops of her breasts. Her shirt was by no means suggestive, but his mind didn't need anyone else's suggestions to conjure images of Bree's naked body. It could do that all on its own.

He shouldn't feel guilty for appreciating a beautiful woman. Tammy had been wildly unfaithful;

he owed her no loyalty. But he still felt connected to her. At the time of her murder, he'd thought they were both in love. He'd gone into deep mourning. Though he shouldn't cling to a memory of something that hadn't existed, convincing his heart to let go was easier said than done.

By the time Eric slid behind the wheel, Bree was buckled in and digging through her purse again. "I still can't find my phone."

"When did you last see it?" Eric was used to asking this question. MacKenzie fretted excessively when she couldn't find one of her toys. She liked to know where all of them were at all times.

"I had it at the café when I stopped in to grab a coffee…."

"You want to swing by there first?"

"Yes. I can't go without my phone. I'll have to start calling you Eric's Taxi Service. But at least I can pick up my car."

"Will you be late for work?"

"Only a little."

Three more minutes and they were at the café. Really, there was nowhere in town that wasn't accessible in the time it took to put on your sunglasses.

"You can just drop me off," Bree said when Eric pulled into a parking space.

"Thought I'd come in and get an iced tea for the road." That was just an excuse, though, to spend another minute or two in Bree's company. What the hell was wrong with him?

"Molly," Bree said breathlessly to the hostess the moment she cleared the door. "Did I leave my—"

Molly was already reaching behind the cashier's desk with a knowing look on her face. "You mean this?"

"Oh, thank God. You know how it is. My entire life is on this phone. Did I just leave it sitting on the counter?" Bree asked as she scrolled through messages.

"Yup. You'd be surprised how many people do that."

"Well, thanks. And can you get Eric a large iced tea to go? On me."

"That's not—" Eric started to object, but Bree held up a hand to stop him.

"Least I could do. Consider it taxi fare." She still was engrossed in her phone. Apparently she did have friends, or an awful lot of strangers who called and texted her.

"Eric." Her voice was suddenly tense with excitement. "You're not going to believe this. Philomene texted me."

## CHAPTER SEVEN

"Really?" A surge of relief rushed through Eric's veins. Although he'd never even met the woman, he would have felt horrible if she'd met with foul play. "When?"

"Just a few minutes ago. I didn't see it right away, because it's a new number. I get a lot of spam, so I check messages from unknown numbers only after I look at everything else."

"What did she say?"

"Here, read it for yourself." She handed the phone to him, and he scanned the few lines of text.

It's me, Philomene. Lost my phone and just now bought a replacement. Sorry I waited so long to call. Please don't worry, I just need to think things through.

"Ugh, I feel so stupid now." Bree pounded her forehead with the heel of her hand. "Running around insisting she was missing, dragging you all the way here."

"It's okay."

"Now I really owe you."

"You don't owe me anything, Bree. The iced tea is payment in full, okay?"

"Considering that we got off to a bad start, you're being awful nice to me."

He shrugged. "I admire that you care enough to *do* something when you feel something isn't right. It's a rare trait. Most people don't bother."

Her face turned a delicate shade of pink. It made him grin to realize he'd caused her to blush.

"Well, anyway, have a safe drive home."

"I'll do my best."

They stood there for several heartbeats, and Eric found himself leaning closer to those plump, strawberry-kissed lips.

Bree didn't shy away from him. She raised her chin a fraction of an inch.

He couldn't resist. He kissed her, right there in the café in front of everybody.

The brush of lips was brief. Bree sucked in a breath and looked at him, surprised.

Eric touched his lips with his fingers. What a strange impulse. He was usually more circumspect.

Bree cleared her throat and stepped farther away from him as a waitress appeared to hand his tea to him. He thanked her, nodded to Bree and turned away before he acted like an even bigger fool.

He was so distracted by reliving that miraculous kiss that he was halfway home before something awful occurred to him. He should have thought of it first thing; even the most green of investigators at Project Justice would have. But now, away from Bree, his brain was working normally again and he had to ask himself: How did they know that text really was from Philomene?

ERIC HAD HOPED to be home before MacKenzie arrived from kindergarten, but she beat him by a couple of hours—and she was cranky about it.

"You said you didn't have to work today." She somehow managed to maintain her pout even while berating him.

"I know, sweetheart, but something came up. Anyway, I'm home now. We can go to PizzaMania for dinner if you want." PizzaMania was the one place he could take his daughter that guaranteed she wouldn't pick at her meal. But he had mixed feelings about the shortage of fruits and vegetables in pizza, so he tried to limit their visits to the kid-friendly restaurant.

"Uncle Trav is making Stroge-noff!" she objected, on the verge of panic.

"Okay, okay. We'll do pizza another night."

"Tomorrow?"

"I may have to…" Stop. Rewind. He'd been getting ready to say he might have to work late. Everyone at the foundation would probably have to work double time to make up for the roach-eradication vacation.

But he'd promised himself when he took this job that he would always put MacKenzie first. He considered himself a good, attentive father. Before

Tammy's death, he'd spent a lot of time with his daughter. Whenever he'd been at home, he'd focused all of his attention on her.

Which might explain why his wife had strayed.

Back then, he'd considered long hours a necessity if he wanted to excel as a real-estate legal eagle. Tammy had made it clear what she expected in terms of his career progress and his income. She'd told him exactly when he should make partner, and the piece of jewelry he would buy her when they celebrated his promotion.

At the time it had seemed like she'd been showing her faith in him, her support of his goals. Now he wondered if Tammy hadn't just seen him as her two-legged cash register.

Things would be different now. He no longer felt the need to rise to the top of his field. Developing and maintaining strong bonds with his daughter, making sure she had what she needed to grow up into a happy, healthy and productive person were the only goals that mattered.

Working ridiculous hours wasn't part of that equation. The generous salary Daniel paid him didn't mean he had to live and breathe his job.

"You know, yeah, let's make tomorrow a date. PizzaMania. And tonight we'll enjoy Travis's beef Stroganoff. But I do expect to see some vegetables on your plate."

MacKenzie wrinkled her nose. But she didn't flat out say no, which was progress. She did seem to be regaining some of her former healthy eating habits. Her therapist said Eric should rejoice in every small step that signaled a return to normalcy.

Eric sat down on the edge of her bed, where she'd stationed herself to pout. "Now, why don't you tell me what you did at school today. Or better yet, show me."

She clamored off the bed and went to the closet, where she had a shelf set aside for her school papers, which she stacked neatly and paper-clipped together. Solemnly she handed him today's stack.

The first paper was a series of pictures of fruits and vegetables. She had filled in missing letters in the names of the fruits and colored the images— brown.

"You really like brown, don't you?" If she hadn't exhibited a love for color before her mom's death, he would have suspected she was color-blind.

"Brown is good. My teacher is Ms. Brown."

"Okay. What's this?" The next picture was a stereotypical stick-figure family—mom, dad, kid, dog. The picture was predictably drawn in brown crayon— except for a dash of purple.

"That's us. There's you and me and Pixie."

"And Mommy." Eric pointed to the obvious stick lady; even though it wore pants, it wore a necklace and had a ponytail.

"No, Daddy," MacKenzie said patiently. "This is Mommy up here." She pointed to a blob up in the sky with wings that he'd thought was a bird.

His heart did a flip-flop. She'd portrayed Tammy as an angel.

"She's in heaven," MacKenzie added. "She's watching us and praying for us."

"Nice." Eric wondered who'd told her that. No one around here was overtly religious, and he doubted any of her teachers in public school taught concepts of heaven and prayer, though he wouldn't object if some sympathetic teacher had attempted to comfort MacKenzie regarding her dead mother. It was also entirely possible another child had said something.

"If that's Mommy, then who is this?" He pointed to the ponytail figure. He figured it was Elena or maybe her teacher; the therapist had said that when a child's family was ruptured at such a young age, she might be fuzzy on the whole concept of family for a while.

"That's Dr. Bree."

"Oh." *In our family?* "I guess you liked her, huh."

"Yeah, she's nice. But she's not Mommy."

"No, of course not."

"There's only one Mommy, right? Except my friend Heather has two, 'cause her parents got divorced and her dad married this other lady, who picks up Heather from school sometimes."

"Well, you only have one. And she is watching over you. And she would be so proud of you. Especially when you eat your vegetables."

Again there was a nose wrinkle. "Heather says

having two is good because she gets twice the presents on her birthday."

Eric was glad he didn't have to negotiate that parental mess. Having a live-in aunt and uncle was about as complicated as it was going to get, and before too long they would find their own place.

"I don't want two mommies," MacKenzie said.

"Well, don't worry. I have no plans to bring home a second one." His thoughts returned briefly to his kiss with Bree. The memory was so delicate it was almost as if it hadn't happened.

"You know why?"

"Why?"

"'Cause they would make me eat twice the vegetables." MacKenzie threw back her head and laughed so hard she snorted. Eric realized with a start that it was the first time he'd heard her laugh like that since Tammy's death.

He hugged her, and she wrapped her warm little arms around his neck. "You're the best," he whispered in her ear. "Best little girl ever."

"You're the best daddy ever," she returned cooperatively.

No, he wasn't. Not by a long shot. Sometimes he felt so helpless, like when she had a bad dream or a tummy ache or when she just cried for no reason. Sometimes she retreated inside herself, and he couldn't reach her.

Then they would share a moment like this.

He wondered again how "Dr. Bree" had earned a

spot in the family portrait, then dismissed the concern. At least MacKenzie had portrayed Tammy as an angel this time, which meant she was coming to terms with the fact her mother was "in heaven." MacKenzie still hadn't grasped the concept of death—the finality of it—but she had at least stopped expecting her mommy to walk through the door just as her daddy had.

Baby steps.

BREE TOOK A long sip of her coffee and looked at the text from Philomene for the umpteenth time. She'd slept badly the previous night, thinking about the missing woman and wondering where she was. Bree had tried calling the new number, but it always rolled to voice mail. So she kept reading the text over and over.

When she wasn't doing that, she was reliving that strange and wonderful moment when Eric had kissed her. She couldn't believe she'd let it happen. But when he'd leaned in, looking at her with undeniable hunger, it had seemed so natural to let the kiss happen.

She wondered who had seen and what they might make of it.

It was just an impulse, she told herself. Not to be repeated, best forgotten. She forcefully returned her thoughts to the text.

Was Philomene in trouble? Had she left some kind of coded message in those few simple words? Something about the text bothered Bree, but she couldn't put her finger on precisely what.

Bree had come early to the café for breakfast because Sheriff DeVille almost always did the same. He had not called her, despite the urgency she'd tried to convey in her note. Her only option was to ambush him.

When she saw Ted Gentry walk through the front door, she thought her patience was about to be rewarded. Ted and DeVille were often seen together, sometimes accompanied by District Attorney Needles. Bree had come to think of them as the Three Stooges, though it was perhaps unfair to lump Ted in with the other two. Of all of them, Ted seemed like the one who had the least to lose if Kelly's conviction were overturned. After all, physical evidence had barely played a role in that case. It was all witness testimony and some other thin circumstantial evidence. The man who had raped Philomene and murdered those other unfortunate women had been very, very careful. He hadn't left so much as an eyelash behind, and certainly no body fluids.

Unfortunately, Ted was alone this morning. She waved to him and motioned for him to join her.

As he made his way toward her booth, he seemed to be placing his steps very carefully, as if he were balancing on a beam.

She'd heard rumors that Ted had been hitting the bottle a little harder than usual lately. But at seven in the morning?

"Morning, Ted," she said amiably. "Join me for breakfast? I just ordered."

"Sure." He slid into the booth opposite her.

"Unless, of course, you're breakfasting with the sheriff this morning. I doubt he'd be too keen to share a table with me, since he's working so hard to avoid me."

"Is he?" Ted asked innocently.

"I have more information to support foul play in Philomene's disappearance. I left him a message yesterday and he hasn't even acknowledged it. If he was too busy himself, he could have at least asked Joan or one of the deputies to get back to me. Personal feelings aside, I am a citizen of Becker County."

"I guess you haven't heard, then."

Bree's stomach dropped, and she set her mug down on the table with a thud. "What?"

"You may think the sheriff is ignoring you, but he got your message." Ted lowered his voice. "Last night he seized Philomene's car and brought Jerrod Crowley in for questioning. They found blood in the trunk."

Bree let that information settle on her for a few moments. "That's…that's awful. Did they arrest him?"

"Not yet. But I thought you'd be glad someone's taking the case seriously."

"I am, but…I guess I was hoping Philomene would be found alive. The presence of blood is a bad sign."

"Well, yeah."

The waitress came by, poured coffee for both of them and took Ted's order. He requested one of those huge "farmer's breakfasts" with eggs, toast, bacon, sausage and hash browns. She wondered how he stayed so lean eating like that. As a doctor, he ought to know better, but she had long ago stopped chiding her friends over their dietary choices.

"I hadn't realized you even knew Philomene," Ted remarked.

"I didn't, not well. But she trusted me, as my patient. She unburdened herself on me. And I felt a certain responsibility toward her."

"It's not like you had anything to do with her boyfriend doing away with her."

"Oh, but I'm not sure Jerrod did it. Not at all."

"Really? You know him?"

"I only met him once. But someone pretended to be Philomene and texted him where to find her car. Someone wanted to make it look like he had something to do with her vanishing."

Ted scratched his head. "How do you know all this?"

"Jerrod told me. And sure, maybe he was lying. Except I received a text, too. Yesterday. Well after Jerrod was seen driving his girlfriend's car. Something's out of whack here."

"Did you tell the sheriff about your text?"

"Not yet. I was hoping to run into him, since he won't return my calls."

"If I see him, I'll tell him to call you. But Bree…

don't get invested in Jerrod's innocence, okay? The guy's a loser with a long rap sheet. You don't need another cause to crusade for."

Great. Ted thought she had some kind of complex, always willing to believe every man accused of a crime was innocent.

"And don't give up on Philomene, either. The blood in the trunk might mean nothing. It's an old car. You never know—someone could have put a deer carcass in there. My cousin did that one time. Hit a deer late at night, decided it was a waste of good venison to just leave it there, so he stuffed it into the trunk of his Buick. God, what a mess."

The waitress brought their food. Bree didn't have much of an appetite left, but she forced herself to eat a few spoonfuls of yogurt and at least some of the fresh fruit.

"Ted," she said after a long silence, "would you do me a favor? Could you let me know what's going on with the investigation? Obviously DeVille isn't going to keep me in the loop."

"Frankly, Bree, there's no reason you should be *in* the loop. It's now an ongoing investigation."

"But I'm the one who reported Philomene missing. And I might actually have information that could help. Yesterday a…friend and I went out to the spot where Jerrod said he picked up Philomene's car—"

"You did *what?*"

"Look, it seemed as if the sheriff wasn't going to do anything, which left it up to me to find her.

No law that says I can't look for someone. Anyway, we found tire impressions. We took pictures." She stopped short of mentioning the whole business about the stolen credit card and cell phone. The last thing she wanted was to get Eric or Project Justice in trouble for illegally accessing private databases.

"That sounds like something the sheriff should know about," Ted said with a worried frown.

"Exactly."

"Can you email them to me? I'll make sure he gets them."

"I don't have them. My friend does."

"That guy you were here with the other day? With the little girl?"

Bree nodded. "Eric. I'll ask him to send you the images."

"If Jerrod really did pick up the car, the tire tracks might simply be from someone dropping him off."

"Then it might verify his story. Anyway, I think it's important."

"Yeah."

And it would give her an excuse to call Eric. She was way more happy about that than she ought to have been, given the circumstances. But she couldn't seem to get him off her mind.

Maybe she'd skip the call and just drive to his office. People found it harder to brush her off or refuse her favors if she asked them in person. Besides, she wanted to tell Eric about the blood and see what he thought. He'd asked her to keep him updated, after all, and she had another errand in Houston she needed to run. A medical supply company there had a type of suturing thread she liked. Since the county hospital wouldn't provide it, she bought her own.

"Are you dating that guy?" Ted asked bluntly. "Because I thought you didn't date."

That was the excuse she'd given Ted when he'd asked her out. Back then, she'd been too busy to have a boyfriend. But it wasn't a blanket policy. She just didn't usually meet anyone she *wanted* to go out with.

"I don't, and he's not a boyfriend. Just a friend. Acquaintance, really." But she couldn't rule out that he might become more.

"COME ON, MACKENZIE, don't cry," Eric pleaded as he pulled out of the school parking lot. The school nurse had called him a few minutes ago with the news that MacKenzie was sick, and someone needed to pick her up. She'd started throwing up and was running a slight fever.

The nurse had said some stomach bug was going around, but that didn't stop Eric from a slight sense of panic he struggled to tamp down. He knew childhood illnesses were a normal part of growing up and that whatever she had, it would probably run its course in a day or two. But MacKenzie had always been so healthy, at least physically. As a toddler, MacKenzie would remain completely unaffected even when both Tammy and Eric came down with colds or flu or viruses. While in prison, he'd gotten regular progress reports on MacKenzie from his brother, and Travis had not once in three years mentioned that the little girl had suffered so much as a sniffle. The kid had the immune system of a rhinoceros.

Eric had tried to contact Elena and ask her to pick up MacKenzie. His sister-in-law had been incredibly helpful watching MacKenzie after school, but she was also helping Travis to organize and expand his construction business, and this afternoon she wasn't answering her phone. She was probably driving and wouldn't check her messages until she arrived. Eric had realized he would have to pick up MacKenzie himself despite an important meeting scheduled for three o'clock—fifteen minutes from now.

He had a sofa in his office, he reasoned. If he could persuade MacKenzie to take a nap, the meeting could go on as scheduled. Eric and the foundation's CPA needed to review some tax documents relating to the building owned by Project Justice, and since real-estate law was Eric's area of expertise, it wasn't a task he could dump on any of the other lawyers.

"My stomach hurts!" MacKenzie complained.

"I know, pumpkin. We'll get you some medicine as soon as we get to my office." One of the cabinets in the break room was filled with any over-the-counter remedy anyone could want, including pain relievers, first-aid cream, antacid and—thank God—Pepto-Bismol. The nurse had said to try that first.

*Please don't throw up in the car.*

"I wanna go home," MacKenzie wailed. "I want Elena."

"Elena is working today, so you'll have to make do with me."

That only made her cry harder.

MacKenzie had been elated when Eric was freed from prison. For the first few days, she'd wanted him to hold her constantly. Although she'd been only three when they'd been torn apart, he represented security to her.

But she'd been in love with the idea of him more than the actual man he was. Although he tried, he wasn't the same man she'd known as her daddy. Prison, not to mention losing his wife in such a horrifying way, had changed him. Sometimes his mind went to dark places, places MacKenzie couldn't go.

Elena, so gentle and loving and great with kids, had quickly bonded with her niece, and all three of them—Elena, Travis and Eric—had done everything they could to give her the love and security and understanding she'd been lacking.

Was she starting to see Elena as a mother figure? Because there was danger in that way of thinking. They wouldn't live with Elena and Travis for much longer. Soon he would have to find a place of their own so that Travis and Elena could get on with the business of being newlyweds. Neither of them had said a word, but if he were in Travis's shoes, he would want some privacy with his new bride.

MacKenzie was still sobbing softly as Eric carried

her through the garage entrance, juggling his magnetic key card and entering the security code. His meeting was in five minutes.

He was still trying to figure out the logistics of caring for his daughter and meeting with the CPA when he entered the break room, intent on finding medicine for nausea. He skidded to a stop. Was he hallucinating?

Bree was sitting at a table drinking coffee and chatting with Jillian.

"Oh, you're back." Bree looked surprised to see him, which didn't make much sense, since she'd come to his place of business. Then he realized her surprise had to do with the bundle of sick little girl in his arms, because her attention was focused squarely on the child rather than him.

"I happened to spot Bree in the lobby a few minutes ago," Jillian said. "You weren't in. I thought she'd be more comfortable waiting here for you."

"Hey, MacKenzie." Bree's voice was all soft concern. "What are you doing here?"

MacKenzie hid her face against her father's neck.

"She's sick. I just picked her up from school."

"And you brought her *here?*"

"I have a meeting in two minutes." He walked past Bree, set MacKenzie on the counter and opened the first-aid cabinet. "It's important. I just came in here to get some— This stuff." He showed her the pink bottle.

"You can't take a sick child to a meeting," Bree

reasoned. "Give her to me. I'll take care of her and you go do your lawyer thing. If I can't find proper medicine and whatnot in here, I have a doctor's bag in my car."

"I'm not sure that's such a good idea…." Foisting MacKenzie off on an almost-stranger when she was sick?

"Oh, don't be such a helicopter dad," Jillian said. "Your kid couldn't be in safer hands. I mean, Bree's a doctor, after all."

"True, but—"

"She'll be fine," Bree said with easy confidence. "Won't you, MacKenzie?"

MacKenzie had stopped crying, at least for the moment. She'd stuck her thumb in her mouth and was contemplating this new threat. Normally Eric fussed at her when she sucked her thumb, but he'd cut her some slack today.

"How about it, MacKenzie?" Eric found a clean spoon and poured some of the pink liquid into it. "Okay if Dr. Bree looks after you for a few minutes?"

MacKenzie's eyes widened with alarm. Mutely she shook her head. Eric held the spoon in front of her face, but she pressed her lips together and shook her head again.

"Come on, pumpkin, the medicine will make you feel better."

In reply, she looked straight at Eric and vomited.

# *CHAPTER EIGHT*

"OH, HELL!" ERIC just stood there holding the spoonful of medicine. He had no idea what to do. All he could think of was that hideous scene from *The Exorcist*.

Bree calmly grabbed a wad of paper towels and started mopping up the mess on MacKenzie's shirt. "Poor baby, you really aren't feeling well, are you?"

MacKenzie shook her head, watching Bree suspiciously.

Bree felt the child's forehead. "She's running a temperature, I think. Has she taken anything?"

"The school nurse gave her some Children's Tylenol."

"Okay. Hopefully that'll kick in pretty soon."

"What else should I do?" he asked.

"Nothing right now. Go on to your meeting," Bree said. "I've got this covered."

"No, really, you don't have to—"

"I deal with this every day," she said, cutting off his lame protest. "Go." Bree deftly placed herself between MacKenzie and her father so the little girl wouldn't see him leave.

But Eric couldn't skulk away like that. Bree might think that was a good idea, but MacKenzie wouldn't. "I'll be back in thirty minutes." Even if he had to get up in the middle of the meeting, he would keep his word. He handed the spoon to Jillian, who had remained sitting at the table watching with barely disguised amusement.

"Hey, how did I get involved in this?" Jillian objected.

MacKenzie didn't disappoint. The second Eric started for the door, she began crying. "Daddy! Daddy, no!"

Bree looked over her shoulder. "Go," she mouthed.

Eric left. As he walked down the hall to the conference room, he decided he was a terrible father. And he would owe Bree big after this.

MacKenzie stopped crying thirty seconds after her father left, as Bree knew she would. Kids loved to manipulate their parents. Children a lot younger than MacKenzie could do it. She saw it all the time in the E.R.

"Let's see what we can do to make you feel better," Bree said soothingly. She worked gently but efficiently to clean up MacKenzie's face and clothes. It would have been better if she could have taken off the little T-shirt and tossed it in a washing machine, but Bree guessed MacKenzie didn't have any extra clothes stashed around here.

The little girl watched her solemnly.

Once MacKenzie was clean, Bree reclaimed the spoon of medicine from Jillian, who appeared to be enjoying the show.

"Do you always find sick children amusing?" Bree asked. She held the spoon in front of MacKenzie and opened her own mouth. "Ahhhhhh."

The child obligingly opened her mouth and accepted the medicine. Little trick she'd learned. Kids would rather be shown what to do than told.

"Oh, no!" Jillian objected. "I'm really sorry you're sick, MacKenzie. I just enjoyed watching your dad and Dr. Bree deal with the situation. I mean, it's not every day we get a barfing kid at the office. Then again, I shouldn't really point and laugh, since I don't have kids. Someday I will, and karma is a bi— I mean... Oh, never mind. Can I help?"

Bree knew Jillian was hoping the answer was no. It was hard to picture the polished, stylish investigator sopping up puke or doling out pink medicine. "I've got everything under control, thanks. Unless... Do you happen to know where a blanket might be?" She felt MacKenzie's forehead again; yup, she definitely had a fever. Bree would keep her warm and watch her for signs that her temperature was going up.

"I can find something."

Bree scooped MacKenzie off the counter and propped her on her hip. It always felt nice to hold a soft, vibrant child, but it was a bittersweet pleasure. Bree never held a child without remembering her own—so tiny she felt more like the size of a puppy than a human baby. She'd been allowed to hold the tiny baby girl for only a few seconds. Then she had been whisked away to a world of Isolettes, tubes and needles.

MacKenzie instinctively put her arms around Bree's neck. Bree stopped at the fridge to grab a bottled ginger ale. A bit more searching turned up a straw. Then she headed to the lounge area where she and Eric had had their first meeting. She smiled now as she recalled him ripping off his shirt and Jillian's stunned look of embarrassment as she'd backed out of the room.

But she quickly sobered. That scar was no laughing matter. It was clearly the result of a serious injury that should have seen stitches but hadn't. Proper medical care would have resulted in a much neater scar and probably would have prevented the infection, too.

Why hadn't Eric gone to the prison doctor to get stitched up? Had he been that afraid of Kelly? If so, why? Could Eric be right? Could Kelly have turned into a different person in prison, a mean, violent man who compartmentalized his less socially acceptable side so that she never saw it? And if that was possible... No. She *knew* him. He hadn't raped Philomene or killed those other women.

Bree settled onto the sofa and snuggled MacKenzie against her. "You want a sip of ginger ale?" It would be good to get some liquids into the child, but she didn't want to do anything that would provoke more nausea.

MacKenzie nodded, and Bree held the soda up so MacKenzie could wrap her lips around the straw. She sucked up a small amount, then smacked her lips, evaluating the taste. "Good," she declared. "What is it?"

"Ginger ale. You never had it before?"

"Uh-uh." She took another small sip, then leaned back. "I'm cold."

Bree was wearing a lightweight cardigan sweater. It wouldn't be much help, but it was all she had. She peeled it off and draped it over MacKenzie's shoulders. "That better?"

"Mmm. Read to me?"

Bree glanced around, but there wasn't any child-appropriate literature handy. "How about if I make up a story?"

"Okay," MacKenzie said uncertainly.

"Once upon a time there was a princess." All little girls liked stories about princesses. "And her parents, the king and queen, wanted her to marry a prince of their choosing. But the princess fell in love with a peasant. He didn't have much money, but he was good at…" What? Motorcycles?

This was a fairy tale she used to tell herself. In her version, the peasant opened his own Harley-Davidson dealership and they lived happily ever after. But that was before the princess got pregnant, and the harsh realities of life put so much pressure on the peasant and princess that they fell out of love. Not the sort of story to tell a sick child.

"What was he good at?" MacKenzie asked.

"Racing horses," Bree finally said. "He had only one prized possession, his noble steed, Harley. Harley was pure black, and a very special horse, the fastest one in the kingdom.

"The king said he would give permission for his daughter to marry the peasant if Harley could beat the fastest horse in the royal stable."

"What was his name?" MacKenzie asked.

"The other horse? Umm, let's see—"

"Billy," MacKenzie suggested.

"Okay, Billy. Now, the king—"

"What color is Billy?"

Bree could tell this story was going to take a while. But that was okay. Anything to keep the sick little girl focused on something other than her upset tummy.

Jillian returned with a lightweight plaid throw. "I found this in someone's office."

"Perfect. Thanks, Jillian." She tucked the blanket around MacKenzie, who was still shivering slightly.

As soon as Jillian left, they resumed the story. "What color do you think Billy is?" Bree asked.

"Pink."

"Okay. Billy the pink horse was really, really fast, because he ate special food and lived in a really nice stable with a feather bed and air-conditioning. He had won many races and he had a hundred prize ribbons hanging in his stall.

"But the peasant wasn't worried. He knew that Harley was still faster than Billy, because Harley—"

"He was magic!"

"How did you know that? Yes, Harley was magic...." And the story went on effortlessly from there. Bree didn't have to work very hard coming up with plot twists, because MacKenzie did it for her. The little girl seemed to enjoy helping craft her own story. Maybe she was destined to be a writer someday.

As the minute hand on her watch crept toward three-thirty, Bree found herself wishing it would stand still. She couldn't remember when she last spent quality time with a child.

Yeah, she saw them all the time in the E.R. But usually they were very sick or seriously injured. Once she got them stabilized, they moved on. She passed out the occasional sticker or coloring book, but she never got to snuggle quietly with any one child for extended periods of time.

This felt way too good. As she and MacKenzie continued with their fairy tale, something deep inside her began to unfurl, a tight ball of petals that had closed up when her own chance at motherhood had so abruptly ended.

Back then, she'd told herself she would never get pregnant again, not even under the best of circumstances. To love a child was like no other emotion she'd ever felt. It went down to the bone—no, even farther. It went soul deep. The pain of losing her precious, tiny baby was beyond description.

She'd locked her pain away in a box that she'd never intended to open. To be vulnerable to that kind of torture—it was too much.

But for whatever reason, the box had opened a crack today.

Why this child, at this time, had gotten through her defenses, she didn't know. But her eyes burned and her voice cracked as she uttered those familiar five words: "They lived happily ever after."

MacKenzie was asleep. Bree noticed a thin sheen of perspiration on the child's skin, which probably meant her fever was going down. If this was the same stomach bug she'd been seeing frequently at the hospital the past couple of weeks, MacKenzie wouldn't truly be on the mend until tomorrow. She would have a hard time keeping anything down, and the fever would return. But hopefully it wouldn't be any worse than that.

Bree glanced at her watch. Eric was five minutes late, but thankfully, his daughter wouldn't know. Meanwhile, Bree was content to sit there quietly with the child tucked up against her, wondering how she was going to stuff all those feelings back into their box, where they belonged.

ERIC HAD BEEN standing in the doorway of the breakroom lounge for a good five minutes, his heart in his throat. He kept expecting Bree to look up, but her attention was riveted on the child snuggled against her as she spun an improbable story about a pink horse named Billy. She didn't have a book open, so the story must have come either from her memory or pure imagination.

But the thing that had shocked him—and the reason he hadn't wanted to interrupt them—was his daughter's response. She was helping to create the story. And despite being sick, she was smiling and even laughed a time or two when Bree came up with a particularly ridiculous detail to add to the story. There was a fairy named Ooga-Booga, who gave someone magic oats that would make his horse run fast, and a princess with a dress made out of spun gold and cotton candy.

This was the kind of scene he'd never come upon when Tammy was still alive. It wasn't that Tammy had been a neglectful mother. She'd made sure MacKenzie had healthy food to eat and clothes and medical care and toys. She had loved MacKenzie in her own way, Eric was sure. And MacKenzie had loved her mommy and had missed her acutely. But Tammy had left a lot of the warm, fuzzy parenting to Eric. At the end of a long day, when Eric had walked through the door, Tammy had handed off their child and disappeared to take a long bubble bath.

Eric had never resented it. He'd loved his time with MacKenzie. But sometimes he'd wondered if his wife and daughter had bonded properly.

And now he wondered what sort of magic touch Bree had, to get his daughter to open up like that. He had to stand on his head and whistle to coax a smile out of MacKenzie, yet with Bree she was relaxed and happy even with the stomach flu. How had Bree managed to get MacKenzie to lose that tense, guarded demeanor she habitually wore like a favorite security blanket?

Suddenly Bree looked up, and their eyes locked silently for several heartbeats.

"She fell asleep," Bree whispered. "And you're late."

"Actually, I wasn't. I just…" Should he just admit he'd been watching them? "I saw she was dropping off and didn't want to spoil it."

"Oh."

"My daughter seems to have taken quite a shine to you. A far cry from that first night when she threw a tantrum because she thought you were going to give her a shot."

"Any port in a storm," Bree said. "I was here, you weren't, and she needed someone." Bree gently eased herself away from the sleeping child and put a pillow under her head. MacKenzie didn't stir. "I think she'll be okay here for a few minutes. We can go in the other room and talk."

Oh, right. Bree hadn't shown up here just so she could care for a sick kid. They both walked into the kitchen area, and Bree reclaimed her nearly un-touched coffee cup. She wrinkled her nose at it.

"Get some fresh. That's got to be stone cold by now."

She nodded, dumped the cup's contents into the sink and poured a fresh cup from the industrial-size percolator that never went empty. Eric hadn't noticed anyone cleaning this room or replenishing supplies, but obviously, someone did.

Maybe Daniel had a legion of elves to do his bid-ding.

Bree took a long sip of her coffee, looking su-premely uncomfortable. "I got some news today. The sheriff questioned Jerrod and impounded Philomene's car. They found trace amounts of blood in the trunk."

"Oh, no. I'm sorry."

"Dr. Gentry said they'll need to do more tests to determine if it's Philomene's blood or if it's even human, but I have a bad feeling."

"So do they think Jerrod did it?"

"He's an easy suspect. And knowing Sheriff De-Ville, he won't look any further if he can pin the crime on the boyfriend."

"Now that law enforcement is involved, it would be better for us to back off."

"I just want to know for sure. I've tried calling Philomene back at her new number, but she won't answer. It always rolls to voice mail, and there's no outgoing message in her voice. I understand why she wouldn't want to talk to me. If she's still alive, she obviously regrets having confided in me and wants to put it behind her. But I can't help but think—"

"What?"

"That whoever the real murderer is wanted to shut her up for good this time."

*Oh, no.* Why couldn't she let this go? "Bree, I know you're really attached to the idea that there's an alternate murderer out there, but think about it logically. How would this mythical real murderer have even known Philomene was going to change her story? Did you tell anyone?"

"Only you and Daniel Logan. But Philomene must have told someone, because the story was out there. Molly, the hostess at the café, even asked me about it."

"Okay, so she told Jerrod. Now Jerrod is spreading it around because he's hoping to get people to focus on someone besides him as Philomene's killer."

"You have an answer for everything."

"Bree, if you came here to try to get Project Justice to reconsider—"

"I didn't," she snapped. "Actually, I came here to get those tire-impression pictures from you. I thought I should turn them over to the sheriff now that he's actually looking into Philomene's disappearance."

"You could have called."

"I know. I had to come to town anyway and I thought I'd just swing by." She said this a little sheepishly, which caused him to wonder—was Bree inventing excuses to see him? Did she feel the same pull he did? Because no matter how many times he told himself he needed to get her and her doomed cause out of his life, he was never disappointed to see her.

And after that kiss…

"I turned the photos over to the lab. We can drop by and see if Beth or one of her assistants has had time to analyze them. But…" He nodded toward the doorway to the seating area where MacKenzie slept. "I can watch her."

"Actually, I thought you might like to see the lab. It's pretty nice. Small, but it has all the latest equipment—every kind of laser and microscope and spectrometer and whatever." He thought as a woman of science, Bree might appreciate the sweet setup they had at their disposal.

"Daddy!" came the panicked call from around the corner.

Eric was at his daughter's side in five quick steps. "I'm here, pumpkin."

"Where's Dr. Bree?"

"I'm here, too." She waved from behind Eric.

"I'm hungry."

"Not too surprised about that," Eric said under his breath, since she couldn't possibly have anything left in her stomach. "Okay, let's get you home."

"But what about—" Bree began.

"I'll take you upstairs and introduce you to Beth, but then I'm out of here. I need to get her home."

"Right."

The lab took up half of the third floor, and it looked like something from a futuristic movie or a space station. Every surface was aluminum or some kind of bright white composite material that was impervious to bacteria. There were gadgets of every description—from monstrous machines with lenses like giant eyes to tiny measuring devices the size of a pen. Glass-front cabinets were filled with mysterious-looking chemicals. One white-coated technician stood at a counter sifting through what looked like vacuum-cleaner dust. Another was putting test tubes into some kind of machine.

Beth McClelland, the lab's director, was in her office—separated by glass walls—peering at a computer screen.

Since the technicians were so engrossed in their work they didn't even look up, Eric went straight to Beth's office and tapped on the door. She jumped, then smiled and motioned for him to enter.

"You brought MacKenzie!" she said with obvious delight. Beth had met MacKenzie at Daniel's house on Christmas Eve—the day Eric had been released from prison and reunited with his daughter.

MacKenzie wasn't interested in making nice. She hid her face in Eric's shoulder, her arms clamped tightly around his neck.

"Actually, she's sick, and I'm taking her home. But I wanted to introduce you to Bree Johnson. The tire impressions I gave you are her concern."

"I was just sending you an email, Eric." She stood and offered her hand to Bree.

"I hope it's okay, doing this for me when it's not a Project Justice job," Bree said.

"It's fine. The lab is an autonomous corporate entity. I take on lots of outside work."

"But you probably get paid for it. I'd be happy to—"

"It's taken care of. So let me tell you the results. The tires are Continental Sport Contact 270/40R20s, most likely from a late-model Range Rover Sport."

Bree gasped. "Oh, my God."

Eric and Beth looked at each other. "I take it this means something to you?" Eric said.

"Only one person I know in Tuckerville—anywhere, actually—drives one of those. Sheriff Bobby DeVille."

# CHAPTER NINE

"THAT IS BAD." Beth looked troubled. "There is nothing more dangerous than a criminal in law enforcement."

"You sound like you speak from experience," Bree said.

"We had a case here last fall. A Montgomery County sheriff's deputy was put in charge of investigating the murder he committed. Catching him almost cost some lives."

"Of course, we might be jumping to conclusions," Eric said.

"Or not," Bree said. DeVille was like a god in Tuckerville. Not everyone liked him, but they all respected him—and some feared him.

"Bree, you could be in danger. The sheriff knows you won't rest until you find Philomene. If he's responsible—"

"Oh, God. But why would the sheriff want to kill Philomene?" Then Bree gasped again. "Because she was going to recant, or he was afraid she would. He doesn't want Kelly's conviction overturned. Catching a serial killer was a huge feather in his cap. Being proven wrong would make him look bad, and that is something he doesn't want, believe me."

"Bree, you shouldn't go back to Tuckerville by yourself."

"What? What am I supposed to do? Move? Leave town, like Philomene supposedly did?"

"Look, we don't know that it was the sheriff's vehicle, and if it is, we don't know why he stopped at the side of the road there. It might not even be related to Philomene's car. We also don't know that Philomene's dead. But I don't want to take chances until we can check things out."

"Talk to Ford or Hudson," Beth suggested. "They're seasoned ex-cops, both of them."

"Right now I need to get MacKenzie home. Bree, come with me. Elena will be home soon—she's my after-school babysitter. Once I get Baby Girl here squared away, we can take a deep breath and figure out our next move."

"I have to go to work," Bree objected.

"Call in sick. Just this once," he added. "I'm not suggesting you go into the Witness Protection Program. But…a couple of months ago, Elena wasn't quite as careful as she could have been and she was almost murdered. Maybe I'm overly cautious—"

"No, I understand. Just this once, I'll call in sick." Truthfully, the thought of going home with Eric intrigued her. She wanted to see where he lived. She felt compelled to figure out what this guy was all about. Maybe his home environment—and his brother and sister-in-law—would help her put more pieces into the puzzle that was Eric Riggs.

"ELENA?" ERIC CALLED as he came through the front door with Bree right behind him. He had mixed feelings about bringing her here to his home turf. How had this situation gotten so complicated?

MacKenzie, at least, was feeling a little better. At least she wasn't throwing up or complaining of a stomachache, though she was even more clingy and whiney than usual.

"Eric!" Elena met him at the door. "I am so sorry. I just got your message. I got this new phone and—"

"Don't worry, it's okay. Elena, this is Bree."

The two women exchanged a cautious greeting.

"Want 'Lena," MacKenzie whimpered.

"Oh, right. A few minutes ago you wouldn't let go of me to sit in your car seat, but now that Elena's here, I'm chopped liver?" Still, he handed his child over to Elena, whose arms were outstretched. He was ready for a break. It was exhausting taking care of a child, especially when she was sick.

"You're not feeling well?" Elena asked as they all trooped from the garage into the kitchen.

"I threw up," MacKenzie said proudly. "Twice."

"Why don't we go change your clothes, then. Okay?"

Elena looked at Eric.

Eric nodded. MacKenzie was in good hands.

"Do you have any ginger ale? Or something similar?" Bree asked. "She should try to sip some liquids."

Eric found lemon-lime soda and poured it into a plastic tumbler, which he set on MacKenzie's nightstand while Elena cleaned her up in the bathroom.

Bree lurked in the doorway. "This room is adorable."

"You can thank my brother for that. At one point he was planning to adopt MacKenzie. He bought this house and fixed it up for her—he's a contractor. Then circumstances changed, and he ended up with the both of us. But it's just temporary," he hastened to add, not wanting Bree to think he was a mooch or that he was incapable of taking care of himself and his daughter. "As soon as I get settled in to the new job, we'll find our own place."

Eric opened one of the dresser drawers and found a nightgown. "MacKenzie's never sick."

"Then I'm sure she'll bounce back quickly."

"It's awful seeing your child in pain."

"Yes," Bree said softly. He thought her eyes looked unusually shiny. Dear God, was she going to cry?

"Bree, don't worry. We're going to work all this out, okay? We'll find Philomene. If anything's happened to her, we'll make sure that person is brought to justice. Nothing's going to happen to you."

She quickly wiped her eyes. "Oh—it's not that. This room is just so— MacKenzie is a lucky little girl to have so many people who love her."

"She hasn't always been lucky," he said grimly.

"But I'm determined to give her the best life I can." Sometimes he wondered, though, if it was even possible to fully heal from seeing your mother stabbed seventeen times.

Elena reappeared with MacKenzie wrapped in a fluffy towel. "I have this under control if you two need to talk."

"Thanks." He looked at his daughter, who was working her way into the nightgown he'd laid out for her. "MacKenzie, you go right to bed."

She didn't argue, an indicator that she really was sick.

"You want me to make some coffee?" he asked Bree as they went downstairs.

"No. Please, don't fuss. I'm not even sure what I'm doing here."

"Because you could be in danger."

"Look, the sheriff is a pompous jerk, but I really can't see him killing anybody. I'll just send him the tire-track pictures like I promised and indicate that I'm turning the whole thing over to him. That should ease his mind if he's guilty of anything and afraid I'll find out."

Eric wanted something to drink even if she didn't. He grabbed a black-cherry soda from the fridge. "Sure you don't want something? Coke? Water?"

"Water, please, if you insist on treating me like a guest."

He got out a glass and ice and filled it from the pitcher of filtered water in the fridge, also giving himself time to figure out where he wanted to go from here.

He'd be the first to admit he was in over his head. He knew a lot about criminal justice from his legal training and his own arrest, trial and appeals. And working for Project Justice was a crash course in investigative techniques. But that didn't qualify him to investigate a crime. He didn't have the tools or the authority or the manpower to do it properly.

"Thanks." She pulled out a chair from the small kitchen table and took a polite sip of her water.

He joined her. "Maybe it's time to talk to the Texas Rangers." Texas's state police force often assisted smaller law enforcement agencies with major crimes, and they also investigated police corruption.

Bree did not look thrilled about the idea. "Great. I'd just love to face off against another round of good ol' boys who will no doubt pat me on the head and tell me to run along and stop imagining things. And you never know who might be a friend of Bobby DeVille's. They probably all belong to the same gun clubs and go to the same shooting ranges."

Damn. He was sure he'd come up with a brilliant solution.

"What if this whole thing is connected?" Bree asked. "What if the real killer found out Philomene was going to recant and silenced her? You have to admit, the timing is suspicious. She vanishes less than twenty-four hours before she was going to talk to you?"

Eric didn't want to admit that. He wanted to tell Bree she was straying close to conspiracy-theory land, and if she started talking like this in front of any cops, they were sure to dismiss her as a nutjob.

But damn it, he suspected she might be on to something. And while he had a vested interest in keeping Kelly Ralston behind bars and safely away from his family, he didn't want to be responsible for allowing a serial rapist/killer to continue running free.

"Have there been any other victims since Ralston was incarcerated?" Eric asked. "There was a string of five, right? Plus Philomene's attempted murder."

"No new cases that I know of. Certainly not in Tuckerville or Becker County. Oh, you think that means the right guy is in jail, right?"

"The thought does cross my mind."

"But maybe the real murderer moved away. Or he got smarter, started spreading out his crimes so the pattern would be harder to discern. Or maybe he started doing a better job hiding the bodies."

All of those were possible. Killers did learn from their mistakes. Their killing styles sometimes evolved.

Bree set down her glass. "I want to talk to Daniel Logan again."

"What? Why?"

"A lot has happened since I last talked to him. I think I can make him change his mind." Bree looked Eric in the eye, challenging him to contradict her.

He had to keep Daniel out of this at all costs. What if Bree succeeded? She was very persuasive, after all.

But even Daniel couldn't understand the visceral fear that Kelly's threat produced inside Eric's gut, even now. Eric couldn't take a chance that Kelly would somehow get released.

"Daniel is a very busy man. Once he makes a decision—"

"I don't have anything to lose. I mean, what's the worst that could happen? He'll say no. He'll refuse to see me."

"Who will refuse to see you?" Elena asked as she swung into the kitchen. "MacKenzie fell right to sleep, by the way," she said to Eric.

"Daniel," Eric replied. "Tell her, Elena. Once Daniel makes a decision, he sticks with it, right? He already turned down Bree's application."

"He might change his mind if there's new information," Bree argued. "Anyway, the only reason Daniel said no was because of you."

Eric groaned. "Let's not go there again."

But now Bree was on the warpath. "You have a personal grudge against Kelly, and I totally understand why. What I don't understand is why you're still involved in this mess."

"'This mess' is finding Philomene. That's a separate issue from getting your friend out of prison."

"Someone's missing?" Elena asked.

"Yes." Bree, perhaps sensing a sympathetic audience, appealed to Elena. "An eyewitness who was going to change her story. She's missing, and there was blood found in her car—"

"Elena doesn't have to hear the whole story," Eric objected.

"Yes, I do. I'm interested. Eric, you could at least offer your guest something to eat." She went to the fridge and pulled out some hummus, pairing it with crackers she poured into a bowl.

"Thanks, that's really nice." Bree nibbled a cracker politely, swallowing quickly. "I'll make it fast. It's possible the local sheriff is involved, which means I can't trust him to find Philomene. I think the timing of Philomene's disappearance is fishy, and I think Mr. Logan might want to reconsider his decision in light of new information."

Elena pulled out a chair and sat down, lazily spreading some hummus on a cracker. "And he turned you down the first time because…?"

"Because Eric told him to. Because he knows my friend Kelly—"

"Boyfriend—"

"Ex-boyfriend, not that it's relevant. Eric knew Kelly in prison and they…didn't get along."

"Do I have to take my shirt off again?"

Elena dropped the cracker and held out both of her palms toward them. "Whoa. Both of you. Eric, obviously you have a bias against the potential client."

"A fair bias. The guy tried to kill me."

"But I think Bree has a point. If there's a dirty cop involved in all this, you should at least talk to

Daniel again and see what he recommends. He may not want Project Justice to take on the case—Eric is right in that he usually does stand by his decisions."

"Thank you," Eric said with a nod for the crumb.

"But maybe he knows a good private investigator or a state senator or a reporter—he knows a lot of powerful people."

"There, you see?" Bree said.

The door from the garage opened and closed. "Anybody home?"

"In the kitchen, Trav," Elena called back.

Great. All Eric needed to make this day complete was for Travis to weigh in on this whole Ralston-Philomene-DeVille mess. Travis might be a big rough, tough construction worker, but he had a soft heart and he would no doubt side with the angelic-looking Bree.

Travis appeared in the doorway from the garage with eyes only for Elena. "Oh, good, you're home. I need to go pick up that radial arm saw tonight, and it's a good two hours away."

"You're going to miss dinner again?" Elena said with a pout.

"I thought you'd want to come with me. I'll take you out to dinner. Eric has a date."

"Not exactly. We'll have to put off PizzaMania. MacKenzie has a tummy bug. But you two do what you need to do. Radial arm saw, huh?" Anything he could do to get his brother and sister-in-law out of the house would at least even the odds.

Elena looked at Eric uncertainly. "I'd love to, Trav, but MacKenzie is home sick and I hate to leave Eric—"

"Don't be ridiculous," Eric said. "I can look after her."

"Are you sure?"

"Of course I'm sure. She's my daughter. And I've got a doctor right here."

Travis looked at Bree for the first time. "I'm sorry. I didn't even see you there."

Eric introduced them without making any explanations. Thankfully, his brother was too distracted thinking about his new saw to question what Bree was doing there.

Elena scribbled something down on a piece of paper and handed it to Bree. "Daniel's private number. Tell him I said you should call him. And whatever you do, don't ever give it to anyone else."

"Thank you, Elena."

Elena grabbed her purse, making a hasty, apologetic departure with her husband, leaving Eric and Bree blessedly alone again.

Bree wasted no time taking out her phone.

"You're really going to call him? Right now?"

"Of course. I don't see the point in wasting time."

"What would it take to get you to not involve my boss?" Eric fished for an argument she might accept. "You can see where this is going, right? The fact I've gotten involved in your…your problems, despite recommending that Project Justice reject your case—

it doesn't look good. I've been working there only a few days. I need this job. MacKenzie sees a very expensive therapist."

Bree set the phone on the table, frowning, and ate another cracker. "I don't want to get you in trouble." Her smooth forehead developed a little crease between her brows as she thought about it. "Okay. If you want me to stay away from your boss, here's what you have to do. You have to talk to Kelly. Face-to-face."

"What?" Just the idea of seeing that monster again made Eric's stomach queasy. "You are out of your mind."

Bree shrugged. "You might see another side of him."

"And he might punch my face in." Eric was hoping Kelly would forget all about Eric Riggs—out of sight, out of mind. Surely he had plenty of fellow inmates onto which he could inflict his brand of pain.

"I guess I can understand why you wouldn't want to go back there. I can't even imagine what it must have been like to lose your freedom. Now that you have it back... Yeah, I'd be afraid to go back. Afraid they might clang the doors shut on me and not let me—"

"I'm not afraid!" The words came out as a knee-jerk reaction. No guy wanted a beautiful woman to think he was a coward.

"No? Then why won't you do it? A pleasant drive, a fifteen-minute conversation..."

"And my job is safe. Yeah, I get it." She was out-manipulating him. Again.

Bree's face softened. "I wouldn't deliberately get you in trouble with your boss. It's just—"

"I'll do it. I'll confront the son of a bitch. And then maybe *you'll* see another side of him." This could work. He could provoke Ralston. Get him to lose his temper. Then maybe Bree would see the real Ralston, the man who thought threatening to dismember a little girl was some sort of joke.

"Really? You'll talk to Kelly?"

"That's what I said."

"Oh, Eric, thank you!" Before Eric knew what was happening, he had a warm, vibrant female pressed against him. Without meaning to, he let his arms slip around her. He wasn't sure what he'd done to deserve her enthusiastic gratitude, but he couldn't seem to turn it down.

Talking to Ralston wouldn't bring Philomene back, that was for sure.

"When can we arrange it?" she asked.

"As soon as possible. I don't want this thing dragging on."

"Sunday? That's the regular family visiting day." She had pulled back enough that she could look him in the eye, but they were still in an embrace, and she made no move to end it.

"Sunday it is."

"Thank you," she said again. "I'm just a major pain in your ass, aren't I?" Then she kissed him. Her lips were soft and warm and filled with…invitation? She showed no restraint, pressing her body against his, letting her hands roam, her fingers muss his short hair.

Eric knew this was wrong on so many levels. But he was unable to push her away or object. Yes, she'd been a major pain ever since she'd appeared in his life, looking deceptively like an angel. But she had also haunted his dreams, day and night, unlike any woman he'd ever known.

He didn't want a woman in his life. He and MacKenzie were just getting started repairing their father-daughter relationship. He had a new job. He needed to find a new place to live.

Even if he wanted a girlfriend, what kind of sucker would he be if he fell for Bree? She was using him. He'd been one woman's patsy, and he wasn't going to do *that* again.

He needed to end this, to push Bree away and tell her he wasn't interested. But how could he do that when his mind was so full of her, the feel of her hair, the scent of her skin, the intriguing pressure of her mouth as he pressed his own against it. She seemed to open up like a flower in the sun.

"Bree," he said on a groan. "We can't…"

"I know," she said, sounding a little desperate. "Not with MacKenzie right upstairs."

That was only part of the reason. "Bree…it's not that I don't want you—I do. But I'm not in any position to…" How could he make her understand?

"You don't have to explain anything. It's not like I'm any prize when it comes to relationship material. I just thought— You're the first man I've met in so long who actually listens to me, who doesn't just dismiss me. You may not agree with me all the time—"

"I almost never agree with you," he corrected her.

"I know. But you listen. You want to help." She looked down and licked her lips. Eric's knees went soft. "Maybe that's no basis on which to form a relationship, or liaison, or whatever the hell I think I'm doing here."

"Relationships have been forged with far less." What the hell was he doing? He needed to shut up.

"If it helps," she said, "I'm not looking for anything long-term. I don't have a lot to contribute. I work all the time, and when I'm not working, I tend to get wrapped up in causes. Well, one cause. Freeing Kelly has consumed my life the last few years. I can't cook. I don't keep house. I make lousy small talk on a date."

"I bet you do some things well." Jeez, why would he say something so suggestive?

"Truth be told, it's been so long I'm not sure I do that well, either. I think I've forgotten how. Certainly this approach lacks finesse." She laughed to herself as she loosened her hold on him.

She was giving him an escape route, but he didn't take it. "Nothing wrong with your approach. There's a distinct…straightforwardness about it."

"So subtlety is not my strong suit."

"Subtlety is overrated. Actually, I like to know what a woman's thinking. I don't like having to guess what she wants. My wife… She played games and I didn't even know it."

"But you still love her," Bree concluded.

"Let's just say I'm still processing. I have a lot going on. You really don't want to saddle yourself with my problems." Not that she had suggested anything of the sort.

"Okay, so it's settled. Neither one of us is a candidate for a relationship. Neither of us would be lucky to have the other. So why are we still standing here in your kitchen holding each other?"

*Good question.* "Because I'm having a hard time letting you go. I may disagree with you most of the time. But I admire your passion and your loyalty. Frankly, I find it an incredible turn-on." That one kiss had aroused him to the point where he didn't think he could walk.

"So does your bedroom door have a lock?"

Oh, God. Somehow he had failed to discourage her. Had he really been trying to? Basically, she was offering herself to him, no strings attached. Just two consenting adults who found each other desirable letting off a little steam.

It had been a long time.

When he didn't immediately say no, she flashed an impish smile and took his hand, leading him toward the stairs. If he didn't stop it, this was going to happen. He knew there were condoms in this house somewhere.

When they reached the top of the stairs, Eric peeked into MacKenzie's bedroom. "Still asleep," he whispered, softly closing her door.

His room was across the hall from his daughter's. He'd never paid attention before, but the door did indeed have a lock. He was awfully glad he'd chosen to make his bed that morning and that he hadn't left any dirty laundry lying around on the floor. Since he was a guest in Travis and Elena's home, he tried to be tidy. But he didn't always succeed.

Still hand in hand, Eric and Bree stopped beside the bed. He sat her down on the edge of the mattress and kissed her on the forehead. "If I step out for a minute, will you still be here?"

"Why wouldn't I be?"

"You might change your mind."

She smiled wickedly and shook her head. "No way."

Nonetheless, Eric was quick as he crossed through the master bedroom and into the bathroom. A hasty search of cabinets and drawers finally netted him what he wanted. He stuck the packet in his pocket and headed back to his own room, his steps light. It shouldn't feel this good, the anticipation. He was about to make love to a woman who wasn't his wife, the first since he and Tammy had married. However long it had been for Bree, it had probably been longer for Eric.

When he opened his bedroom door, he almost fainted. Bree was in his bed and she was naked.

"Well."

"Well, indeed. I thought maybe you were the one about to change his mind."

"And you thought you'd make it a little harder for me to do that."

She nodded. The covers were drawn up just over her breasts, revealing her creamy white shoulders, a stark contrast against her black hair, which hung artfully over her flesh. His mouth went dry.

"Are you going to join me? Or do I have to get up and undress you?"

He let his mind linger on that mental image for a few moments—Bree's lovely, delicate hands working the buttons on his shirt, sliding beneath the starched cotton to his heated skin. He would love for her to undress him. But maybe another time. Because appealing as that thought was, the thought of lying beneath the covers with her, both of them naked, was even better.

He undressed in record time. Shirt, tie, shoes, pants—all of it was peeled off and ended up in a pile on the floor. All the while he undressed, Bree watched, her eyes filled with admiration. He wasn't sure why. Although all of his life people had told him he was handsome, he hadn't felt that way since before prison.

When he'd first gotten out, he'd gone straight to take a shower and change clothes. He'd examined himself critically in the bathroom's full-length mirror for the first time in years and had been shocked at what he saw. Despite working out in his cell on a regular basis, he was skinny. And pale. His face was gaunt, his hair dull and ragged. The running joke was that the prison barber had learned how to cut hair by trimming trees.

A few weeks had passed and Eric had put on a few pounds. His hair had grown, and he'd gotten it cut by a decent barber. But he was still no one's pinup model—especially not with that puckered scar across his chest.

Eric pulled back the covers and slid between the sheets. At first he didn't touch Bree; he just looked at her, and she did the same. He couldn't believe this was happening, and she seemed a little surprised by the turn of events herself.

Finally she raised her arm and touched his shoulder, then ran her fingertips softly across the scar tissue, from one end of it to the other. He sucked in a breath, almost expecting it to hurt. But the wound had finally healed, and her touch felt amazing.

"This must have hurt something fierce," she said.

Eric didn't remember the pain so much as the fear. His body must have been pumped with so much adrenaline that the pain had been irrelevant.

He grasped her hand and pulled it away from the scar. "I don't want to think about that right now. Someday I hope my time in prison will seem nothing more than a bad dream. But right now it's still too fresh."

"I'm sorry."

"You don't have to be. I think the thing to do is to create new memories, better memories, that will push out the bad ones."

"I'm all for that."

They kissed again. This time Eric held nothing back, practically devouring her with the force of his desire. She opened her mouth greedily, welcoming the intrusion of his tongue. His hands were all over her. Her breasts— He was holding one of her breasts and if he hadn't already been lying down, he'd have fallen. There was just nothing like the feel of a woman's breast. Bree's weren't large, but they were round and firm and just about the nicest thing he'd ever put in his hand.

Bree's hands were busy, too, testing, exploring.

It didn't take her long to find the evidence of his desire. He was unapologetically hard for her—how could he not be? He would've been more than happy to plunge himself inside her anytime she said. But he wasn't a caveman, never mind his eagerness. This wasn't the sort of lovemaking session that would go on for hours—not with MacKenzie asleep across the hall. But neither did he want to rush Bree. If this was going to be their only time in bed, he wanted it to be good for her. He didn't want her to regret what they were about to do.

She wrapped one hand around him and he gasped

with pleasure and delight over her boldness. She was certainly not shy.

"I love that I have this effect on you," she whispered in his ear. "You seem so...stoic. I didn't imagine you would be this responsive."

"Are you kidding? How could any man not be responsive to you? You're like...perfect. The first time I saw you, I thought you looked like an angel."

She laughed at that. "Oh, right. I'm so angelic."

"Well, maybe not your personality."

She swung one leg over him and climbed on top, brushing her neatly trimmed bush against his erection in a definitely purposeful way. "Not angelic, hmm?"

"The jury's still out. But right now you're more devil than angel."

"Is that so?" She leaned down and kissed him, and her hair fell in a dark curtain around their faces.

He wrapped his arms around her, holding her close, wishing he'd never have to let her go. It felt so incredible to just stop thinking and feel for a change. He couldn't remember the last time he wasn't actively worried about something. But with his mind and his senses so full of Bree, there was no room for worry.

He wasn't even worried about his performance. It didn't matter how long he'd been celibate; his instincts took over. Every touch, every caress, came naturally to him. Their lovemaking was a graceful dance—no fumbling, no rushing. It was like eating an ice-cream sundae, savoring each bite, but a whole lot better.

They switched positions, and he spent several minutes just kissing her amazing breasts and listening to her breath quicken. Sometimes she made little noises of surprise when he playfully nipped her, or sighed softly when he gently sucked one nipple to an excited peak.

As he ran his hands over her flat abdomen, he noticed something that gave him pause: stretch marks. They were faint but undeniable. He was familiar with stretch marks because Tammy had sported a few after giving birth to MacKenzie.

So Bree had a child? Hadn't she told him she had no kids that night at the diner?

"Hey. Where'd you go?"

He realized he'd gone still. "Sorry. I was just…taking it all in. You're so beautiful it's overwhelming."

"I'm past the point of needing pretty words," she said meaningfully. "I need more. I need all of you."

*Need* was the right word. He needed her just as badly. Kissing, licking, stroking—all were good but not enough. He needed to possess her.

There was no awkward fumbling, no second-guessing. She grabbed the condom package from where he'd dropped it near the pillow, opened it and sheathed him with no fuss. She didn't tease him, just opened her legs and welcomed him inside the safe harbor of her body.

They fit together well, and the sensations were

novel and familiar at the same time, as if they had done this before.

Everything just felt right.

"Oh, this is good," she said with some surprise in her voice.

"You thought it was going to be lousy?"

"Of course not. I just didn't imagine…" She closed her eyes and sighed deeply. "I didn't imagine it would feel so right."

A chill wiggled its way up Eric's spine. Bree had read his mind. Talk about two people being on the same page.

Bree wiggled, adjusting their bodies to a slightly different angle. The movement was subtle, but it sent a surge of pleasure coursing through Eric's whole body. If he wasn't careful, this was going to end way too soon. He bit his own lip until he was sure he had complete control again.

*Ice cubes. Freezing showers. Ah, better.*

They started moving, slowly at first, savoring each sensation, each degree of friction. But soon that wasn't enough, and the dance accelerated until he was pounding into her hard and fast. She gripped his biceps, her blunt nails digging into his flesh as she whispered a frantic "yes, yes, yes."

Then he finally crested the top of the roller coaster. One breathless moment poised at the top, then he was plummeting down at the speed of sound and holding on to only enough sanity that he didn't scream.

He was panting like an Olympic sprinter by the

time it was over, and Bree was laughing with tears in her eyes.

"Holy cow," she said.

He rolled onto his back and pulled her on top of him, laughing with her. How long had it been since he'd found something funny or delightful enough to provoke such a reaction? His laughter sounded rusty.

"'Holy cow'?" he said when he found his words. "That's the best you can do?"

"Let me think on it. I'm sure I can do better. But my brain is all full of…hormones and stuff."

"It's okay. You don't need to say anything more. I think we're in agreement."

"No, no, wait, it's coming to me. Euphoric. It was eu—"

A scream from across the hall cut her off.

## CHAPTER TEN

ERIC WAS OUT of bed as though someone had put him into fast-forward. He jumped into his pants and threw open his door, then MacKenzie's door.

"Daddy!" She held out her arms to him. He sat down on the bed and pulled her against him.

"What's wrong, pumpkin?"

"I had a bad dream."

"Oh, I'm sorry." He caught his breath as relief poured over him like hot fudge. "Dreams can be scary." Especially when you have a fever, which MacKenzie definitely did. He could feel heat radiating from her little body.

"What's wrong?"

Eric looked up to see Bree standing in the doorway, dressed, more or less. She was barefoot, but at least she had on a shirt and pants. "Bad dream," Eric said. "I think her fever's up."

"Maybe we should try some ibuprofen. MacKenzie, sweetie, how does your tummy feel?"

"Okay."

"If you go through the master bedroom and into

the bathroom," Eric said to Bree, "you'll find a medicine cabinet with children's ibuprofen."

Bree left the room and Eric continued to comfort his daughter. "You want to tell me about the dream?"

"There was a bad man. He had a knife."

Oh, God. Why couldn't she dream about monsters under the bed, like other kids? He'd been worried about this moment ever since Tammy's murder. She had always said that she didn't remember what happened that day, couldn't recall seeing anything. Her therapist had warned Eric that she might have repressed memories of the event and that she could start remembering at any time—or not at all.

"It was just a dream," Eric said. "He can't hurt you."

"He was all bloody," MacKenzie said.

"Was the man someone you know?" Eric asked, disturbed by the graphic nature of the dream.

"I don't know." She sobbed, and he realized he shouldn't have asked her that question. He wanted to know whether she'd actually witnessed the murder, but not at the expense of encouraging her to dwell on the unpleasant dream.

"It's okay. Stupid question. Just try to forget about it, okay?"

Bree returned with two bottles—one of children's ibuprofen and a green bottle he didn't readily recognize. "I brought her something to reduce her fever, and this stomach medicine, in case her tummy gets upset again."

"I don't want any more medicine," MacKenzie said.

"Ah, but the pills are orange flavored," Bree said. "And the other medicine is cherry flavored."

"I'll go get a cool washcloth," Eric said. And he would put on a shirt and hope that MacKenzie wouldn't ask too many questions about why her father was parading around half naked with "Dr. Bree."

BREE DOLED OUT first the orange tablets, then the antinausea medicine. This was good stuff—she remembered her own mother dosing her with it when Bree was a little girl.

MacKenzie took the pills and liquid with no further complaint.

"You had a bad dream?"

"Uh-huh. There was a bad man with a knife and he was chasing me."

"Oh, no wonder you were scared. But you know what I do when I have a bad dream? I change the way I remember it. Like, I had an awful dream about a week ago where I wrecked my car. So I thought about the dream, and I went through it second by second like a movie in slow motion. And when it got to the part where I hit the other car, I swerved and slammed on my brakes." She acted out driving and swerving. "And I didn't hit the other car. And then I just pretended that was the dream."

She seemed to digest Bree's suggestion.

"It's still scary."

"Well, sure it is. I'd be scared, too. But when I feel scared, I just remember that I'm strong. And you're strong, too. You've been through a lot—losing your mommy, having your daddy in jail, but you survived it. So when you're scared, you just remember that whatever it is that's scaring you—whether it's a dream or the dark or a mean person—you tell yourself you're strong, and you're smart, and you're gonna be just fine. It's like going through a tunnel. It's dark inside, but you always know you'll come out on the other side. You just have to hold on and be strong and brave. You understand?"

MacKenzie nodded.

Bree wasn't sure if what she said made any sense at all. But she encountered a lot of frightened children in her line of work—scared, in pain. She found that a lot of them just wanted someone to take an interest in their feelings. She could stitch their cuts and set their broken bones, but trauma went deeper than that. A car accident or a fall or an assault, especially to an impressionable child, could be a shadow that hung over them for life. She liked to think that she at least started those fragile minds on the road to emotional healing.

"Can I have some soda?" MacKenzie asked.

"Ah, I see the crisis is being defused, if she's asking for soda."

Bree moved aside and let Eric sit beside his daughter. "Lie back, honey, and let me put this cool wash-cloth on your head. It'll feel nice. And I'll bring you a soda in just a bit."

She did as he asked. Eric fluffed the little girl's pillow and smoothed the covers over her, then tenderly placed the damp washcloth against her forehead.

"Do you feel better?" he asked her.

She nodded.

"You want me to bring Elena's tablet in here, and you can watch Muppets?"

Again she nodded, and a small smile found its way onto her face.

Something happened to Bree's heart. It felt suddenly heavy, then light as if it were going to float out of her chest. There was something so special about a father's love for his child. It moved Bree every time she saw it, but especially with *this* father and daughter, who had been through so much. Seeing how they carried on, it was easy for her to believe that love *could* conquer all.

It hadn't worked that way for her and Kelly. Their love hadn't been strong enough to withstand what fate had dished out. Maybe she didn't have what it took to form a lasting pair bond. Her mother had always said she was too selfish, too focused on her own interests, to be a good wife.

Her growing feelings for Eric weren't a healthy development. Even if she were a good candidate for a lasting relationship, Eric wasn't in the right place. He'd been out of prison less than two months. He was just getting to know his daughter again. No one should interfere with that.

"Eric, I think maybe I should go."

Eric turned abruptly to face her. "What? No."

"I think we overreacted to the news about the tire tracks," she said sensibly. "There must be dozens or hundreds of Range Rovers out there. Or maybe the sheriff was there for some perfectly legitimate reason. It's possible he spotted the car before we told him about it and chose not to reveal that. He might have pulled up behind it to run the license plate."

"But why take a chance?"

"What am I supposed to do, stay in a hotel?"

"Don't you have a friend you could stay with?"

Sadly, she didn't. She had work friends and lots of acquaintances in Tuckerville. But no one she would impose on. She shook her head. "Even if there was someone, if the sheriff wanted to find me, he could. The town is not that big."

"Then stay in a hotel. Although it would be easier for you to just stay here." As the objection was about to leave her lips, Eric rushed on. "You could sleep on the sofa, if you're worried about Trav and Elena asking too many questions."

"Daddy." MacKenzie tugged on his sleeve. "You said Muppets."

"I'll get the tablet."

While Eric got his daughter set up watching what was apparently her favorite movie, streaming from the internet, Bree hardened her resolve. She never should have gotten Eric involved in this, even if he was the only person who had ever listened to her. What if her plan backfired? What if Kelly and Eric argued during their visit?

With MacKenzie's attention firmly locked on the tablet, which she had propped up against her knees, Eric took Bree's elbow and gently guided her out of the room, closing the door.

"Now, what's this about leaving?"

"I'm intruding. I'm even having second thoughts about you visiting Kelly."

"Because you're afraid I'm right about him."

"You're not. But maybe…maybe I should take a step back and let the police handle the investigation into Philomene's disappearance. If they drop the ball, I can rethink the decision—"

"You've already decided? Just like that?"

"No, I've been mulling it over."

"But…was it because…?" He nodded toward his bedroom door. "Because that shouldn't change anything."

"It changes everything." She headed for the stairs with Eric right behind her.

"You think it was a mistake?" He sounded insulted. Maybe even slightly outraged.

"I think it wasn't very smart. I was feeling vulnerable. I was grateful you agreed to talk to Kelly—"

"Yet now you don't want me to. You're not making sense."

She stopped in the middle of the living room, not

sure where she'd been heading or what she wanted to do.

"You want to pretend it never happened?" Eric asked, challenging her.

"How can we?" Tears pressed against the backs of her eyes, hot and insistent. She didn't want to cry. "I'm just going to go home. And work. I'll be careful. My apartment building is very secure. I'll be fine."

She went to the kitchen and found her purse, digging through it until her hand wrapped around her keys.

"I feel a little used."

She couldn't tell if he was kidding or not. Most men were more than happy to have sex with no strings. But Eric wasn't most men, she reminded herself.

She turned to face him, to face up to her actions. "I didn't mean for it to be that way. We got caught up in the moment, that's all. I didn't think you wanted any entanglements."

"I'm not sure I do. I'm a little confused myself. But that doesn't mean I want you to walk out that door, out of my life, right this second."

"What *do* you want, then?"

"I want to finish what we started. I want to find out what happened to Philomene. And if there's a criminal posing as sheriff of Becker County, I want to remedy the situation. I want to make sure no one is coming after you."

"It's not even your fight."

"Um, news flash—you made it my fight."

"So do you still want to talk to Kelly? By your way of thinking, it's not related. And despite what I said, I don't want to hold your feet to the fire. I won't call Daniel. And you can do what you want."

"I said I'd talk to him, and I will. What do I have to be afraid of?"

SUNDAY DAWNED BRIGHT, cool and clear, a perfect winter day. Eric was driving through the countryside with a beautiful woman in the passenger seat. Life should have been great. Except for the fact that the woman hadn't uttered a single word to him in the past fifty miles.

It didn't seem as if she was angry; she just seemed determined not to speak to him. Even when he tried to engage her, asking direct questions, she answered with monosyllables or by shaking or nodding her head. Her gaze remained firmly focused out the window, never at him.

He felt as though he'd done something wrong, but he couldn't figure out what. He hadn't coerced her into bed, hadn't even wheedled her there. He thought the decision had been a mutual one. The experience had blown his mind, yes, but it seemed to have thrown Bree for a real loop. He thought *he* was the one with issues.

He should just be grateful she hadn't called Daniel and leave it at that. But like it or not, he was involved in this mess for the duration. Today he was going to face the man who had nearly killed him.

Eric was curious to see how Kelly and Bree would interact. She had emphasized that their love affair had been over years ago, and all that remained was an abiding friendship. But he had always been suspicious of *friendships* between men and women. True, he considered Elena a friend, and he was getting to know and appreciate a number of women at work— he admired their minds, their passion, and he enjoyed their company without feeling a particular sexual pull. Maybe this was a state of being that came with maturity.

But Kelly and Bree—the thought of those two together turned his stomach. Eric had a hard time overlooking Bree's former intimacy with that cretin. How could she have been attracted to someone like Kelly, then someone like him? Did she have a thing for bad boys, and the fact that Eric had served time, even if the conviction had been overturned, put him in that category? Or had it, in fact, turned him into someone who was, if not bad, at least not as good as he should be? Someone filled with rage, someone who lied, someone who resorted to physical violence?

Suzy the GPS told them they had arrived at Huntsville Prison. But Bree directed them to a different entrance, and he followed her directions, gratified to at least hear her voice.

The guard at the gate checked their names against a list, then carefully scrutinized their IDs before allowing them access to the parking lot. He handed them a list of rules, which Bree set aside without looking. Clearly she knew them all by heart.

At his questioning look, she shrugged. "You're not wearing open-toed shoes or a short skirt, are you? Planning to bring any cigarette lighters or sharp metal objects into the visiting room?"

"Nope."

"It's all commonsense stuff. You can't even bring food in—no birthday cakes that might have a file inside, I guess. There are vending machines available if you want to buy someone a snack."

Eric wasn't planning to buy Ralston a snack, that was for sure.

They had to negotiate another checkpoint, with a metal detector, and a guard carefully searched through Bree's purse. Then they had to wait. Bree had requested a face-to-face meeting rather than one with a glass partition and a phone, and there was a line.

Finally a guard motioned that they should follow him. They were taken to a small windowless room with a table and three chairs. Eric swallowed back the bile creeping up the back of his throat. He'd done okay so far, feeling only mildly anxious walking through the gates into this hell that had been his home for three years. The waiting area, with its semblance of cheerfulness in the form of pictures on the walls and magazines to read, hadn't seemed so bad.

But this room definitely felt like prison. It smelled

of prison, a noxious blend of body odor, urine and hopelessness that he had never encountered anywhere else.

Eric broke out in a sweat.

"Hey, you okay?" Bree asked.

He'd been hoping she wouldn't notice. "I'm okay. It's just…"

"Oh, God, Eric, I hadn't even thought about that. I was so focused on seeing Kelly and helping him that I forgot what kind of effect this place might have on you."

He didn't want her pity. "I'm okay. Let's just get this over with and get out of here." He sucked in a breath and followed Bree into the cheerless room, glad that at least the guard hadn't recognized him. The man didn't look familiar to Eric, so perhaps they'd never met.

After a few minutes, which they spent in silence, the door opened again and Kelly Ralston entered.

Eric kept his gaze downcast, not quite ready to look at this man he had so hated—and feared. Yes, despite what he'd told Bree, he felt fear.

"Bree." The voice was familiar yet not. That was because it held a note of fondness, certainly not a tone Eric had ever heard coming out of this man's mouth.

"Kelly, you're looking well."

"In the prime of my life. For all the good it does."

Eric forced himself to look up. He had tried to prepare himself for this moment, but it was still a shock to the system seeing Ralston again, sitting not three feet away as if it were no big deal.

Ralston met Eric with an even gaze and a placid expression on his face. "Eric Riggs. Bree told me you were coming, but frankly, I had a hard time believing her. I thought you were dead."

"Alive and kicking." Eric had decided during the drive to Huntsville that he would say very little, allowing Bree to orchestrate the meeting however she wanted. He wouldn't do anything to deliberately provoke Ralston, but neither would he placate the man or make any friendly overtures.

"So," Ralston said, returning his attention to Bree. "What's this all about? You said you had some news?"

"It's not good, Kelly," Bree said. "Philomene turned up missing."

Eric tensed, waiting for some kind of explosive response from Ralston. Eric remembered how it felt every time a glimmer of hope for his release had been snuffed out.

But Ralston merely shook his head. "I knew it was too good to be true." He shifted his gaze back to Eric. "What does this have to do with him?"

"Eric works for Project Justice."

"I'm not here in that capacity," Eric said quickly.

"But that's how we met," Bree said. "I went to the foundation to try to get them to accept your case—"

"Well, no wonder they turned you down!" Ralston actually laughed. Eric was sure he had never heard his fellow inmate make that noise, either.

"So I guess it's true you two knew each other?" Bree said.

The question irritated Eric. "You thought I was lying?"

"No. But, Kelly, I do want to hear your side of things."

Ralston shifted in his chair and refused to meet Bree's earnest blue-eyed gaze. "Whatever he told you, it's probably all true."

"You cut him?"

"Yes."

"Kelly...why would you do something like that?"

"I don't think you understand what it's like in here. Every day is a fight for survival. The strong do everything in their power to stay on top. The weak..."

"I understand the need to defend yourself," Bree said. "So did Eric attack you?" The question came out awash with disbelief.

"No. He was trying to break up a fight between me and another guy. I didn't cut him on purpose."

Bree looked between her former lover and her more recent one. "Eric? Is that what happened?"

Eric shrugged. "What he says is true, technically. I was trying to break up a fight, and I can't honestly say your friend meant to slice me open like a cut of meat at the butcher shop. It's what happened afterward that colored the incident for me."

"And that was...?" Bree asked impatiently.

"Okay, about that." If anything, Ralston looked even more uncomfortable. "That was for your own good, Riggs. You know that, right? You were green back then, maybe, what, a week in?"

"Something like that. But how can you imagine that threatening my family, my child, was for my own good?"

Bree gasped. "Kelly. Please tell me you didn't…."

"I had to say something that would get to him—fast. He was about to go to the guards. Do you have any idea what happens to stoolies in this place?"

Bree winced and shook her head.

"Trust me, you don't want to know." He returned his attention to Eric. "I remembered what it was like to be new and scared. You were young, pretty—I imagine you were terrified."

"Of course I was. And what you did made me feel so much more secure."

"If you had tattled to the guards about your little injury, you might have gotten some short-term satisfaction. But you'd have gotten a label. The worst kind. It would have made you look weak. And once the guys in here figure that out… Even if your body had survived, your mind wouldn't have. I was *saving* you."

Bree looked back and forth between them as if she were watching a Ping-Pong match. Now she was waiting for Eric's next volley.

"Someone told the guards," Eric said.

"But it wasn't you. I know that. You damn near went to your grave with the secret. But once you went to the infirmary, word got out. I spent a week in the hole. No biggie."

Eric couldn't believe this. Had he really gotten this all wrong?

"You could have just told me. Might have saved me almost dying. I could have gotten medical attention without telling who cut me. Instead I let it fester. They had to find me unconscious in my cell."

"Maybe I could have handled it differently," Ralston said gruffly.

"You didn't have to threaten to kill my baby daughter."

Bree didn't just gasp. She turned white as whipped cream. "Kelly. Dear Lord, is he telling the truth?"

Ralston just looked away.

"Oh, Kelly…"

"It wasn't like I was ever going to do it, for Chrissake. Even if I ever get out of this godforsaken hellhole, which is looking less and less likely."

Bree said nothing.

"I had to make an impression," Ralston tried again. "It was for his own—"

"To threaten a man's child was for his own good? In what universe? I can't believe this. Eric told me there was a side of you I didn't know, but I didn't believe him."

"He's right. To survive in this place, I have to show a different face than I do to you."

"So was it all a lie, then? That sweet, gentle, sensitive guy I once fell in love with—"

"I'm still me, Bree. But you don't know what it's like in here."

"I think we're done." Bree got up and headed for the door, reaching for the buzzer that would summon the guard. In mere seconds it would all be over. Bree's faith in Kelly had been destroyed. She wouldn't continue with her attempts to prove his innocence.

"Bree, wait." Eric couldn't believe he was doing this. She turned and looked at him, her eyes filled with unshed tears and questions.

"He's right."

"Excuse me?"

It had taken Eric a few moments to process Ralston's explanation, but to his chagrin, it made perfect sense. "What he said. It's true. If I'd ratted him out to the guards, I'd have been labeled a snitch and punished in ways you can't imagine. I had *victim* written all over me."

"So you're taking his side? You're excusing his behavior?"

"*Excusing* isn't quite the right word. But let's just say I now understand why he did it. And in some ways, he did me a favor. After I got out of the hospital, I was put in a different cellblock. The guys saw that gnarly scar on my chest and they didn't cross me, didn't think about using me, even if I was pretty."

"For the record," Ralston said, "I'm sorry. I didn't mean for any of it to happen. I especially didn't want you going through life thinking I was coming after your kid. That's horrible."

Bree folded her arms and returned to her chair. "You might think about that next time you're tempted to threaten someone's child. Jesus, Kelly."

"I'm sorry, Bree. I hate disappointing you. You're the one person who hasn't turned their back on me."

Bree seemed to shake off her outrage. "Let's move on. I brought Eric here because the only way Project Justice will take on your case is if we convince him you're innocent. Now that I understand why he wanted to keep you here, I'm not sure why I'm bothering."

"Because I'm innocent, and you know I am."

Bree didn't look as positive of that fact as she previously had been. "What about the bragging? Eric said—"

"Inmates say a lot of things," Eric swiftly interrupted. If he didn't take over this conversation, his lies would take center stage and he had no desire for Ralston to know Eric had so viciously slandered him to the one person who believed in him. "To gain stature, to make ourselves more frightening. We don't have to rehash it."

After a moment, Bree nodded tightly. "That's true. Nothing would ever make me believe you could rape or kill anybody."

Suddenly Ralston smiled at Bree, and Eric was shocked by what he saw. The smile transformed him from hardened criminal to...a man worthy of

Bree's admiration. The look exchanged by the two of them, though fleeting, spoke of more than admiration, though. Eric saw love, a universal love that transcended the hell these two people had gone through.

Eric couldn't explain it, but in that moment he'd seen all he needed to see.

"No convincing necessary, Kelly. I believe you're innocent."

"What?" Bree and Ralston said at the same time.

"I don't think you did it. Bree was right. The person I knew behind bars is different than the one she knows."

"Just like that? There's no catch?"

Eric shook his head. "If Philomene was pressured by anyone—the D.A., the sheriff or a janitor—to pick Ralston as her attacker, and if she was going to recant, her disappearance takes on a more sinister air. Something needs to be done. Immediately."

"Yes. Thank you. Finally. So you'll talk to Daniel?"

Did he have a choice? He'd backed himself into a corner, and he had no one to blame but himself, for lying in the first place. He should have known no good would come of it. But he wouldn't let an innocent man continue to suffer as he had suffered. Even if that meant losing his pride, his job, his license to practice law.

Even if it meant losing Bree to her first love.

## CHAPTER ELEVEN

BREE'S STEP FELT light as they left the prison. She hadn't felt optimistic on her way in. She'd expected an ugly scene between the two men. But she never would have guessed the tide would turn so quickly, that Kelly would convince Eric of his innocence in a few minutes' conversation.

But Eric was a lawyer, and she supposed he was used to sizing people up at a moment's notice, determining who was an enemy or an ally, who was lying and who was sincere.

As soon as they cleared the prison gates, Eric slid down his window and took several gulps of the fresh air.

"You okay?" Bree asked.

"I need that stink out of my nose. It took me two days to get rid of it after my release."

The place did have a distinctive odor, but she'd never thought much about how it would be to live with that smell, day in and day out.

"Now that we're outside the fence, you aren't going to change your mind, are you? You'll still talk to Daniel?"

"You don't have much faith in my word."

"No, I do. I'm sorry."

"You know what puzzles me? You thought I was lying about how I got that scar. But you slept with me anyway."

"I…um…I wasn't thinking about that when we… I mean, you had agreed to meet with Kelly, even though I knew you didn't want to. That said a lot about your character. And the way you were with MacKenzie, such a good dad… What?"

He wasn't smiling. "It just occurred to me that you might have gone to bed with me to seal the bargain. You know, make sure I didn't go back on my word."

"Wow. You really think I'm that calculating?"

"No. No, not really. But it was clear that once it was over, you wanted to forget it happened."

"That's not true. I'm not likely to forget it anytime soon."

Once again they were drenched in an uncomfortable silence as they hurtled down the highway in Eric's car.

Bree was going to have to admit she'd blown it with Eric. Any goodwill or warm feelings they'd created had been obliterated by her manipulations. Threatening to go to Daniel, pressuring him to return to the prison where he spent three obviously hellish years, had yanked him right out of the friendly state of mind he'd been in.

*You got what you wanted.* Eric was going to talk to Daniel and get him to accept Kelly's case.

But now that she was away from Kelly, she was filled with doubts about whether she was doing the right thing. Did she really know Kelly? *Was* he innocent? She'd always been convinced he wasn't capable of rape or murder. But until a few minutes ago, she'd been convinced he wouldn't stab a man with a homemade knife or threaten him and his family with bodily harm.

Even if Kelly was innocent of the crimes for which he'd been convicted, had prison ruined him, corrupted him to the point where he couldn't be redeemed?

Whatever the final outcome of this, it would be on her head.

ERIC'S MOUTH WAS dry as he descended the stairs into the lair. He had always thought it was amusing before, referring to Daniel's underground home office as if he were some wild animal holed up in a subterranean cave.

But Daniel could be a dangerous man—everyone said so. Right now comparing him to a lion or bear didn't seem all that funny. Eric couldn't escape the feeling that he was about to be ripped to shreds.

"Ah, Eric," Daniel greeted him, standing and extending his hand from behind the gigantic U-shaped desk that dominated his command center. He had two laptops open as well as his phone. Above them on the walls were three TVs, each set to a different news broadcast. Thankfully, the sound was muted on all but one, on which a somber-voiced anchor discussed a plane crash.

"Daniel. You're looking well." Tanned, anyway. He had somehow avoided that late-winter pallor everyone else sported. Probably from playing polo no matter what the weather.

"You, too. I heard you visited my barber."

"Felix worked wonders with the post-prison haircut. I'm feeling a lot better, too." Physically, he hadn't felt this fit since before prison. Travis had some weights in the garage, and the two of them had been working out in the evenings and sometimes running in the mornings.

"How about in here?" Daniel tapped his temple with his index finger. "I know I healed physically a lot quicker than mentally. Even eight years later, I'm still fighting a few demons."

"Yeah, of course. Having MacKenzie back in my life has gone a long way toward healing me, though. I'm more worried about *her* emotional scars than mine. But she's improving—opening up, talking more, not quite so scared of strangers."

"Glad to hear it. Being responsible for the well-being of another human being—it's huge. I'm about to find out what it's like."

"It can be pretty terrifying. But so worth it. Apparently my marriage was a sham, but I've never once regretted bringing MacKenzie into the world."

"Aren't you going to sit down?"

Eric was too nervous to sit, and this cordial chat

made him even more on edge. He had to get to the point soon. Daniel was a busy man. There were people in the world who would pay a million dollars to have Daniel's ear for thirty minutes, and Eric had it for free.

"It's about Kelly Ralston."

"The guy in Huntsville? I thought that matter had been decided. The business we're in, you can't spend too much time second-guessing yourself. We have limited resources and we have to spend them on the candidates most deserving of freedom, as best we can determine. A guy who brags about his crimes in disgusting detail doesn't sound like someone I want out on the streets."

Eric could have continued lying. He could have said that he believed all that jailhouse bragging was simply a way for Ralston to up his status, establish him as a tough, scary guy and make sure he stayed on top of the pecking order.

But the lie had been weighing heavily on him. His conscience constantly reminded him that he had wronged the man who had essentially saved his life by intervening with the governor and vouching for Eric. He'd also given Eric a job and referred him to his barber. A man didn't share his barber with just anyone.

Daniel trusted Eric. And Eric had repaid him with an egregious lie.

"Ralston never confessed to his crimes—not to

me or anyone that I know of. He has always maintained his innocence."

Daniel looked momentarily confused. "You lied?"

Eric nodded.

"Good God, Eric, why on earth would you do that? Did you even know him?"

"Yes, I knew him—for about two weeks. During that time, he sliced open my chest with a shiv, then threatened to kill me if I ratted him out."

"The injury that landed you in the hospital?" Daniel's voice and expression were carefully neutral. Eric had no idea what he was thinking. He was probably one helluva poker player.

Eric nodded. "That wouldn't predispose me in his favor, but the real issue is different. He threatened to go after MacKenzie...." He repeated the whole disgusting story. "So you can imagine how I felt when I saw that man's face on the screen in the conference room. I would have done just about anything to keep him behind bars, where I firmly believed he belonged."

"Even lie."

"Even lie to a man who certainly didn't deserve that from me, not after everything you've done."

Daniel was silent for a time. Eric couldn't tell if he was angry or not, but he looked troubled.

"I'll understand if you fire me. I'd probably fire me if I were you."

"Believed," Daniel said suddenly.

"Excuse me?"

"You said, you *believed* prison was where Ralston *belonged*. You used the past tense. Does that mean you've changed your mind?"

"I'd be lying if I said I looked forward to the day that man walks out of prison. But he did give a plausible explanation for why he threatened me. He said he was trying to protect me—to keep me from getting labeled a snitch. I'm guessing you know what my fate would have been if that had happened."

Daniel nodded. "Not a pretty picture. So you went to visit Ralston?"

"Yes."

"Might I ask why you did such a thing?"

"Let's just say Bree Johnson is a persuasive woman."

"Ah. Brianna. That explains it."

"Really?"

"I did talk to her on the phone. She was…insistent. Very passionate in her belief in Ralston's innocence. Frankly, the reason I had you give her the bad news was because I didn't want to. I knew she wouldn't give up without a fight."

"Combine that personality with the looks of a sexy angel and you'll understand why I found it hard to refuse her anything."

There was a moment of silence during which Eric relived his initial meeting with Bree—how hot she'd looked, how uncomfortable he'd felt because she was the first woman he'd wanted since Tammy came into his life.

"Oh, dear God," Daniel said. "You slept with her."

"Hell, how did you know that?"

"I'm impressed you didn't try to lie about it. I probably would have."

Eric shrugged. "I don't see the point. If I'm gonna lose my job anyway."

"If I fired people for having sex with inappropriate partners, my whole staff would be gone. And I'd have to resign myself. Makes me wonder if someone's pumping hormones into the water pipes."

Eric tried not to laugh. He wasn't sure if Daniel was kidding. "Maybe that explains the size of the cockroaches there."

"So what's the bottom line?" Daniel asked. "You obviously came here today hoping for a certain outcome."

"I'd like for you to reconsider taking on Kelly Ralston's case. The woman who claims she misidentified Ralston as her rapist?"

"Philomene Switzer, yes. What about her?"

"She's gone missing." Eric gave Daniel a quick rundown of the evidence they'd amassed so far. "I'm afraid Bree might be next. If someone got to Philomene, they undoubtedly know that she confided in Bree. And if the sheriff is involved…"

"Bree certainly can't depend on the local law enforcement to adequately investigate Philomene's disappearance."

"Exactly."

"Where is Bree now?"

"At home, I think. I tried to get her to stay with

me until I talked to you, but she insisted she would be careful. Stubborn woman."

"All right. Since a woman's life might be at stake, I'll put Joe Kinkaid on this. He just concluded another case, so he can jump right on it."

"Really?"

"I'd already approved this case before you deep-sixed it. Seems like the right thing to do is resurrect it and give it the attention it deserves. The victim threatening to change her story, then vanishing sounds ominous—requiring some type of urgent action."

Something tight inside Eric's chest unwound, and he took a deep breath. Thank God. Daniel *got it*. Eric might be unemployed, but at least someone would be looking out for Bree. And poor Philomene. She would either be found alive...or avenged.

"Thank you, Daniel. I'm very grateful. I'll go clean out my office."

"Did I fire you? I don't think so."

"Oh. Aren't you going to?"

Daniel softened his tone. "Come on, man, I'm not that much of a hard-ass. You were trying to protect your daughter. When it comes to family, I'd do just about anything for them—including killing someone, and obviously you would, too. That's the kind of guy I want on my payroll."

This was unexpected. "Thank you, Daniel. I don't even know what to say."

"You can say, 'Daniel, next time I'm faced with

some kind of ethical dilemma like that, I'll confide in you instead of lying.'"

"Done."

"I just have one question. Did you lie to Bree, as well?"

"I had to give her some kind of reason for the foundation's change of heart."

"Have you told her the truth?"

Eric shook his head.

"Nothing will be right between you until you do. Tell her what you told me. She might be angry at first, but if she's a woman worth your time, she'll understand. Eventually."

"I plan to tell her." *Eventually.*

BREE HAD THOUGHT she was being brave and sensible when she'd marched away from Eric the previous day, declaring she could take care of herself. She'd convinced herself that she wasn't in danger, that calling in to work sick and hiding from some imaginary threat was a severe overreaction.

But when she'd left the hospital in the predawn hours, physically and emotionally exhausted from caring for the victims of a multicar accident, she'd noticed something that filled her with unease. A strange car—a beige Acura, several years old—had been parallel-parked in the street adjacent to the staff parking lot.

No one ever parked there at night. There was nothing around except a couple of houses that had plenty of parking in their driveways. Hospital visitors and patients had their own lot, which always had spaces available.

The suspicious car had tinted windows, so Bree hadn't been able to see if anyone was inside. But she'd felt as if she was being watched.

She'd shaken off her feelings, convincing herself she was just tired. But when she'd awakened from a restless sleep at close to noon, she'd looked out her front window and seen the same car, now parked on her street.

Was she being stalked?

Bree walked downstairs to pick up her newspaper, which the carrier always left for her in the lobby. While there, she peered out the front window, where she could get a better look at the car. From this angle it didn't appear that anyone was behind the wheel.

She breathed a sigh of relief. This whole business with Philomene had made her far too jumpy—and had impeded her judgment, apparently, given how easily she'd succumbed to her attraction to Eric. Her heart twitched inside her chest at the memory. She couldn't recall when she'd ever meshed with someone so seamlessly, so perfectly. Everything had felt *right,* like two longtime dance partners who could anticipate each other's moves without words.

But afterward—she'd behaved badly. Horribly. Okay, so she'd panicked, and she was desperately out of practice when it came to romance and sex etiquette. The moment they'd joined their bodies, she'd realized the whole "no strings" idea was a nonstarter. She already had feelings for the man, and a longing to be part of a family again that made her stupid.

Putting a quick, decisive end to the episode and returning to a business-only relationship had seemed like the wisest course of action.

But when was it ever wise to hurt someone? Rather than exhibiting gratitude for being spared the awkward after-sex tap dance, Eric had acted hurt and angry. So clearly not all men appreciated no-strings-attached sex.

Did that mean Eric *wanted* strings? Or was he simply miffed that he hadn't been the one to declare there would be no repeat performance?

Her fridge was empty, so Bree decided to make a trip to the market. Maybe a pint of Chunky Monkey was in order. Wasn't that what her friends always did when they had man problems—eat a large quantity of ice cream right out of the carton?

In the end her medical training won out, and she compromised with low-fat frozen-yogurt pops. By the time she was stuffing her bags in the trunk of her car, she'd all but forgotten about the beige Acura—until she spotted it again, parked at the end of her row.

This was no coincidence. It was the same car—she'd taken note of a scrape on the right rear fender.

Someone was keeping tabs on her.

She was too scared to drive home. What if this guy lay in wait for her, surprised her? He could disable her before she could get to her cell phone. No one would hear her scream.

She didn't see anyone behind her as she drove home, but he didn't have to follow her; he knew where she lived.

Oh, God, she was being paranoid. Wasn't she?

He probably hadn't beat her home, because he hadn't passed her. So she could go inside, lock all the doors, set her security alarm.... But then what about the next time she had to go out? She could call in sick to work. But how long could she do that? How long would four small bags of groceries last her?

When she let herself in through the security gate, she noticed that the keyhole had scratches all around it. Had those always been there? Or had someone picked the lock?

Okay, that was it. She wasn't going home by herself. She chucked her groceries back in the trunk, got in her car and got the hell out of there.

After several minutes of aimless driving, trying to figure out where she would be safe—a motel? A friend's house?—she did what she'd known she would do all along. She turned the car toward the interstate and headed for Houston. Eric might be mad at her, but he wouldn't turn her away. He would never propose that she put herself in danger. He cared for her at least that much.

ERIC'S DAY HAD been long and tedious. After leaving Daniel's place, he'd met with Joe Kinkaid, an investigator who had played a key role in proving Eric's innocence and getting him released from prison. Eric liked Kinkaid. The guy was former Secret Service, and at first glance he seemed like the buttoned-down, by-the-book agent—military haircut, bulky dive watch on his wrist, rigid posture. But a few minutes' acquaintance soon revealed a rebellious streak a mile wide. The guy dressed in dark conservative suits, but his ties were definitely nonregulation. Today's had a picture of a cartoon woodpecker on it.

Debriefing Kinkaid had taken a couple of hours. Then they'd spent another couple of hours setting priorities—keeping Bree safe from any repercussions resulting from their investigation was number one. Next was finding Philomene. If she could be found alive, they would convince her to visit Dr. Claudia Ellison, the foundation's on-call psychologist, who was a nationally renowned body-language expert and hypnotherapist. She was especially adept at recovering suppressed memories. If anyone could help Philomene remember the true identity of her rapist, Claudia could.

Then there was the whole angle of possible law enforcement involvement in the crimes perpetrated against Philomene. Kinkaid had a contact in the Texas Rangers; he'd promised to talk to that guy and see if the Rangers might get involved, perhaps on an advisory basis.

Recruiting any kind of law enforcement was a tricky business, Eric had discovered. Getting more people to work for the home team was good. Unfortunately, cops tended to take over. And if they decided to, they could order Project Justice investigators to stand down—which meant the foundation's priorities could get derailed.

It was all enough to make Eric's head spin. He wanted to keep working, but he also wanted to get home to MacKenzie. She'd stayed home from school today just as a precaution, but she seemed completely recovered from her stomach bug. Elena, bless her heart, had agreed to stay home and babysit, but now it was Eric's turn.

His heart jumped when he saw a strange car in the driveway. Then he realized it wasn't so strange, after all.

Bree.

He'd been looking forward to calling her and giving her an update. He'd also planned to convince her to take her safety more seriously. Now he would have the pleasure of doing so in person.

Seeing her was dangerous. Now that Kinkaid was on board, Eric ought to turn the whole thing over to him and be done.

But the thought of staying totally away from Bree was about as attractive as putting his arm under his brother's new saw.

Eric parked behind Bree's little red Fiat and loped inside. The front door was unlocked—he'd have to speak to Elena about that. Just because Tammy's murderer had been caught and locked up didn't mean other crazies weren't running around. He found Elena in the living room folding laundry.

"Look at you, domestic goddess."

"It's not so bad. Not that I'd want to quit working, but I don't mind doing the house-and-kids thing once in a while."

"Where's MacKenzie? Is she doing okay?"

"She's doing great. Good appetite, eating better than I've ever seen her. I've had to pace her—don't want her overdoing it right after being so sick. But she seems fine. No fever, no stomachache, nothing. Now, aren't you dying to ask me where Bree is? I know you saw her car."

"My kid first. Then Bree. She is here, isn't she?"

"Yes. She offered to keep MacKenzie entertained while I attacked our mountain of laundry. They were in the backyard last I checked. Bree was pushing MacKenzie on the tire swing."

The mental image that came to mind was sweet— Bree and MacKenzie laughing, Bree's skirt blowing in the wind, clinging to her shapely legs…. "Do you know why she's here?"

"She didn't offer an explanation and I didn't interrogate her." Elena lowered her voice. "But I'm guessing she's here because she likes you."

Eric smiled, though he thought *like* was a pale verb to use when describing what was going on between him and Bree. "I can't thank you enough for watching MacKenzie. Dinner's on me tonight."

"Great, because I haven't pulled anything out of

the freezer. Oh, but Bree brought groceries. She put a few things in the fridge, anyway."

What the hell?

He peeked out the window that faced the back-yard, but Bree and MacKenzie weren't there. The tire swing was still.

His first thought was that they'd disappeared. Immediately he counseled himself to stop jumping to ridiculous conclusions, but every cell in his body was on edge until he climbed the stairs and heard the high-pitched tones of MacKenzie's voice and Bree's more dulcet tones.

He found them in his daughter's room. MacKenzie sat at her little desk with papers and pencils and crayons spread out in front of her. Bree had dragged in a chair from Eric's room so she could sit beside the little girl.

Eric stood quietly in the doorway, observing.

"So we've got three pieces of pie here and two pieces of cake and one cookie. How many desserts does that make?" Bree asked.

MacKenzie counted laboriously on her fingers. "Six!" she announced proudly.

"Excellent. So write the number six in that box."

Using her special fat pencil that was supposed to encourage her to hold it correctly, MacKenzie filled in the box. Her teacher had said that MacKenzie was reading, writing and spelling on a first-grade level and progressing well at math, too.

"Okay, next one," Bree said. "We have one mommy,

one daddy and two children. How many people are in that family?"

MacKenzie touched each of the family stick figures with her index finger. "I don't have a mommy," she said softly, sounding sad. "She got killed. That means she's never coming home."

Eric sucked in a breath.

"I heard about what happened to your mother," Bree said. "That's very sad."

"She's in heaven now. She's an angel and she's watching me."

"I bet she's very proud of how smart you are. You're doing all these papers by yourself. I'm hardly helping at all."

"Are you a mommy?" MacKenzie asked innocently.

Bree's expression changed abruptly from one of compassion to an almost palpable sadness. "I am. But my little girl—she's in heaven, too."

Eric stopped breathing. *Oh, my God.*

# CHAPTER TWELVE

MacKenzie's eyes widened. "Hey, maybe she knows my mommy!"

"Maybe she does." Bree seemed to be struggling to hold herself together, and Eric realized he shouldn't be lurking here, watching and eavesdropping when neither party had noticed him.

He knocked briskly on the doorframe. "Knock knock, anybody home?"

"Daddy!" MacKenzie popped out of her chair and launched herself into Eric's arms. "Dr. Bree and me is doing—"

"Dr. Bree and *I are*..." he corrected her gently.

"Bree and I is—are doing homework."

Bree was hastily dashing her eyes with the back of one hand. "One of MacKenzie's classmates dropped by with the day's worksheets."

"That was nice of Ms. Brown to make sure you didn't miss anything important."

"Uh-huh. Dr. Bree says big kids do homework after school."

"Well, you're getting to be a pretty big girl."

Bree stood up. "I'll just— Um, bathroom." She made a hasty escape.

Eric let MacKenzie show him all the day's "worksheets," which consisted of coloring, connect-the-dots puzzles, spelling and math. She had done them all except for that last problem with the stick-figure family. He gently returned her attention to the family, and she gave the correct answer of four and wrote in the numeral with no extraneous emotion this time.

Meanwhile, Eric was absorbing the fact that not only had Bree given birth to a child, but that the child had died. Losing his mother had been heart-wrenching; losing his wife had been excruciating. How much worse to lose your child, your flesh and blood?

How did anyone survive it?

His respect for Bree and her strength of spirit rose another notch.

"Daddy, look, I colored a puppy."

Eric looked at the paper his daughter so proudly showed him and was mildly surprised. The puppy was pink and purple. How ironic that the one thing she probably *should* have colored brown or black had turned into her breakout art project. "That's beautiful, sweetheart. I love the colors."

"Except puppies aren't really purple," she said with a giggle.

Again Eric was struck by how much he missed MacKenzie's laughter. He remembered when she was a baby how she would laugh and laugh when he made funny faces at her. He didn't know what Bree was doing, but MacKenzie was showing some definite improvement. Or maybe it was simply that time was healing her, and Bree's presence was purely coincidental.

Still, obviously MacKenzie liked "Dr. Bree," who seemed to have a natural affinity for kids. What a tragedy that she didn't have her own. It must be hard to see other little girls and wonder what hers might have turned out like, if only.

"Since you've done such a good job finishing your homework, would you like to watch TV?"

MacKenzie nodded.

"You can watch in the living room. And maybe you can help Elena fold laundry."

"Okay." She slid off her chair and walked to her bookcase, where her toys were lined up with meticulous care. She checked to make sure they were all present and accounted for, then chose a hand puppet of a giraffe to take downstairs with her. She was still worried someone would take her toys away. He wondered if that was an insecurity that would follow her to adulthood.

Bree returned from the bathroom and looked around. "Where's MacKenzie?"

"I told her she could watch TV for a little while. I figured you might want to talk in private. Or did you come just to see my daughter?"

She smiled ruefully. "It's certainly no hardship

spending time with her. She's so sweet." Bree dropped her gaze. "You were listening to our conversation."

"Guilty. I didn't want to interrupt. I love seeing her happy and engaged, talking to someone. For a while I worried that she was hopelessly introverted. So yes, I did hear you. And I'm so sorry. I can't even imagine…"

"I think maybe you can. You did almost lose your little girl. Isn't that what happened? She was almost adopted?"

"Yeah, by the son of a bitch who killed her mother. That was horrible. But not the same." He wanted to know more. Like when had this happened? And who had the father been? Was it Ralston's? But he figured she would open up about it when she felt comfortable, not before. Meanwhile, he had no business trying to drag it out of her.

"Yes, she was Kelly's," she said abruptly. "I was eighteen when she was born. We were planning to get married. Her name was Casey, after Kelly's mother. She was born premature, weighed four and a half pounds and lived six hours and twenty-five minutes."

Eric had nothing to say. Any platitude he came up with would be stupid. So he just put his arms around her.

"Mostly I've learned to deal with it." Her voice was thick with tears. "But every once in a while, something will set me off."

"Like my daughter asking intrusive questions."

"Actually, Casey was already on my mind. She would have been a little older than MacKenzie. I was just feeling sorry for myself that I couldn't help my own little girl with her schoolwork." She pulled away. "I'm okay, really." She cleared her throat. "You're probably wondering why I'm here."

"I guess it's too much to hope that you couldn't stay away from me?"

She smiled beguilingly but then quickly grew serious. "Eric, someone is watching me. Stalking me."

Eric's pulse jumped. "Jesus. Who?"

"I have no idea who it is. It's just a car with tinted windows, and I see it everywhere—near the hospital's staff parking lot, on my street, at the grocery store." Bree was obviously shaken.

"You're sure about this?" he asked sharply.

"You mean, do you think I'm imagining things?" She shook her head. "It's the same car. He even tried to follow me out of town."

"He didn't—" Eric swallowed back the panic.

"No, no, I made sure there were no cars behind me when I got off the freeway."

But plenty of people had seen them together recently. If someone was really stalking Bree, he or she might think to check Eric's address. It wouldn't be that hard to find, especially if the stalker was law enforcement. Bree wouldn't be safe anywhere. And if they followed her here, MacKenzie wouldn't be safe.

"You believe me, right? I'm not delusional."

"Of course I believe you. And I'm glad you came

here. I won't let anything happen to you, Bree. We're going to get to the bottom of this. And we don't have to do it alone. The Kelly Ralston case is officially on the roster at Project Justice."

Bree smiled through the last of her tears. "That's wonderful news!"

"The case is getting priority consideration, given Philomene's precarious situation."

"I've tried calling and texting her. I've reassured her that I just want to be sure she's okay, that I won't pressure her to do anything she's uncomfortable with."

"And?"

"No response. Also, there's something else. I looked at that last text message supposedly from her. The spelling and grammar are perfect. I compared it to another text she left. She used shortcuts like T-H-X for *thanks* and the numeral four to mean F-O-R. It seems pretty clear to me she didn't write that text."

"I agree. Joe Kinkaid is the investigator assigned to the case. This afternoon he and I went over everything we know and came up with a strategy. Obviously, finding Philomene is near the top of our list. We used satellite maps to examine the area around where her car was found. There are lots of places to hide a body—woods, water. We're going to bring in searchers and dogs."

"I want to help search."

"Of course. We'll need all the people we can round up. There's a lot of ground to cover."

Bree stood, suddenly filled with nervous energy. "When is this going to happen?"

"Wednesday."

She paused and pressed her lips together. "Sheriff DeVille isn't going to like this."

"He was the first person we contacted. He'll be in charge of the search. Or at least, he'll *think* he is."

Bree's look of surprise would have been comical if the situation weren't so grim. "But why…?"

"He has to at least pretend to be grateful that an organization with the resources of Project Justice is trying to help locate a woman missing from his town. With the finding of the blood, he has to at least admit the possibility Philomene met with foul play."

"Plus, if he's involved, he might be able to orchestrate the search to his advantage."

"Or he might already know her body isn't there, so what's the harm of pretending cooperation?"

She laughed unexpectedly. "I'm so relieved not to be in this alone anymore. I should call Kelly and let him know." She whipped out her phone from her pocket, but Eric stopped her.

"It's taken care of. Thanks to his existing appeals attorney, I've been put on the list as part of his legal defense team. I can get access to him when necessary."

"Did you talk to him?"

Eric nodded. Dealing with the man who had nearly killed him wasn't his favorite part of the current situation. But it was his job now. "He was grateful."

So grateful, in fact, that Eric had found it hard to remember who this guy was. What if it was all an act? What if Ralston didn't believe Eric when he said he hadn't ratted him out? What if Eric ended up being the one responsible for securing Ralston's release, and his efforts caused some harm to befall MacKenzie?

Eric knew how counterproductive it was to live in a state of fear and paranoia. He had to believe he was doing the right thing. He had to believe in Bree and her faith in the man who had fathered her child.

"And everything's okay between you?"

"Bree, if I seriously believed he intended harm to me or mine, I wouldn't have taken up his cause." That was the bottom line, he supposed. Even if Ralston was pure evil, Eric doubted he'd be stupid enough to finally get out of prison, then do something to put himself right back in.

"I'm glad."

Eric sensed that she wanted to say more, maybe *do* more—like put her arms around him. But in the end she clasped her hands behind her back.

"So I brought a carload of groceries with me. Since I'm too freaked out to stay at home by myself, I'm throwing myself on your mercy and offering to feed you in exchange for a safe haven."

"You don't even need to ask, and no payment is necessary."

"How does everyone feel about hamburgers?" she asked as if he hadn't spoken.

He smiled and nodded. "Sure. Want me to fire up the grill?"

"As long as you let me do the cooking. I want you and MacKenzie to spend quality time together and leave everything else to me." She whisked past him out the door and trotted down the stairs.

Eric frankly enjoyed the thought of Bree preparing their dinner. As though they were friends. Family, even. It was an intimate thing to do, even if it was only hamburgers for the whole gang.

He went out onto the patio to make sure the grill was clean and showed Bree how to light it. Then he joined Elena and MacKenzie in the living room, where MacKenzie and her giraffe puppet were purportedly helping Elena fold laundry. In reality they were probably a hindrance. MacKenzie hadn't bothered to turn on the TV—she was engaging with Elena, another positive sign.

When Eric had first been reunited with Mac-Kenzie, she'd spent a lot of time in front of the TV, watching cartoons she'd seen a million times. Her therapist had said she was comforted by the familiar and to let her soothe herself that way. As she'd become more secure with her new living situation and caregivers, she had gradually cut back on TV all on her own, as the therapist had hoped. Dr. Fredricks was considered something of a miracle worker when it came to helping traumatized kids, and with MacKenzie he hadn't disappointed.

"Need more help?" Eric asked. "Bree offered to fix dinner, so I'm off the hook."

Elena laughed. "Think again. You'll cook tomorrow night. It's so your turn."

"I'll do it anytime. But my cooking sucks when compared to Travis's." Travis had practically raised him and had learned to stretch the grocery money by cooking meals from scratch rather than buying TV dinners and frozen pizza. He'd found their mom's recipe box, which had come from their grandmother, and taught himself.

"Well, the laundry is pretty much done. So you can just...play."

"Gee, thanks, Mom." He would be forever grateful to Trav and Elena for everything they'd done, but he was going to have to fly on his own, sooner rather than later. He could cash in a couple of bonds and get enough money to put down a deposit and pay first and last month's rent. If he lived nearby, Elena would most likely still be available for after-school care. Then he would just have to find a backup babysitter.

When he'd first gotten out of prison, logistic tasks such as finding childcare had seemed a huge challenge. Even shopping for groceries or fixing a meal had taxed him. Now Eric wasn't bothered by the prospect at all. Maybe MacKenzie wasn't the only one coming out of her shell.

Following Elena's directive, he sat down next to MacKenzie. "How about we play Go Fish?"

MacKenzie nodded enthusiastically and ran upstairs to get the deck of cards.

"Okay, what's the deal?" Elena asked. She sounded curious, not confrontational.

Eric gave her the *Reader's Digest* condensed version of recent events. "Bree is really spooked, and I don't blame her. You don't mind if she bunks here a couple of nights, do you?"

"Of course not. Especially if she's going to buy groceries and cook. Where's she going to sleep?"

The deceptively innocent question took him by surprise. "I'll take the sofa, of course." Much as he might like Bree to share his bed, he wasn't ready to send mixed signals to MacKenzie—or to Bree herself, for that matter. He certainly wasn't ready for a live-in girlfriend, not that Bree had given any indication she wanted to play that role.

As he and MacKenzie played cards, Eric's mind wandered, and he found himself imagining what it would be like going to sleep with Bree in his arms, waking up with her next to him. He had enjoyed being married. He missed simple domestic pleasures. He missed having that one person he thought he could rely on.

But it would be a long time before he trusted any woman the way he'd trusted Tammy.

BREE WOKE UP disoriented in almost total darkness, and it took her a few moments to remember that she was staying with Eric—sleeping on the lumpy living room sofa at her own insistence. But her thoughts kept drifting to Eric's comfy double bed with its down comforter and the hot guy that came with it.

She knew why they weren't sleeping together, and she was okay with it. She was the one who had thrown up barricades to begin with, so she could hardly complain that Eric was being a complete gentleman. But two nights spent on this sofa seemed an eternity.

She had to forget about the amazing sex and move on. She had her priorities—first, to not get herself killed. Then she had to find Philomene and get Kelly's conviction overturned. Anything else was just a distraction, especially when she had to work fifty hours a week. The E.R. supervisor hadn't been all that happy that she wanted a couple of days off, but at least he hadn't said no.

What time was it, anyway? She was snuggled way down deep under her blankets. As she reached out to find her phone, which she'd left on the coffee table, she realized she had more blankets than when she'd started. Someone—Eric, no doubt—had placed a down comforter over her. Her heart warmed at the thoughtful gesture. When was the last time any man cared about something so trivial as whether she was chilled?

It was four-thirty—almost time to get up if she and Eric planned to make it to Tuckerville by sunrise, around seven-thirty. That was when all of the searchers were gathering out on Curry Road.

The sound of rustling in the kitchen brought Bree to full attention. She sat up straight. No lights were on, yet someone was definitely moving around.

All senses on alert, Bree quietly slipped out from under the covers. She grabbed the first thing she saw that might ostensibly be used as a weapon—a glass bowl full of papier-mâché fruit on the coffee table—and crept toward the kitchen. As she reached the open doorway, she moved the bowl to her right hand, ready to lob it at the intruder and run, then switched on the light.

The shirtless intruder whirled around with a yelp of surprise and Bree issued an abbreviated shriek.

"Jesus, Bree, you scared me half to death." It was Eric.

"I thought you were a burglar."

He nodded toward the bowl in her hands. "And what were you going to do, pummel me with paper fruit?"

"I was going to throw the whole bowl at you and run," she confessed. "It was all I could find on the spur of the moment." Now that she'd spoken it aloud, her plan seemed pretty lame.

Eric stepped closer and relieved her of the bowl, setting it on the counter. He put his arm around her shoulders. "For the record, if you think there's a burglar in the house, you scream bloody murder and then get out of the house. You don't throw stuff at him."

"Oh, right, and leave the rest of you to deal with him? How cowardly would that be?"

"Then call 911 and hide."

She could have done that, she supposed. Her phone had been right there. "Guess I wasn't quite awake or thinking clearly." She still wasn't thinking clearly, not with him standing so close and not wearing a shirt, just a pair of jeans that rode low on his slim hips.

Just when she was about to turn toward him and snuggle into his light embrace, he released her. "I was trying not to wake you. I thought I'd put together some kind of breakfast to eat in the car."

"Okay. Where's your shirt?"

"Oh. The clean laundry never quite made it up-stairs yesterday." He walked around her into the living room, found a laundry basket filled with folded shirts and grabbed one at random. It was a long-sleeved knit shirt the soft gray of a mourning dove. Bree said a silent goodbye to that gorgeous naked torso—scar and all—as he dragged the shirt over his head.

"You can go get dressed if you want," he said. "I've got breakfast handled. Unless you'd prefer something besides fruit, cheese and granola bars?"

"No, that's fine." She looked down at herself, grateful she was wearing a pair of perfectly respect-able man-style pajamas, though she was braless un-derneath, and she was pretty sure her hard, tight nipples showed through the pink cotton. "Don't forget the coffee."

"Right. The most important part of breakfast for you." He'd prepared the coffeemaker last night; all he had to do was push a button.

Bree had bought a few necessities before arriving here yesterday. Now she grabbed her shopping bag and retreated to the bathroom to change. She'd showered last night so she could get ready quickly this morning. A hasty teeth brushing, a splash of water on her face and a comb through her hair, and she was ready.

They tiptoed out of the house, and by five-thirty they were headed toward Tuckerville.

The weather had turned overnight; the temperature was a chilly thirty-eight degrees, which reminded Bree: "Thank you for covering me up last night. I hope *you* didn't give me your only blanket."

"I was fine."

"Well, it was thoughtful of you. I really appreciate you taking me in."

"Stay as long as you like. I'm sure Elena actually enjoys having another woman to talk to."

"Yeah, well, she might like it okay now, but she won't if it drags on."

"Actually, Daniel has offered to provide you with a bodyguard."

"A bodyguard? Really? Just because I've seen a strange car?"

"He takes that kind of thing very seriously. The

guy who killed my wife and almost killed Elena—he started out following Travis around, painting graffiti threats. He escalated quickly, and it's a lesson we all took to heart."

A chill ran up Bree's spine. Elena had told her in detail what had happened when MacKenzie's foster father took issue with Travis stopping his attempt to adopt the little girl. John Stover had taken Elena hostage, planning to kill her as an act of revenge against Travis. Fortunately, Travis had shown up just in time to prevent that from happening.

It must have been incredibly terrifying for both of them.

"I'm glad my complaints about this stalker are being taken seriously. But a bodyguard? Does Daniel often make such generous offers?"

"Actually, he does. He says what's the point of being a billionaire if I can't throw money around? Also, a trained bodyguard might be able to find out who your mystery stalker is—confront him, even."

"I'll think about it." She didn't really want some stranger watching her every move, sleeping in her apartment, shadowing her at work. But what choice did she have? Other than taking an indefinite leave of absence from work and hanging out at Eric's for the rest of her life, and she didn't think that was an option.

When they reached the intersection where Philomene's car had been found, they discovered they weren't the first to arrive, not by a long shot.

More than a dozen cars were parked haphazardly along the side of the road, and twice that many people were milling around in the early-morning cold, their breath fogging. Men, women, even children had come to help look. Whether their volunteering was due to a genuine desire to help or a more prurient interest in finding a dead body, Bree didn't care to know. She was just glad they were there.

Unfortunately, Sheriff DeVille was already there with his bullhorn, organizing the volunteers.

"Great," Eric muttered as he got out of the car.

A clean-cut guy wearing creased khakis and a neat blue button-down strode toward them, hand outstretched. "Glad you could make it, Eric."

"Of course. I wasn't going to miss it. Joe Kinkaid, this is Bree Johnson."

"Ah." Bree shook the man's hand; his grip was just short of bone crushing. "I can't tell you how grateful I am that you've taken this on."

"I'm gonna do my best." He lowered his voice. "Your local sheriff isn't making it easy on me. He was very clear on the fact that this is his investigation, and if I start trouble, he'll slap me with an obstruction-of-justice charge."

"Of course he wants to control every aspect," Bree said. "So he can hide any evidence that points to him."

"Or he might just be a typical territorial cop. I saw it all the time when I was Secret Service, and I see it now, too. We have to be careful not to jump to any conclusions."

Bree, for one, was going to let DeVille know she was involved and watching his every move—without clueing him in that he was a suspect. She walked brazenly to where he was organizing the volunteers into groups and explaining how a grid search worked.

"You'll proceed in straight lines, one step at a time, so that every inch of these woods gets an eyeball on it," he said through the bullhorn. "Don't be in any hurry. You're looking for anything that might indicate a human being was here recently, from a footprint to a piece of trash, a piece of clothing, a cigarette butt. You're also looking for ground that appears to have been disturbed or like animals have been rooting or digging."

Bree winced, hoping that if Philomene's remains were nearby, the animals had left her alone.

"Now, if you do see something, do not touch it. Not even to get a better look at whatever it is. You wave to me or one of the deputies here." Three uniformed deputies raised their hands. "If we aren't close enough to signal, you send your partner to find one of us and bring us to you. Do not move away from the thing you saw until one of us in uniform has checked it out. Everybody get that? Do I need to say it again? Do. Not. Touch. Anything. Very important."

Bree stood only a few feet away from him now. She did her best to adopt an eager I-want-to-be-of-service expression instead of an accusatory I'm-keeping-my-eye-on-you glare.

Finally he looked at her. "Bree. Glad you could join us." He didn't sound very glad at all. "Do you have a partner?"

Eric stepped up beside her. "I'm her partner."

His words put an inappropriate warmth deep in her chest. *Get a grip, Bree. He means search partner. Not any other kind.*

"Okay. Deputy McClusky, the doctor and the lawyer will be joining your group."

Deputy McClusky, the only woman on the sheriff's staff, motioned for them to join her and a motley group of about fifteen people. "We're gathering over here."

Ted Gentry was a part of their group. He smiled a greeting at Bree. "I thought I'd see you here." Bree could smell mint mouthwash on his breath. She recalled how he'd had trouble walking a straight line when she'd seen him at the café and wondered again if he had a drinking problem.

"Ted, you remember Eric?"

"Sure." The two men shook hands. "Thanks for coming all the way out here. Long drive so early in the morning."

"It's kind of my job now."

Bree explained. "Project Justice has taken on Kelly's case. Finding his supposed victim is key to the case."

"Of course, of course." Ted nodded vigorously. "I'm hoping she's still alive, though."

"Me, too," Bree said. "But the blood in her car trunk…"

"Oh, actually, I have some news about that. It hasn't been released publicly, so keep it under your hat, but that blood? It's not human."

"Really?" Bree felt a ray of hope. "That's encouraging."

"It's still good we're doing this search, though, even if it's just to rule out that she was lured out here and murdered. Hey, you notice one person who's conspicuously absent?"

Bree hadn't taken inventory of every single person here, so no, she hadn't. She shook her head.

"The boyfriend. You know, Jerrod Crowley. Maybe he knows what we'll find. Or maybe she's buried somewhere else and he's not worried. Still, you'd think he would show up for appearance's sake."

Just then a pickup truck with a camper top came to a screeching stop, veering to the side of the road at the last minute. A young, solid-looking man hopped out, then ran to the back of his truck and opened it, releasing a lanky black Labrador retriever.

"Hey, hey, hey!" the sheriff objected, marching over to the newcomer. "I said no pets. You have any idea how much damage a dog can do to a crime scene?"

The young man looked confused. "I'm with Project Justice." He made this announcement as if that explained everything, but apparently it didn't to the sheriff.

"What part of 'no pets' did you not understand?"

Joe stepped between the two men before they came to blows. "Excuse me, sheriff, Ian is here at my invitation. And this dog—"

"She's not a pet," Ian said indignantly as he hunkered down to curl a hand around one of the dog's floppy ears. "Violet here is the best damn cadaver dog you'll ever run across. She's found bodies for the FBI, the ATF and just about every major police department in the country."

"That so? Well, she's not gonna muck up my crime scene, if there is one, which I doubt."

Bree couldn't keep silent any longer. Why was the sheriff being such a lunkhead? She walked over to the group of men and tapped DeVille on the shoulder. "Sheriff, anyone who watches TV knows how helpful a properly trained dog can be when it comes to locating human remains. How can you turn down this man's offer to help? Don't you want to find Philomene?"

She had him in a corner and he knew it. He pressed his lips together in a thin line, then sighed. "All right." He waved a forefinger in her face. "But if that mutt runs off with a leg bone or pees on a footprint, I'm holding you personally responsible, Dr. Johnson. You're the one who brought all these outsiders to town with your crazy talk about Kelly

Ralston being innocent. Sometimes I gotta wonder...
what makes you so damn sure? Maybe when we're
done here, I'll haul *you* in for a little interrogating."

# CHAPTER THIRTEEN

"WHOA, WHAT WAS that about?" Ian asked as he attached a lead to Violet's collar. He was a little older than he'd first appeared, with his baggy jeans and black hair flopping boyishly over his forehead.

"Sheriff's a jerk, that's all," Bree said dismissively. She leaned down to pet Violet. "You ready to go to work, girl?"

"We got woods on this side," Joe said to Ian, pointing, "and a farmer's field with a stock tank over there. I talked to the farmer this morning. He's not too keen about a bunch of trespassers on his land and even less excited about dragging the tank for a body. Plus, there's cows everywhere. So I say start with the woods."

Eric lightly touched Bree's elbow. "We better get back to our group. Ian, let us know if Violet gets a hit."

"Will do," Ian said.

The actual process of searching was tedious—one step at a time, first through tall grass, then trees and brush. A couple of guys with machetes were cutting back the brush only as much as necessary for the searchers to pass, with the deputy watching closely to make sure they didn't obliterate any evidence.

"I don't think the murderer would have hiked through all this brush," Bree said. "The farmer's field makes more sense to me. The dirt is already disturbed from the farmer planting his broccoli. Late at night, maybe the cows were penned up, so they wouldn't be a bother." She stopped to peer at a rotting log, then stepped over it as their line of searchers moved forward another few inches. "I sure hope all the ticks are dead this time of year."

"Ticks?" Eric's brow furrowed.

"You're such a city boy."

"No, I'm not. I mean, yeah, I grew up in Houston, but I used to go camping and fishing and hunting. I just hate ticks."

Bree shivered. "Me, too. In the summer people actually show up at the E.R. with ticks on them, expecting *me* to remove them. I'd rather stitch up a bloody gash any day of the week."

As they made their painstaking progress across their assigned sector, they caught occasional glimpses of Ian and Violet whipping back and forth through the trees. Apparently they were working some sort of grid system, too, but not the one the sheriff had laid out. And they were covering ground a lot faster.

"Hey, look, there's something." Bree could see a flash of something bright yellow in the grass. She and Eric both leaned down to take a closer look. She got a whiff of his woodsy aftershave, and for a few seconds she was mesmerized by how handsome he was. The sun had just risen over the horizon, and it glinted off the blond streaks in his hair, making them look like burnished gold and throwing his face into chiseled relief.

"It looks like a little piece of drawstring from a plastic garbage bag," Eric said. "And…is that duct tape stuck to it?"

Pulled back to the matter at hand, Bree bent closer still. "I think it is."

They both straightened and raised one hand to alert Deputy McClusky, but she had already seen them and was on her way over.

"Got something?"

"Maybe."

The deputy removed her hat and leaned down. "Good catch, y'all." She whipped out a camera from her black canvas messenger bag and snapped a couple of pictures, then some wider-angle shots of a couple of landmarks—a tree, a telephone pole—to establish the position of the evidence. "You don't have to stay here. You can move on. The rest of the line is getting ahead of you."

Bree had been interested in watching how a real cop collected evidence, but she and Eric took the hint and moved on as McClusky put on her rubber gloves.

"Do you think it'll turn out to be something important?" Bree asked as they continued their visual search.

"Hell if I know. Sites like this, the cops sometimes

collect a ton of trash because they don't know what's going to end up helping solve the case or providing evidence to help convict someone. But garbage bags and duct tape are two things used when disposing of a body, and there's not much other trash out here, so it could be significant."

She shivered. "I don't want to think about bodies in garbage bags and duct tape. It's so horrible. How can people be so evil?"

"That's why you became a healer instead of a criminal or a cop. People like you aren't meant to have to deal with this kind of thing. I mean, not that you're squeamish or fragile. I'm guessing you deal with some pretty horrific situations in your line of work. But—"

"But I help them *before* they die. I could never... I just don't understand how anyone..." She stopped before she got choked up. She wasn't close to Philomene—she'd only chatted with her a few times. But now that they were facing the very real possibility that she'd been murdered—that her body might be right here, within a few feet of where they stood— it got to her.

Eric slid an arm around her shoulders. He was so warm, so solid. "We'll get through this, Bree. One step at a time."

From somewhere not too far away they heard Violet barking.

Bree went on alert. "Does that mean anything?

That she's barking?" Up till now the dog hadn't made a sound.

"I don't know," Eric said. "Different dogs have different ways of alerting."

Seconds later Eric's phone rang. He dragged it out of his jeans pocket. "This is Eric." He listened, nodded a couple of times. "Okay." He hung up.

Bree waited for him to explain.

"That was Kinkaid. Violet *was* signaling. She seems to think there's a body in the stock tank."

"Can a dog really detect the scent of human remains under water?"

"I know, it seems beyond believability, but Ian's very confident in her abilities."

The rest of their group was still searching, so Bree and Eric kept at it, too, though Bree was dying to know what was going on at the stock tank.

"They'll have to get a diver to go down and have a look," Eric said. "It'll take time to get someone here."

"I bet Daniel Logan knows someone."

"He does. Kinkaid already offered to bring the guy in, but the sheriff nixed it. He wants to use his guy, some dude who works out of a nearby county sheriff's office."

"Control freak," Bree murmured. "Doesn't he realize we're all on the same team? Ultimately we all want the same thing—to find Philomene. To make sure guilty people pay for their crimes."

"No. He's interested in proving he was right all along. He's an elected official. His whole career rides on his public image. He doesn't want to look like an idiot."

Bree could understand that, but the man had been elected to represent justice in Becker County. It seemed to her he should have *some* interest in doing what was right.

"Hey, what's that?" Bree pointed to something yellow, but when she leaned closer, she shook her head. "Never mind. Leaf."

"We'll continue to that fence line," Deputy McClusky announced. "Then we'll meet back at the staging area and see if the sheriff has another area he wants us to work."

"Thank God," Bree murmured. This work was tedious and her back hurt. She'd have never made it as a cop or a CSI-type person. She had actually briefly considered being a lab scientist if she hadn't been accepted at medical school. But she probably wouldn't have liked it. She was much better with real live people than test tubes and petri dishes.

When they returned to the intersection where everyone had parked, the sheriff was sending people home.

"Thanks so much for your time, Jerry, Ruth," he said to a middle-aged couple.

"Of course," the woman said. "I'm sorry we didn't find anything useful, but at the same time...I'm grateful we didn't find anything, you know?"

"Yeah. No cop wants to find a dead body. We

haven't had a murder in years, not since they locked up Kelly Ralston."

Bree stiffened. "How dare he! Kelly was never even tried for those other murders, much less convicted. That's slander." She started to march over and give the sheriff a piece of her mind, but Eric grabbed her arm and stopped her.

"Bree, don't. I know you hate to hear your friend maligned, but we need to foster cooperation from the sheriff. Right now he's letting us in, providing information, keeping us in the loop. But he doesn't have to. We have no legal standing and he could kick us to the curb anytime he pleases."

"Oh, all right," she huffed. "I won't antagonize the jerk. But when this is all over and Kelly is exonerated, I'll make him eat his words. Ha! He's up for reelection soon."

The place was clearing out as one car after another drove off, leaving a plume of dust behind it. After a few minutes, only a handful of people remained—the sheriff's department personnel, Joe, Eric and Bree. Ian was still milling around with Violet.

"Are we waiting for the diver?" Bree asked Deputy McClusky.

"Actually, we're waiting for a warrant. Tierney chased us off his property."

"You're kidding. Toby Tierney?"

"Yeah. If you ask me, he was acting kinda suspicious. I mean, why wouldn't you want to help solve a crime?"

"Let me talk to him," Bree said.

"Your funeral," McClusky said with a shrug. "He's pretty bent out of shape over one little dog."

"Come with me," Bree said to Eric. "I think he'll be impressed that Project Justice is involved."

"Sure."

Rather than tromping across the farmer's field, they drove Eric's car around and came up the driveway. A ferocious-looking German shepherd greeted their arrival with a frenzy of barking and growling. Bree opened her door.

"Whoa, wait a sec," Eric said. "Do you want to get eaten alive?"

"That's just Bert," Bree said. "He's all bark and—Well, you know." She climbed out of the car, and the dog stopped barking to sniff her. Then he wagged his tail in recognition and she gave him a pat.

Eric joined her, allowing the dog to sniff him, as well. "You really are just a big teddy bear, aren't you?" He scratched Bert behind his ears, then hunkered down and wrestled with him for a few seconds.

Bree couldn't help her reaction—her heart swelled. She'd never seen Eric playful before.

"You like dogs?" she asked as they resumed their path to the front porch.

"Of course. Mom wouldn't let us have a dog when I was a kid, though. We really couldn't afford one."

"Pets are expensive."

"My wife had a little dog when we got married. Pixie." His smile was bittersweet. "He was a little

Chihuahua mix. Not the kind of dog I'd normally go for, but he was a character. And MacKenzie loved him. He was so good with her, even when she was a baby. You know how babies squeeze too tight and pull ears—they don't know better. Pixie never once objected."

"What happened to him?"

"Tammy's killer let him out. He disappeared and we never saw him again. I can only hope someone found him and took him in. MacKenzie still talks about him."

"He was in the picture she drew," Bree said, suddenly remembering. They ended the conversation because Toby Tierney had come out onto his porch to meet them. He was a tall, thin man with a face weathered from the constant sun and thinning brown hair starting to go gray at the temples. He wore overalls—the farmer's cliché. "I told you folks to get off my— Oh, Doc Bree. Sorry. Thought you were one of the sheriff's people at first."

"Actually, I am. I mean, I'm with the searchers. This is Eric Riggs—he's with Project Justice. You know, the foundation that—"

"Those folks that get innocent people out of jail?" Tierney gave Eric a curious once-over, then extended his hand. "Didn't know y'all was involved in looking for that missing girl."

"She's an important witness," Eric said.

"Toby," Bree began, getting to the point, "it's incredibly important that we get access to your tank."

"No way. Word gets out there's a body in my tank, no one will buy my cows. Plus, I don't want all those people trampling my broccoli."

After Bree explained about the warrant, Toby finally agreed to the search.

"But I want you there to supervise," he said.

"Me?"

"Yeah, you. I know you'll look after my interests. I'd do it myself, but I got work to do. Just came up to the house for a bit of lunch. You can bring four people with you. That's it. More than that, you'll need that warrant."

"Thank you, Toby. I'll do my best. But if they do find a body—"

"Then I'm screwed." He shrugged. "Then we'll have the coroner and CSI and a cast of thousands tromping around. I guess I can't get around that." He turned and disappeared back into his house with Bert.

"So which lucky four people ya gonna bring with you?"

"The diver, of course. You and Joe and…the sheriff, I guess. He'll be insulted if I don't."

"You were good with that guy."

"Sometimes being nice goes a long way toward getting what you want."

"And sometimes you have to be mean. Luckily, you can do both."

"I wasn't mean."

Eric opened her car door for her, then just looked at her.

"Okay, maybe I did go off on you a little bit."

"Threatening to rat me out to Daniel. That was cold."

"I guess I do what's necessary."

JUST WHEN ERIC thought he was getting a handle on Bree, she showed a different side of herself. Her warm and gentle way with the cranky farmer was a far cry from that avenging angel she'd shown him on their first meeting.

They were standing next to Tierney's livestock tank. The sheriff, of course, wanted to be in charge, and Bree let him think he was. But the diver and even Kinkaid were quietly deferring to her, he noticed. She had this quiet authority about her that was compelling and sexy as hell. She had asked everyone to walk between the rows of planted broccoli, and amazingly, even the sheriff had complied.

The diver was in the water now. It was a big tank, not some little puddle that could be searched in thirty seconds. It was more like a very small lake. The diver, a guy named Niko, surfaced every few minutes to give them a thumbs-down.

Bree worried her lower lip with her teeth, causing Eric's stomach to swoop as he recalled all the talented things those lips and teeth could do. "Do you think the dog was wrong? I really *don't* want to find her, not like this. I mean, I'm the one who pressured her into coming clean about her misidentifying her attacker. If I'd just left her alone—"

"Bree, you can't blame yourself for this. If Philomene has come to harm, it's the fault of whoever hurt her."

"Realistically I know that. But still, if I hadn't pushed her…"

"He's got something!" DeVille yelled.

Bree whirled around to look. Niko had surfaced, and he pulled off his mask. "There's something down there. The water is so murky, it's hard to tell. But it looks like something wrapped in a blue tarp."

Eric's stomach sank. That sounded as if it could be a body. "Can you bring it up?"

"It's pretty heavy. I think it's a two-man job. If I do it by myself, the package might come apart."

The sheriff snorted. "Well, let's get you a helper, then."

"I can call in a buddy, but it might take some time."

Eric raised his hand. "I can do it."

The sheriff looked at him skeptically. "You gonna swim in your skivvies and hold your breath?"

"I got extra gear in my van," Niko said. "Keys are in my bag. You certified?"

Eric nodded. He and Tammy had honeymooned in the Bahamas, where they'd both taken a scuba certification course. He didn't have a lot of experience, especially in low-visibility water, but he could make this work.

Because everyone had waited around long enough,

Eric jogged across the field to the road, where Niko's van was parked. He found the wet suit, mask, flippers, regulator and fully charged tank without any problem. He tried to remember if Niko had been wearing a weight belt, because he didn't see an extra one. But in freshwater, with his low body-fat ratio, he probably would sink like a stone with just the tank.

He was glad to make some material contribution to this investigation, too. He was honest enough to admit he wanted to impress Bree. He hoped she would see him as something more than the lawyer guy who had spent three years in prison.

As he waded into the water holding his fins, he could almost feel her gaze on him. He looked over his shoulder and met her gaze, gave her a thumbs-up, pulled the mask over his face, slipped on the fins and swam out to the middle of the pond where Niko waited for him.

"The package is about six feet long and two feet wide," Niko said. "I'll take the leading edge, and you can take the trailing one. Try to put a hand at each corner, and we'll keep it as level as possible. I think the easiest way to do this in a body of water this small is just swim it nice and gentle to the edge, rather than try to lift straight up to the surface."

Not that they had much choice. They didn't have a boat. "How deep is this thing?"

"About ten feet. Surprisingly deep for a little puddle like this. Ready?"

Eric nodded, put the regulator in his mouth and

made sure it was delivering good air, and they went under. He cleared his mask, took a couple of trial breaths. It had been years since he'd dived. The first thing that struck him was how little he could see. He caught a glimpse of the yellow stripe on Niko's fin and followed it, fighting the slight sense of claustrophobia as the light faded.

Niko had a flashlight, at least. When they reached the tarp-wrapped bundle resting on the sandy floor of the tank, Niko pointed the beam of light first at one corner, then another. Eric took his cue and grasped the corners, trying not to think of what might be hidden inside. Whatever it was, it was heavy.

A few moments later, Eric felt a tug. He lifted his end of the bundle, which resisted slightly as it struggled to break free of the muck. Finally it did, and he guided it like a wheelbarrow, barely twitching his flippers as they made their slow, gentle way up and out to the shore. It took only a few seconds and their heads were breaking the surface. The floor of the pond was closer than Eric thought; his knees hit first. Somehow he got his flippered feet under him and stood. Kinkaid, barefoot and with his pants rolled up to the knees, had waded out to help with the burden, as had one of the sheriff's deputies.

The crowd at the edge of the water had grown well past the original four; all of the deputies, the coroner and a couple of his helpers. Bree had obviously ceased to care about the farmer's field; her eyes were glued to the mysterious package coming out of the water.

It was heavy—had to be at least a couple of hundred pounds. Moving awkwardly with his flippers, Eric literally duck-walked out of the water. The air was chill, but he was so filled with adrenaline he hardly noticed. The atmosphere seemed to be pregnant with anticipation as they laid their burden gently onto the ground.

Dr. Gentry stepped forward at the exact same time as the sheriff. "Bobby?" Gentry said in a genial tone of voice. "Body's my domain."

"Well, we don't even know if it's a body yet, do we?" the sheriff said, just as friendly, though perhaps with a bit more of an edge. If he was the guilty party, he probably wanted to be the one to unwrap the package and obliterate any possible evidence while he was at it. Also, if he put his own fingerprints on everything, any found by CSI could be explained away.

Eric pulled off his mask and flippers. Someone handed him a blanket, but the wet suit was pretty good insulation.

"Thanks for stepping in, man." Niko held out his hand, and Eric shook it. "Good job."

"No problem. I like diving—except for the dead-body part."

Bree and Kinkaid joined them. Bree offered an admiring smile. "I had no idea you could do that."

Kinkaid laughed. "Better not let Daniel know you

can dive. He can get a lawyer any day, but not a certified diver."

"How often could a situation like this possibly come up?" Eric asked.

"You'd be surprised how often we look for evidence in bodies of water—just a few weeks ago we found a murder weapon in Buffalo Bayou."

"You must be freezing," Bree said. "Why don't you go get dried off and change back into your clothes?"

"In a minute." An evidence guy with a camera was taking video as the sheriff slowly unknotted the ropes holding the tarp around its contents. "The sheriff doesn't seem to be struggling with the knots very much."

"Because he's the one who tied them in the first place?" Bree whispered.

"Maybe. Those knots look pretty complicated."

Kinkaid chimed in. "The kind of knots someone ties can be a signature. I already asked the CSI guy if we can get a copy of his video—if this turns out to be what I think it is."

Finally the ropes were off. Then there was duct tape to contend with. The CSI guys collected it carefully. Eric knew that convictions could be based on matching duct tape samples to a roll in a suspect's possession or finding fingerprints or saliva stains on it. The last two were no doubt obliterated due to the water, but the tape could still be analyzed and identified. Beth could do it. She had all the appropriate testing equipment and databases at her disposal.

Finally the tarp was ready to be folded open. The farmer's field got very quiet as everyone seemed to hold their breath. Sheriff DeVille whipped his hand back in a flourish.

A fetid smell wafted up, engulfing everyone within twenty feet. Bree took one quick look, then turned and hastily walked some distance away. There was no doubt as to what was inside that tarp, though it bore little resemblance to a human being at this point.

Eric looked at it long enough to ascertain that it was, or used to be, human. A woman, if the strands of green-tinged blond hair clinging to the partially skeletonized skull were any indication. In her current state of decomposition it wasn't easy to recognize the features from Philomene's photograph, which he'd committed to memory. But the hair was right, and the fingernails. Bree had described long, elaborately decorated acrylic nails. Most of the dead woman's nails were broken, possibly in her struggles with her killer. But enough remained that Eric could make out a crazy red-and-white zebra pattern and one rhinestone that glinted in the sunlight.

He turned away and tugged his running shoes onto his bare feet, then followed Bree, who had moved well away from the crowd of people around the remains. She had her back to everyone, her head bent low and—God help him—her shoulders were shaking.

"Bree?" he said softly, leery of intruding on her moment of grief. "You okay?"

"I knew she was dead." Her voice was thick with tears. "In my heart, I knew. So I don't know why this should come as some big surprise."

Eric's thoughts flitted back to the day he'd come home from work to find his wife lying on the kitchen floor with seventeen stab wounds. Even the memory made his throat tighten and his eyes burn.

Bree dabbed at her eyes with a tissue. "I guess some little part of me still believed I might be wrong, that she would turn up, surprised that everyone made all this fuss."

Eric wanted to draw Bree close and comfort her, but he was wet and cold. Hugging him would be about as pleasant as hugging a six-foot frog. He settled for taking her hand and squeezing it. "I'm sorry it didn't turn out differently."

"At least if we'd found her alive, she could have told us who she was afraid of."

"She'll be able to tell us a lot. There's a whole truckload of evidence in that tarp, starting with the tarp. The cord, the knots, the body itself."

"Yeah, but after it's been underwater? Fingerprints and DNA—gone. Plus, even if there *is* evidence, look who's investigating the crime."

"Those evidence techs seem to know what they're doing. Plus, Project Justice will offer the services of our lab and our experts. They're the best money can buy."

"Unless DeVille destroys all the evidence. You know, almost nothing was recovered from the serial killer's victims. And even if we find Philomene's killer, that doesn't help us with Kelly. I'm afraid she was our last hope for proving his innocence."

"I have an idea about that. Those murders, the ones you were just talking about—how many were there?"

"Three for sure. Four if you count the one over in Hollings County, but it occurred several years earlier, and it didn't seem to exhibit the same care and attention to detail."

"So maybe it was our perp's first murder, and he was less sure of himself. Murderers do learn from their mistakes. They evolve."

Bree thought about it. "As I recall, there was some DNA recovered from that crime."

"So if we come up with a suspect in Philomene's murder, we can compare his DNA with what they collected at the Hollings County murder. That's one way the crime could be solved. There may be others. Don't lose hope. I may be new to Project Justice, but they have an enviable track record. Daniel has a knack for picking cases that can be won."

Bree returned Eric's hand squeeze. "Thanks for the pep talk. I'm better now. And you're freezing."

Now that the adrenaline had worn off, Eric was acutely aware of the cold.

"Go change your clothes," Bree said. "I have something to take care of."

# CHAPTER FOURTEEN

JOE THOUGHT THEIR next step ought to be lunch at the Home Cookin' Café. "It's on me," he announced. "I've got an expense account."

Bree didn't feel much like eating, not after seeing—and smelling—a dead body. But nothing much affected men's appetites. She'd discovered that in med school when some of her fellow students thought nothing of eating a sandwich while dissecting a cadaver. She wasn't exactly squeamish or she wouldn't survive in her line of work. But she still couldn't summon much of an appetite.

Ian and Niko—who had quickly allied himself with the Project Justice group—joined them. They all crowded into an extra-wide booth, but Bree still found herself squeezed rather cozily between Eric and Joe. The testosterone level at their table was running high. The men ordered chicken-fried steak, barbecued ribs, meat loaf and half-pound burgers. When Bree asked for only a bowl of chicken noodle soup, they thought she was kidding.

Apparently Joe couldn't resist ribbing her. "I hope you're not one of those women who can't eat in front of anyone. My last girlfriend was like that. At a restaurant she would order a salad and nibble on the lettuce. Then when she got home, she would pig out on potato chips and ice cream. She thought I didn't know."

The other guys laughed—all except Eric. "Hey, c'mon. She just saw her friend's remains. Cut her some slack."

Bree shot Eric a quick, grateful smile, and he squeezed her hand under the table.

The rest of the guys sobered immediately. "Sorry, Bree," Joe said. "You've been working so closely with us on this case, I forgot for a minute you weren't one of us."

"Yeah, you know how it is with cops," Ian added. "They work pretty hard at detaching themselves from the more gruesome aspects of the job."

"Thank you for worrying about my delicate sensibilities, but I'm not squeamish. I'm just…sad. Not only did some jerk snuff out a young life, but he pretty much killed my best chance to get Kelly out of prison. Please, don't censor yourselves on my account. I hope everyone will be candid with me."

They talked strategies while sipping on drinks and waiting for their food. Bree nursed her usual black coffee.

Joe stepped away from the booth to take a call. He came back a few minutes later, smiling. "Daniel has a contact at the Hollings County Sheriff's Department. He thinks it won't be any trouble getting the physical evidence from that case transferred to our lab. It's colder than a witch's—"

Eric cleared his throat.

"—um, a witch's nose," Joe finished. "They'll probably be grateful for anyone to take a fresh look at it."

"The case is, what, eight years old?" Bree said. "DNA testing has progressed since then. If there's enough of the biological material to resample and test again, you might get more detailed information."

"If it's possible, Beth can do it," Joe said.

"With that in mind, I have a present for you." She reached into her purse and pulled out a plastic bag and an old envelope. Each of them contained a cigarette butt.

Joe looked at her impromptu evidence collection bags, then back at her.

"The one in the baggie came from Sheriff Bobby DeVille. The other was dropped by D.A. Sam Needles."

"Needles? You think he's a suspect?" Eric asked.

"He's worked awfully long and hard to thwart my efforts to get at the truth. Plus, he and the sheriff were together the night Philomene disappeared. I figure it couldn't hurt to have it, right?"

Joe accepted her offering but looked skeptical.

"Look, I know the evidence would never stand up in court, but I figure they might come in handy."

"If we get a viable sample from Hollings County,

we can compare them anyway. It's a long shot." Joe pulled a Sharpie from his pocket and labeled the two bits of evidence.

At least no one had laughed at her playing detective. "I'll have a third sample for you in a minute or two." She'd spotted Jerrod Crowley in a booth by himself, eating a hamburger.

"What about Dr. Gentry?" Eric asked. "He was with Needles and DeVille that night."

"He'll be in the system," Kinkaid informed them. "All MEs have their DNA on record because they handle so much evidence. We might as well compare his DNA, too."

"I'm going to formally request to review the evidence in the other four cases," Eric said. "Since I'm now on Ralston's legal team, and those murders are believed to be linked to the crime for which he was convicted, Needles ought to comply."

"If the evidence hasn't been 'lost.'" Bree sighed glumly. Still, by the time the meal was over, she felt a little better. They weren't defeated, not yet. Kelly still had a shot at freedom, though at this point it was more like a shot in the dark.

As promised, Joe picked up the check, and Bree covertly delivered to him a plastic straw plucked from a cup on Jerrod's empty table.

Molly, the hostess, pulled Bree and Eric aside. "Is it true?" she asked breathlessly. "They found a body, and it's Philomene's?"

"I'm afraid so," Bree said. "I mean, the coroner will have to confirm her identity, but I feel pretty certain it's her. I'm so sorry."

Molly's eyes filled with tears. "I knew Jerrod was no good. I told her a million times he was just a low-life freeloader. I mean, he stole money from her. What kind of boyfriend does that?"

"So you two were close friends?"

"Pretty close. I mean, we go to—went to—the same church. Sang in the choir together."

That surprised Bree. She hadn't pictured Philomene as the churchgoing, choir-singing type, though she wasn't sure why. "We talked sometimes," Molly continued. "She didn't have any family close by, and I don't think she liked any of those snooty Realtors she worked for. I think she was kind of lonely."

Bree had gotten that impression, too. She had seemed as if she'd needed someone to confide her secrets to.

"Do you have any reason to believe Jerrod would want to kill her?"

"I know she was thinking of breaking up with him. She was going to confront him about the money he stole. Maybe the argument got out of hand.... I don't know."

"How well do you know Jerrod?" Eric asked.

"Not well. I only met him a couple of times. But it was easy to size him up. Phil was nothing but a mark to him, someone he could use because she was insecure and needy. And I'll tell you something else.

Jerrod Crowley will never get convicted in this town. He's the D.A.'s nephew."

*Oh, great!* Even if DeVille did a competent job investigating the murder, would Needles prosecute it? Or would he find some way to let his relative off the hook?

"I wouldn't be surprised if Needles helped Jerrod cover up the murder."

Eric raised his eyebrows.

Molly shrugged. "He's corrupt. Everyone knows that. If you're his friend, you can do anything in this county and he'll somehow make it go away."

"Is the sheriff part of that club?" Eric asked.

Molly thought about it. "I think he's got a conscience, at least. If you want to catch Phil's killer, you better get the FBI involved. I'm just sayin'." She stepped away to greet a customer.

Eric and Bree looked at each other.

"If it's Jerrod," Bree said, "then it's probably unrelated to Philomene recanting her testimony. And we really have nothing."

"But if it's him, we need to know." Eric looked at his watch. "I have an appointment with Dr. Gentry in a few minutes. Want to come?"

"Oh—when did that happen?"

"I called him a few minutes ago and asked if I could come in today and chat about the autopsies from those old cases. Maybe something will catch my eye. You don't have to come."

"Of course I'll come. You're a lawyer. I'm a doctor. Which one of us do you think has the stronger stomach?"

"But you didn't eat—"

"I'm upset, okay? Anyway, I've seen the photos before."

"Oh." He sounded disappointed—probably because he thought he was covering new territory.

"Believe me, over the last few years I turned over every stone I could get my hands on. But I'm willing to look again. You never know when something will jump out at you."

ERIC WASN'T AS blasé about seeing dead bodies—or pictures of them—as he pretended. He did it because he had to. But Bree was right—law school hadn't exactly prepared him for in-depth discussions of hyoid bone fractures and petechial hemorrhages.

But Dr. Gentry was patient. He was good at explaining what was in the gruesome photos in terms a nonmedical professional could understand—he probably rocked when it came to testifying in court.

"This is the last victim before Philomene was attacked," Gentry said, placing a new photo in front of Eric. They were in the coroner's office, which was different than any physician's office Eric had ever seen. Antique anatomy charts decorated his walls, and one bookshelf was devoted to archeological artifacts—Egyptian scarabs, a mummy's finger and the skull of a prehistoric hominid of some kind. Eric supposed he shouldn't be surprised that the good doctor would be interested in body parts and grave goods from the past, but it seemed kind of creepy.

Eric placed his attention on the photo, which was of a young woman, naked, laid out on an autopsy table. Each set of photos started like this—the victim intact. If he squinted, he could convince himself she was merely sleeping, though the bruises around her throat were a giveaway.

"Like the others, Patrice Baxter was raped, then strangled with an item of her own clothing—in this case, her brassiere. Like the others, an item of her jewelry was taken. You can see here the bruising on the back of her neck. The individual links of the chain made a pattern, so it was pulled off postmortem. Her mother said she was missing a silver chain, if I remember. Like the others, there was no DNA recovered."

"How were the bodies found?" Eric asked. "Were they hidden? Posed?"

"In all four cases, the bodies were found in their beds. They were redressed in their nightclothes and posed on their backs, arms folded over their chests, a pillow under their heads, blankets pulled up over their heads."

Here was something he hadn't heard before. "Like a shroud?"

The doctor seemed pleased Eric had caught on. "Yes. They were posed as if ready for burial."

An image flashed in Eric's mind. Philomene had

been resting on her back, her arms folded across her chest and duct-taped.

"Is this something you've seen before?"

"No. It's very distinctive. There's no doubt in anyone's mind that the last three murders were committed by the same person."

"And what makes everyone so sure Philomene's rape was part of this pattern?"

"There were a few similarities. She was a single woman who lived alone. Her attacker came through a window late at night when she was asleep. He didn't have intercourse with her, but he violated her in… other ways. And he wore some kind of cap so he wouldn't shed hair—the sort of care the serial killer must have taken with his victims, given the lack of DNA. We think he would have killed her if a neighbor hadn't heard her screaming and banged on the door. But the kicker is, he grabbed her necklace just before he fled. But there's really no way to know for sure because he didn't kill her. Frankly, it strikes me as a little careless that he chose a victim whose neighbors were home. The other women were much more isolated."

"And the other murder, the one in Hollings County—why is that one ruled out?"

"At first it appeared to fit the pattern. The woman was single, living alone. She was raped late at night and strangled with a ligature, and she was found in her bed. But there the resemblance ends. The victim wasn't redressed. She wasn't posed. There's no indication the perpetrator took jewelry."

"And he left DNA."

"Right. Not as fastidious or careful as our serial killer. Plus, the crime occurred four years before any of the other ones. Our guy was pretty consistent—killing one victim per year. Oh, another thing—our victims were all killed in early December. The Hollings County woman died in May. So all in all, it really doesn't fit."

"They never found a match for the DNA?"

"Nope. Maybe it was a one-off, and the guy never killed anybody again. Maybe he died. Hard to know."

"When will you have results in Philomene's autopsy?"

"We're not even sure it's her, you know. I'll start this afternoon. Might have preliminary results tomorrow morning, but obviously, test results will take a while. I'm at the mercy of our lab."

Helluva coincidence if it turned out not to be her, in Eric's opinion. "Any guesses as to cause of death?"

Gentry shook his head. "There was nothing obvious—I didn't see any signs of strangulation, no bullet or stab wounds. Might be blunt-force trauma, suffocation, drowning, poison—won't know until I get in there."

"Okay."

"Ted," Bree said, "I really appreciate you being so candid with us. I realize you don't have to talk to us—and that the sheriff probably won't be too happy if he knows you're sharing information with us."

Gentry shrugged. "Bobby isn't too happy with the whole situation. I know he was as surprised as anyone when Philomene actually turned up dead—if it's really her," he added quickly. "He thought you were just blowing smoke."

"It's understandable. A homicide like this, regardless of who the victim is, isn't something any sheriff wants in his jurisdiction."

"On the other hand, if he solves it, takes some dangerous predator off the streets, he's a shoo-in for reelection."

Bree smiled. "Good point. I'll remind him of that if he starts giving me grief. Ted, let me ask you something. How close are the district attorney and Jerrod Crowley?"

"You mean how far would Sam Needles go to protect his nephew? Not very far. I mean, yeah, Jerrod's his family and all, and they're both members of the good-ol'-boy network. But I can't see Sam protecting a murderer." He shook his head. "No way. He might look for other suspects, he might do his best to see Jerrod got a fair trial and all that, but he's not gonna cover it up. You don't have to worry about that."

She nodded. "Good. But I don't think Jerrod was the doer anyway. I can't see him being cool or clever enough to hide the body so thoroughly. Or lying about his guilt so convincingly. No, I think the serial killer knew Philomene was gonna change her story, and he shut her up."

Gentry stood. "I hope we find out whether you're right or wrong. Now, if you don't mind, I have a date with a dead blonde."

"WHAT DO YOU make of that guy?" Eric asked once they were in the car. "He seemed pretty forthcoming."

Bree agreed. "Not like he's protecting his buddy the sheriff. Hey, would you mind taking me by my place before we head back to Houston? I want to pick up my mail and water my plants."

"Sure."

Bree gave him directions. After only about half a mile, they turned onto a pleasant shady street lined with large turn-of-the-century homes. This was obviously where Tuckerville's wealthiest citizens lived. E.R. doctors must do okay.

But she didn't stop on the first block or the second. On the third block he saw several small apartment buildings sandwiched between houses that were still nice, but smaller.

"It's the one on the right at the end of this block."

He pulled up to the curb right in front of her white stucco two-story building and parked. "Nice. How many units?"

"Just six. I'll only be a minute. Or…maybe you'd like to come in?"

Eric was already halfway out of the car. If someone was stalking her, and she believed they'd tried to break into her building, he didn't want her entering her apartment alone.

The property had a driveway with an electronic gate and a sign that said Resident Parking. There was a wall around the building itself and another gate, decorative wrought-iron with a sturdy-looking lock.

Bree had a key card that opened it. "See the scratches? It looks like someone tried to pick the lock."

"Are you sure they weren't there before?"

"Well, not positive. But the manager here keeps things immaculate."

She let him in and they approached the front door, which she also unlocked. The placed seemed pretty secure.

"Honestly?" Eric said. "If I wanted to break in to this place, I would try to slip in after someone drove into the parking area. And then I would hide until one of the residents came in, and I would slide in after them, before the door slammed shut. Also, you'd be amazed how many people just let strangers into their secure building. Guy says, 'I'm here to see Bree.' Smiles a disarming smile and they just let him right in."

"And you know this how?"

"When I was in law school, I was a part-time process server. I learned all kinds of clever ways to gain access to people's homes and offices."

"If it's that easy, why do we bother with all the security?" she groused.

Bree checked her mailbox, which was in the lobby, looking over the thin stack of envelopes before stuffing them into her purse. She threw a grocery store circular into a recycling bin, then headed up the stairs. "Actually, my neighbors are a pretty suspicious lot. They know not to let people in."

"A good con man can look and sound so innocent they can get past just about anyone's defenses."

"Thanks. Now I'm really creeped out."

"You haven't seen that car again, have you?"

"No. But I didn't imagine it."

"I never said you did." But he'd thought it. With a murderer running around loose out there, it was easy to let your imagination get the best of you. Still, he didn't want to take any chances, in case Bree was right.

They entered her apartment, greeted by the light floral scent of room freshener with a slight trace of... cigarette smoke? "Bree, you don't smoke, do you? On the sly?"

"What?" She laughed. "No."

Eric looked around, unable to mask his curiosity about the sort of place Bree had chosen to live in. It was classic, with dark wood floors, crown molding and many-paned windows. Old gas fixtures, now defunct, he imagined, still graced the walls.

The colors were soothing—soft blues and greens with a touch of gold here and there. With all the frenzied activity at her job, she probably needed a calming haven to retreat to when her shift was over.

Bree suddenly went still. "Something's not right."

"What?"

"Someone's been in here."

Eric looked around. Nothing appeared out of place to him. "Are you sure?"

"Yes. Someone's been touching my things." She paused in front of an antique desk that displayed a collection of glass animals and trinkets—an angelfish, a deer and an elaborate carousel. She picked up a blue glass swan. The head fell off.

She gasped. "This wasn't broken. I just dusted this shelf a couple of days ago and no one else has been in here."

"What about the manager?"

"She would never come in here without telling me. If they were going to do any kind of maintenance, I'd have been notified. No, someone's been here."

"That might explain why I smelled cigarette smoke."

Bree took a big sniff. "Really? I didn't smell it. Then again, I think I've trained myself not to register smells. You wouldn't believe how bad people can smell in the—"

"Um, Bree?" Eric's heart felt like the pounding of a sledgehammer. He'd lifted the skirt of a tablecloth, looking for…he wasn't sure what. But he'd found it.

"Oh, my God, is that a bomb?"

"Looks like one."

"But why—"

"We can wonder about that later. We might have triggered it by coming through your front door. We have to get out of here." He grabbed her arm and all but dragged her out the door.

She skidded to a stop in the middle of the staircase. "Wait. We have to warn the others."

"Bree, we don't have— Damn it!" She was heading back up. She went straight to her neighbor's door and pounded on it. "Mrs. Hampton? Are you home? We have to evacuate the building."

"Here, this will work a lot faster." Eric had spotted a fire alarm in the hallway. He broke the glass with his elbow and pulled the red handle, and immediately an ear-piercing siren reverberated through the whole building. "Now will you come on?"

"But Mrs. Hampton and the others—"

The blast cut her off and her front door blew off its hinges and flew through the air all the way across the landing, missing Bree by inches. Without another word of objection she headed down the stairs.

## CHAPTER FIFTEEN

"The blast probably wasn't strong enough to hurt anyone who wasn't in your apartment," Eric reasoned as he pulled his phone from his pocket and dialed 911.

"Or below me. The bomb was sitting right on the floor."

"Police and fire," Eric said to the dispatcher, "and maybe ambulance. A bomb just went off in my friend's apartment."

As they pushed their way out the front door, Eric caught a glimpse of a beige Acura speeding down the street.

"There, there!" Bree said excitedly, pointing as the car retreated. "That's him!"

They both ran toward the street, but by the time they got there, the car was too far away to read the license plate.

One by one, Bree's neighbors came out of the building looking shocked and worried but uninjured. The elderly Mrs. Hampton was first to appear, followed by a couple who were only slightly younger, a young woman with two children and a middle-aged man in a cardigan who reminded Eric of Mr. Rogers. They were all shouting excitedly.

"It was a gas explosion," Mrs. Hampton said, "I'm sure of it. Bree tried to warn me. Did you smell gas, dear? Was that it?"

"I, um, I'm not sure," she mumbled, probably not wanting to alarm them. Then she looked around frantically. "Where are Jules and Patrick?"

"I think they're both at work," the Mr. Rogers man said.

"Oh, thank God." Then Bree's knees started to wobble.

Eric grabbed on to her just as she sank to the ground.

"I can't believe it," she whispered to Eric. "Someone really did try to kill me. My stalker is a hit man."

BREE STILL FELT WOOZY. Maybe it was the fact all she'd had to eat today was a granola bar and a bowl of soup.

She and Eric were in an interview room with Sheriff DeVille as well as two ATF agents, and they'd been questioning her for two hours. If this was how they treated victims, she sure would hate to be a suspect.

Or maybe she *was* a suspect. Maybe they thought she set the bomb herself, to shore up her theory that Philomene's killer was after her, too, and it was all tied to the crimes Kelly Ralston was believed to have committed. Everyone seemed to be mystified as to what had triggered the bomb to blow when it did. The ATF guy said it would have been more normal for the door to have triggered the firing mechanism.

In Bree's opinion, the only possible explanation for someone wanting to kill her was her recent association with Philomene, and she had said so—repeatedly.

"If Philomene was killed because she was going to change her story, maybe the perpetrator thought Philomene had already told me something."

"And did she?" the sheriff asked eagerly. A little too eagerly, Bree thought.

"No. All she said was that when she identified Kelly Ralston in the lineup, it was a mistake. She hadn't seen her attacker well, because it was dark and he had a stocking over his head. She just picked Kelly because she felt pressured."

Bree didn't add that it was the sheriff himself who had pressured Philomene to make an identification, and that he had given her subtle clues as to which suspect in the lineup she should pick.

"But she continued to point the finger at Ralston," the sheriff objected. "She pointed him out in court."

"She said once she started lying, she was afraid to stop. But she'd been feeling guilty about it ever since and she wanted to set the record straight."

"And you can't think of anyone else who might want you gone? Jealous boyfriend? Have you lost a patient in the E.R. recently? Someone whose relative thought you did a bad job?"

"No, really, nothing like that. I can't think of anyone who's mad at me."

"Sheriff DeVille," Eric interjected, "this has gone on long enough. Bree's tired. She's upset. She needs to rest."

The sheriff shot Eric a dirty look. "She's got a mouth. Why don't you let her decide when she's tired?"

"Because I'm her lawyer," Eric said.

"And you think she has something to hide? That why you're protecting her?"

"Oh, good grief," Bree grumbled. "Eric is right. I'm tired and I can't even think straight. I'm happy to make myself available to you or any other law enforcement who mistakenly believe I have something to add. But tomorrow, huh?"

The sheriff exchanged glances with the ATF agents, then nodded. "Okay. Where will you stay? With your folks?"

"Oh, God, no way." Crap, had she said that out loud? "I don't know yet where I'll stay, but you can always reach me on my cell." She sent a nervous glance to Eric, who, thankfully, said nothing. It might look a bit odd if people knew she was living with the Project Justice attorney working on her case.

She wasn't planning to stay with him anyway. No way was she leading a hit man who liked to plant bombs anywhere near Eric's family. She would stay at a hotel.

"What about my apartment?" she asked. "The door was blown off."

"We'll be processing the scene for a couple of days," one of the ATF agents said, "and we'll make sure the doors and windows are boarded up before we leave. But frankly, there's not much left in there worth stealing."

That was a glum thought. But possessions could be replaced. If Eric hadn't spotted that bomb—if she hadn't realized someone had been in her apartment— they would both be dead or maimed.

Once they were back in Eric's car, he asked, "Are you sure you don't want to call your parents? I know you said you weren't close, but you might at least let them know you're safe."

"Eric, they didn't even visit me in the hospital when I had the baby. They didn't come to Casey's funeral. Eventually, when they realized I wasn't going to come crawling back to them, repentant and groveling, they apologized and I pretended to forgive them."

"Did you move in with Kelly?" Eric asked, though expressing his curiosity about Bree and Kelly's relationship was like probing a sore tooth.

"Yup." She shook her head. "God, what a disaster. We lived in a mobile home in Kelly's cousin's backyard. We lived on rice and beans and peanut butter and food from the food bank. I was trying to graduate. Kelly was working at a garage. We were poster children for the campaign against teen pregnancy."

"I can't imagine.... I mean, I would hope Mac-Kenzie wouldn't grow up to fall in love with the wrong guy and get pregnant in high school. But if she did, I would never kick her to the curb."

"My parents were just so humiliated by their pregnant daughter. My dad didn't run for reelection because he thought I had shamed him so thoroughly no one would ever vote for him."

"So how did you swing college? Medical school?"

"Ah, a little thing called a college fund, in my name, courtesy of my grandmother. She was the peacemaker, actually. She got us all talking again. My parents tried to sweep what they did under the rug once the baby was out of the picture and Kelly and I broke up. But I knew in my heart that if our baby had lived, if I'd stayed with Kelly, they never would have accepted either of them.

"Now, with me championing Kelly's cause—well, you can just imagine how that sits with them. I can't be with them ten minutes before one of them brings it up and tells me how stupid I am."

"Why are you so passionate about Kelly's situation?" Eric asked. "Are you still in love with him?"

She looked at him sharply.

Yeah, there it was. The question he never should have asked. He blundered on, trying to justify the question. "You conceived a child with him. You went through an awful lot together. That can create some pretty strong bonds."

"No, I'm not in love with him! Jeez, isn't it enough

that I see injustice and I want to make it right? Honestly, you men always want to assign some sexual meaning to every move a woman makes. Don't think you're the only one who has this notion that I'm helping Kelly get out of prison because I'm in love with him. Jeez!"

"Okay, I'm sorry I asked."

"Are you still in love with your wife?"

Eric looked stunned that she would ask, and she was immediately contrite. "God, I'm sorry, Eric. That was uncalled for. But you and I, we both have these tragic romances in our past, and we wouldn't be human if we didn't wonder whether we can get past that. I mean, would you even care if I had feelings for Kelly if you didn't have feelings for me?"

"This conversation has gotten completely out of hand."

"Agreed. Hey, there's an Embassy Suites up ahead. Why don't you take me there? I can't keep staying with you. It's out of the question."

"I'll take you to Daniel's. It's secure as Fort Knox."

"Are you sure that's okay? I barely know him."

"He has houseguests all the time. Think about it. Our investigators are always stirring up hornets' nests. They deal with some unsavory characters. Our clients, their friends and relatives, often get caught in the cross fire and need a safe haven. Daniel's estate is perfect for that."

"I guess when you put it that way, it's really the

safest choice. At least maybe I'll be able to sleep tonight." Though she wondered if she'd ever get a good night's sleep again until they caught whoever was trying to kill her.

ERIC HADN'T FELT quite right about just dropping off Bree at Daniel's house. At least he knew she would be safe there. But she was in despair, and he wanted to be the one to comfort her.

He needed to get home. He wouldn't neglect his little girl, no matter what the cost.

As he drove home, he kicked himself for his own stupidity. Why had he asked Bree if she was still in love with Kelly? If she was, she wasn't going to answer honestly. She might not even realize the depth of her feelings for the man with whom she had shared the bond of parenthood.

He certainly hadn't liked it when she turned the tables on him, asking him if he was still in love with Tammy.

Was he?

She had been dead for years, yet it seemed like his feelings for her had been in some kind of suspended animation, and he was fully processing her loss only now that he was out of prison and back with Mac-Kenzie. He had only recently learned of her infidelity. Before she died, if he had known of her affair, his love for her would have withered and died a natural death. He felt certain he would have divorced her.

But it was a lot harder to hate a woman who had been so cruelly murdered, a victim of her own excesses.

If he felt pangs of jealousy over Bree's former relationship with Kelly Ralston, she might have the same sort of feelings about him and Tammy.

Maybe she was right. Even if they cared for each other, maybe neither of them was ready for a new relationship.

The thought of giving Bree up forever made his chest ache, as though a two-ton weight sat on his heart. He tried to imagine saying goodbye, walking away from her for good once this case was concluded. If Project Justice succeeded in freeing Kelly Ralston, Bree would have her hands full helping him reintegrate into society. Lord knew he would need help, just as any ex-con did. Eric didn't know how he would've survived without Travis, Elena and MacKenzie showering their love on him.

This was true even if Bree and Kelly were just friends. Eric would only be in their way.

The whole crew met Eric at the door as he entered the house; MacKenzie jumped into his arms while Elena and Trav both tried to hug him at the same time.

"Thank God you're okay," Elena said.

"We've been watching the news," Trav added. "It looked like the whole apartment was destroyed. Were you really right there when it happened?"

Eric wasn't too crazy about discussing this in front

of MacKenzie. He didn't want her worrying about him being at risk at work—she was already anxious whenever they were apart. So he soft-pedaled the danger.

"We had just left," he said in as cheerful a tone as he dared. Even a child as young as MacKenzie could spot it when an adult faked an emotion. "Neither of us was injured at all."

"Thank God," Elena said again. "Bree must be terrified. Why would anyone want to hurt her?"

Elena knew exactly what she was talking about. Not so long ago, someone had tried to kill her.

"She's scared, of course. But Daniel is personally looking after her safety."

"Then she'll be okay until they catch the bas—" Travis stopped himself and changed course "—the jerk who wants to hurt her. Eric, is there anything we can do?"

"I appreciate the offer, but Daniel's on the warpath. You know how personally he takes it when any of his employees find themselves in the line of fire. I haven't been working there long, but he considers me one of the gang and he's not going to take this lying down. Every resource the foundation can muster will be put to use finding whoever did this, whether it's directly related to the case I'm working on or not.

"And now I think we should stop talking about this in front of the little pitcher and change the subject, okay?"

"Good idea," Elena said. "Travis has been smoking

a brisket all day, so we're all in for a treat at dinner. And I bought some pineapple ice cream for dessert."

MacKenzie clapped her hands together. "Yay, my favorite kind!"

Eric was happy to see that all the talk of killers and bombs and danger had for the most part gone right over MacKenzie's head. She was more interested in showing her daddy her new coloring book than talking about his day.

As he spent a couple of quality hours with MacKenzie before dinner, his thoughts strayed to Bree and the baby she lost. Suddenly Eric felt like one hell of a lucky guy. He might not have parents, but he had a brother and sister-in-law and a child who all loved him to distraction. He got to see them every day.

Bree didn't seem to have anyone. Maybe that was why getting Kelly out of jail was so important to her. At least she had a connection there.

Damn it, he'd never wanted to see justice done so badly. He wanted to do this one thing for her, to prove that bastard Ralston was innocent and get him out of jail. At least then he could part ways with Bree knowing she had someone in her life.

His stomach churned, though, at the thought of parting with Bree.

BREE TOOK SOME vacation time, and for once her boss was completely understanding. Whether he actually cared about her welfare or he just didn't want to chance Bree bringing all kinds of negative publicity to the hospital by being murdered at work, she didn't know. But she'd take it. She doubted she could be focused and sharp enough to perform emergency medicine anyway.

Staying at Daniel's was like vacationing at a four-star resort—she didn't have to worry about anything. Not only did Daniel provide her with every toiletry and cosmetic item she could possibly want or need, her room had come complete with a closet full of clothes in her size and dresser drawers filled with lingerie, pajamas, socks, scarves, gloves, you name it. She was now more fashionably— and expensively— dressed than she'd ever been in her life.

If she needed exercise, she could walk around the beautifully manicured grounds or take advantage of the workout room in the basement, complete with sauna and whirlpool.

Daniel had lots of people to take care of his various needs—a barber and a masseuse who made house calls, a solicitous personal assistant and, of course, a full kitchen staff.

The degree of luxury and pampering far surpassed anything she'd experienced. Her parents were considered one of the "first families" of Tuckerville. They drove luxury cars, had a country club membership and took exotic vacations. But even they would have been shocked at Daniel's level of wealth. He owned his own string of polo ponies, for God's sake.

Yet he wasn't a snob. He and his wife, Jamie, the district attorney of Houston, were some of the most gracious people she'd ever met, treating her more like family than a guest.

She felt as if she ought to be doing something more proactive. She was so much in the habit of devoting her every spare minute to taking some kind of action to help Kelly's cause or at least thinking about what her next step could be. But for the first time in a long time, she had nothing to do. Finally, someone else was working toward the same goal. Daniel had said that while he appreciated her willingness to help, none of his people wanted to have to worry about her safety while she was out and about. She understood the wisdom of staying behind locked gates even if she didn't particularly like the isolation.

It might have been easier to take if she knew what was going on. Eric had undoubtedly turned over those DNA samples from their three suspects to Beth. How long did DNA processing take? It used to be weeks back in the old days, but she thought it could be done pretty quickly now. And what about the physical evidence from the Hollings County case? Had it arrived yet?

She was ashamed to admit she was also hungry for any contact with Eric. She missed MacKenzie, too.

She'd convinced herself this wasn't the right time for her and Eric. But was there ever a "right time" for anything? If you were lucky enough to stumble on someone so perfect, someone you could forge a deep connection with, wasn't it stupid to walk away because you were afraid things wouldn't go smoothly?

Deep down maybe she feared *she* wasn't strong enough to make a relationship work.

Eric and MacKenzie had been abandoned once. They needed a wife and mother who could go the distance this time.

And yet no relationship, not even one between the two healthiest, most stable people in the world, came with ironclad guarantees.

As she sipped her coffee at the breakfast table on the fifth day of her enforced vacation, she decided to talk to Eric, open up to him about her fears and doubts. If her worries about her own fitness as a potential mate and mother gave him cold feet, she would have her answer.

"Bree, you're unusually quiet this morning," Daniel commented.

"I'm just wondering when I can go back to having a normal life," she said wistfully. Her normal, sterile life with nothing but work to fulfill her. She'd once thought that would be enough.

"We're having a staff meeting this morning. Usually I attend via video conferencing, but today I thought I'd join everybody in person. Would you like to go with me? It will be perfectly safe. My limo has bulletproof glass and a driver trained by the Secret Service. And the Project Justice office… Well, let's just say no one gets past Celeste."

Bree smiled, recalling the foundation's formidable receptionist, who apparently did far more than merely "receive" visitors. "I would love to come."

Her heart thrummed as she thought about seeing Eric again. It wasn't the teenage-crush type of excitement she remembered from when she first started seeing Kelly at age sixteen. This was more mellow, a warm acknowledgment of the connection they shared. Less like anticipating a hot-fudge sundae and more like knowing she was about to sip a fine burgundy wine.

A few minutes later Bree found herself in the back of Daniel's limo. The last time she'd ridden in such luxury was at her junior prom, and then she'd been sharing the car with several of her girlfriends and their dates, with the stereo blasting out rock music.

This experience wasn't quite the same. Instead of guzzling booze smuggled from her parents' liquor cabinet and listening to pulse-pounding guitars blasting from the speakers, she sipped Kona coffee from a travel mug while music from a string quartet surrounded her and Daniel.

"Is this case solvable, do you think?" She realized she ought to take advantage of these few minutes she had with Daniel.

"Philomene's murder, you mean? There's no such thing as a perfect crime. It's true that a body submerged in water for several days isn't ideal. But there's still a ton of evidence to go through.

"The question is, does the Becker County crime lab have the equipment and expertise to decipher the clues? Or will they muck it up? The sheriff is unfortunately not anxious for any help. He wants to solve this murder on his own."

"And what about the bomb at my apartment? Solvable?" She knew in her heart it was all connected. Pull one thread out and the whole scarf would unravel. They just needed one thread—one!

"At least the ATF is involved in that investigation. If anyone can figure it out, they can."

"But it's not like our bomber blew up an entire building or even injured anyone," Bree pointed out. "Will they devote that much time and effort to it?"

"They take bombers very seriously. Let this one get away, and his next bomb might take out a twenty-story building or a jumbo jet. I've been assured they're analyzing every scrap of evidence. Probably digging into every aspect of your past, too, well beyond what they've asked you about."

She shrugged. "Let them dig."

The limo pulled into the secure garage behind the historic brick building. Daniel's driver hustled them both from car to door, subtly placing his body between them and any threat that might come from the other cars parked there. She would hate to have to live with this degree of paranoia every day as Daniel did. No wonder he'd developed agoraphobia, though apparently he had overcome it to some degree.

The conference room was abuzz with animated conversations, the smell of coffee and a plate of pastries that made Bree wish she hadn't eaten such a large breakfast. She scanned the people in the room for Eric, but there was no sign of him.

She did find Joe Kinkaid, however. "Joe. Do you know where Eric is?"

Joe glanced at the clock on the wall. "I'm sure he'll be here shortly. Sometimes getting the munchkin off to school can take more time than anyone plans for."

Poor little MacKenzie, still so insecure about being separated from her father. Was that a problem that would follow her her whole life?

Daniel got the meeting started promptly at nine. Bree listened attentively as several of the foundation's top investigators gave progress reports on various cases, making liberal use of the huge video screen to project images from their smartphones or tablets. It was like having a front-row seat watching one of those crime shows on TV, except this was real. These people were certainly passionate about their work and good at what they did.

Finally it was Kinkaid's turn to give a progress report on the Ralston case.

"I'd hoped Eric would be here before I gave my report," Joe said.

"I got a text from him a while ago," Daniel said. "Apparently his car got a flat tire overnight. I thought he would be here by now, but he's not, so go with what you've got."

Bree relaxed slightly. A flat tire. Nothing terrible. Eric would probably be here any minute. She listened as Joe related the latest developments. Everyone knew about the bomb, of course, because it had been on the news. But a lot had happened since then. As the minutes stretched on and Eric failed to appear, Bree started feeling unsettled again.

Eric was always prompt. It wasn't like him to be more than an hour late for a meeting. Where the hell was he?

"MACKENZIE, COME ON!" Eric called up the stairs. "We're already really, really late."

He should have just changed the damn tire himself. Waiting for the auto club had been a mistake, as the fifteen minutes they'd promised to arrive in had turned into forty-five. And then the guy who'd come to change the tire had had no clue what he was doing, and Eric had ended up helping him—and getting dirt on his white shirt, which was what he'd been trying to avoid in the first place.

"I'll go see what's keeping her," Elena said, running up the stairs.

Lord only knew. Yesterday morning she'd turned the bathroom sink into a Barbie doll hot tub when she was supposed to be eating breakfast.

Elena came back downstairs almost immediately, looking bewildered. "She's not there."

"Maybe she's in my room."

"No, I looked in all the rooms."

Alarm slithered up Eric's spine. "Maybe she went out to the tire swing." The swing had turned out to be a big hit with MacKenzie. Since the backyard had a high privacy fence, he'd been known to let her go out there by herself, but she usually asked for permission before going outside.

Eric strode to the back door and stepped out onto the porch. "MacKenzie? Where are you? We're late—we need to go!"

Nothing.

Elena met him at the door as he returned inside. "I can't find her downstairs, either."

"Could she be waiting in the car?" Maybe she'd slipped out the door when he was dealing with the auto club paperwork.

They both went out to look. No MacKenzie.

Back inside, they searched again. "MacKenzie!" Eric bellowed. No matter where in the house she was hiding, she would be able to hear him. "This is no time for hide-and-seek. You come out this instant or you'll be punished!" God, he never punished MacKenzie. She was eager to please and never disobeyed.

"Did she seem worried about going to school today?" Eric asked Elena.

"No. She went right out with you the first time you tried to leave."

"Elena, what the hell's going on?"

"Let's search the house again, then outside. She wouldn't leave the property by herself, would she?"

"I don't think so." MacKenzie wasn't by any stretch an adventurous or rebellious child.

They had just resumed their search when Eric's phone rang. Probably someone at the office wondering where the hell he was. He was missing the weekly staff meeting. "Eric Riggs," he answered distractedly in between calling for his daughter and looking under furniture and in closets.

"Missing something?"

"Missing something..."

## *CHAPTER SIXTEEN*

ERIC WENT COLD. "Who is this?"

"Never mind that. If you want your daughter back
safely, you'll do exactly as I say. Do not call the police. Do not tell anyone except Dr. Johnson. I assume
she's with you?"

"What do you want? If you harm one hair on my
daughter's head, I will hunt you down like an animal and—"

"Simmer down and listen," the voice growled. It
didn't sound natural; it had been electronically al-
tered. "Wait to hear from me. When next I call, I'll
have very specific instructions for how to get your
daughter back."

"If it's money you want, I don't have any. Mac-
Kenzie is the heir to some money, but she doesn't
have it now."

"Disobey my orders, even a little, and I'll send
MacKenzie back in little bitty pieces."

"You do that and you'll be—"

But the caller had hung up.

Eric's head was spinning. He wanted to hit
something—someone. But he had to calm down.

MacKenzie needed him. He took a few deep breaths. Better.

There was no way he was going to just sit by and passively wait for the kidnapper's next move. But he was terrified of angering the kidnapper by refusing to follow directions. It didn't sound as if the guy was a sexual predator, more that he intended to demand some kind of ransom. Eric had to pretend to go along so the guy wouldn't get pissed off and take out his frustration on his hostage.

He could hear Elena's footsteps coming up the stairs. "Eric? Did you find her?"

She entered MacKenzie's bedroom, where Eric had been searching when the phone call came in. He didn't even remember sitting down on the bed, but there he was.

"Eric, what's wrong?"

He had no choice but to tell Elena. "She's been kidnapped. Someone just called, said he would call back and tell me what to do to get her back."

"Oh, Eric."

"He said not to call the police."

"They always say that. But we're not going to call the police. We're calling Project Justice. Come with me."

Numb with shock and terrified down to his marrow, he followed Elena downstairs.

"When I was working for Daniel, I went to a special school where they train you what to do in the event of kidnapping or hostage taking. The first rule is that you never try to handle it by yourself. Daniel will know what to do."

"Elena, he said he would…he would…cut her—"

"They always say that. But just in case, we'll take precautions so there's no way he could know you've called anyone." Elena led him to the kitchen and opened a drawer. "When I first quit working for Daniel, I got one of those cheap throwaway phones. There are a few minutes left on it." She scrolled through the contacts. "There's Daniel's private cell number. Call him."

Gradually Eric felt his senses returning. He took the phone and waited for Daniel to answer.

"Elena?"

"Daniel, it's me, Eric. MacKenzie's been kidnapped." He told his boss exactly what had happened and when. He related the caller's words as closely as possible. "This has to be connected to the case," he concluded. "Otherwise, why would they have told me I could confide in Bree and no one else?"

"Agreed. He must not know who is in the house with you. He doesn't have eyes on it right now. He knew Bree was staying with you last week but he doesn't have current information. So we're probably dealing with one guy, no helpers."

Eric was impressed with Daniel's cool, logical conclusions. The guy might have inherited a fortune, but he was also smart enough not only to hold on to his wealth but to build on it.

"So he might just assume Bree is living with me,

therefore she already knows…. No, that's not right. He said I could *tell* Bree."

"We don't have time to argue semantics. I've got to get Mitch busy tapping into your phone so we can trace where the call came from. The kidnapper is no doubt using a throwaway phone, but even those sometimes can yield information. Meanwhile, on the off chance our guy *does* have eyes on your house, I'm sending Bree in. She'll have an untraceable cell phone we can use for communications. We'll set up a situation room here. Give me a few—" The call cut off; Elena's throwaway phone had run out of time.

"What did he say?" Elena asked anxiously.

Eric paced the small kitchen while relating the conversation to his sister-in-law. His nerves felt raw, his stomach about to reject the Cocoa Puffs he'd had for breakfast.

How could this happen to him? Hadn't his family suffered enough? His wife murdered, himself imprisoned for three years for something he didn't do, Elena beaten in an attempted abduction by the man who had killed Tammy.

Now, just when MacKenzie was starting to smile again and Eric felt he might be able to return to a normal life after all…this.

"MacKenzie won't survive this."

"Eric, of course she will! Whoever this is, he's not interested in hurting her. He wants something from you. You'll appear to give it to him and you'll get your daughter back. Daniel is very, very good at this sort of thing."

He nodded. Daniel would do everything he could do, of course, but what if it wasn't enough?

WHEN MACKENZIE WOKE UP, she was in a dark place. She tried to move, but her arms and legs wouldn't obey her. Something was tied around her hands.

She didn't like the dark. Her eyes filled with tears as fear welled up in her chest. "Daddy? Daddy!"

Usually if she woke up in the night after a bad dream, all she had to do was call once, and Daddy would come to her. He would wrap her in his big arms and hug her tight and tell her again and again that she wasn't alone, that she was safe, that dreams couldn't hurt her.

This wasn't a dream. At least, she didn't think so. And she wasn't in her bed. She was...in a car. She could hear the motor and feel the bumps in the road. But why was it so dark?

She tried hard to remember. She'd gotten ready for school, she'd had her breakfast—Cocoa Puffs with strawberries—and then she and Daddy had gone out to his car. She liked it when Daddy took her to school, which he did most days. She still didn't like saying goodbye to him, but at school, with other kids around her getting out of their cars and saying good-bye to their moms and dads, it seemed a little easier.

But he hadn't taken her to school, because of the flat tire.

They'd both gone back into the house while they waited for something called auto club to come fix the tire, and Daddy had told her she could play for a little while. She'd gone out into the backyard to swing.

The puppy! That's when she'd seen a white puppy huddling near the fence.

She loved animals. She still missed Pixie. People didn't think she could really remember the dog, because she'd been only three when he ran away, but she did remember.

The puppy had looked scared, and MacKenzie had gone right over to it. Where had it come from? Was it lost? She'd pet it, and it had licked her hand, making her laugh.

Then... Oh, yeah, the man. He'd talked to her through the fence. He'd said it was his puppy and it had run away, and he'd asked her to bring it to the gate and let it out so he could take it home. She'd happily picked up the trembling puppy and done as the man had asked, though she'd wanted to play with it. She'd unlocked the gate and opened it—and the man had grabbed her. He'd put a cloth over her face with something stinky on it, and that was all she remembered.

"Daddy?" she tried again. But no one was answering. Daddy wasn't anywhere near. This car was taking her farther and farther away from him.

Everybody always told her not to talk to strangers. Now she knew why. But he'd sounded so worried about his puppy....

She felt sick to her stomach, so sick she almost couldn't be scared. It smelled bad here, like rubber and dirty carpeting. Her stomach rolled; she didn't want to upchuck, because then she would be lying in it. She tried moving. Maybe she could sit up. But with her hands tied up it was hard.

She scooted her knees under her body and tried to raise up, but she hit her head on something. Oh, she was in the trunk! Daddy was going to be really mad that she wasn't in her car seat. She was never, ever supposed to ride in a car without her car seat.

No way around it—she was in trouble. First she'd talked to a stranger, then she'd gotten into a car with a stranger—also a big no-no—and now she was riding in a car without even a seat belt. When this car stopped and she got out, she was going to yell at that bad man who was getting her in so much trouble.

Her daddy had told her that if any person ever made her afraid, she had to stay calm and tell a grown-up what was going on, or she should call 911 and tell the police. Dr. Bree had told her she was smart, and she shouldn't let anyone bully her or make her do something she didn't want to do, that no one had a right to hurt her or take her things.

When that bad man let her out of his car, she was going to yell at him real good. And she wasn't going to cry anymore, because she wasn't a baby. Dr. Bree said it was okay to cry sometimes, but that if you were sad or scared, it was much better to *do* something to make yourself feel better. MacKenzie liked that idea. She liked it that she could do things, make things happen.

She was going to make that bad man take her home to her Daddy.

BREE'S STOMACH FELT like a cold, hard rock inside her. Daniel had whisked her back to his home so she could pick up her car, because it might look weird if she showed up driving a different vehicle. He'd said he wanted to be sure the kidnapper knew nothing of Project Justice's involvement.

Now she was behind the wheel of her Fiat, amazed she could drive without having a wreck.

Poor MacKenzie, poor little girl, in the hands of some monster! And poor Eric. Hadn't he been through enough? Whoever had taken her had known how to strike where it would hurt most. Eric would die a thousand times before he would let anyone harm so much as a fingernail of his precious child.

She was terrified at the responsibility she'd been given. She would be Daniel's eyes and ears; with the super-safe encrypted silver phone he'd given her, she and Eric could talk freely to him.

Her speedometer had inched up in the past few minutes. She slowed. A speeding ticket wouldn't help matters. She glanced into the rearview mirror. A plain-looking silver Honda followed her. Joe Kinkaid was behind the wheel along with Jillian. They would park somewhere near Eric's house and see if they could figure out who was watching, if anyone was.

If no one was watching the house, then they would come in and hunt for evidence. Beth had assured her that the kidnapper had left *something* behind—a hair, a footprint or perhaps a witness. The lady next door was a big snoop, always peering out a crack in her curtains. Though Eric had been cleared of all crimes, she had made it known she didn't want "those Riggs boys" living next door to her. One day when Bree was taking out the trash, she'd had the misfortune to run into the unpleasant neighbor, who had mistaken Bree for a housekeeper and confided her theory that Elena was sleeping with both brothers.

Bree had disabused her of that notion.

Maybe the old biddy would be useful for something, after all.

As she pulled into Eric's driveway, her heart started to pound and her palms grew damp. Would she always have this reaction to him? Ever since she'd realized she was reluctant to get involved with Eric because of fear, she'd been nervous about seeing him again.

She wanted to take the chance. But would he, since she'd been acting like a split personality? If anything happened to MacKenzie, she wondered if he'd ever believe in anything again.

She opened her car door and started to get out, but the front door of the house opened and Eric stepped out onto the porch. "Bree. Don't get out."

"What?"

"Just drive around to the garage. There's a spot for you."

He seemed a little intense about where she parked. Did he not want anyone to see her car there?

She drove around to the alley, and a few seconds later she pulled into the open garage. As soon as she got out she found herself wrapped in Eric's arms.

"Jesus, Eric, I'm so sorry. I'm so, so sorry I got you involved in this." Then the tears came. She started crying and couldn't stop. It hadn't hit her until this moment, but *she* was responsible for MacKenzie's kidnapping. If she hadn't pressured Eric to take on her cause, this wouldn't have happened.

"It's not your fault, baby," Eric said softly, stroking her back as they stood there in the garage.

"But this has to be related to Philomene's murder and all the rest."

"Maybe not. I'm not sure if I've mentioned it, but MacKenzie is the sole heir to a huge fortune, something like $17 million. That fact was in the news. Someone might have gotten the idea that I have access to that money. I don't. It belongs to her great-grandmother, Tammy's grandmother, who's in a home and completely senile. The money is untouchable until she dies."

Bree got herself under control and dried her tears with a tissue from her purse. "Who handles her money now?"

"She gave some nurse at the home her power of attorney. We are very fortunate the woman is a responsible, honest sort who is using the money strictly for Granny's care."

"Who would inherit the fortune if MacKenzie was…?" Bree asked as they went inside.

"A second cousin of Tammy's. Somebody is looking into that angle."

In the living room, Bree found Elena and Travis sitting on the sofa, holding hands. The kidnapper had specified that Eric tell only Bree, but it had been impossible to keep it from his brother and sister-in-law. When Travis called to ask why she hadn't shown up at a job site with some paperwork, Elena had told him what was going on and he'd come straight home.

Bree hugged them both. They had been so kind and welcoming to her, and she knew they couldn't love MacKenzie any more if she were their daughter.

"So why did I have to park in the garage?" Bree asked.

"It occurred to me," Eric replied, "that whoever wants to harm you has lost track of your whereabouts and would like to find you. By kidnapping MacKenzie, they've drawn you back onto the radar. I just didn't want to take a chance that someone would take a potshot at you when you got out of your car."

Bree shivered. "I never even thought of that. I was so focused on MacKenzie…."

"That might be exactly what someone wants. We've all got to be careful. Someone who stoops to kidnapping a child might do anything. Which brings me to the question—have you talked to your parents lately, Bree?"

Bree sank into a chair. She was always at odds with her mom and dad, but that didn't mean she wanted them to come to harm.

She couldn't deal with them right now. So she called her aunt Terry in Corpus Christi and asked her to let her parents know that she had become the target of a killer and they needed to be extremely careful.

She was relieved to learn they were currently out of town, on a cruise.

Next, Bree checked in with Daniel using the encrypted phone.

"I take it you haven't heard anything from the kidnapper?"

"No." It was twenty minutes until noon.

"I'll make sandwiches," Elena said.

"I'll help," Bree offered. It wasn't that anyone was hungry, but Bree needed to do something with her hands. She couldn't just sit there staring into Eric's haunted eyes.

Bree spread mayonnaise on bread while Elena stacked slices of ham, turkey, cheese and lettuce. By the time they were done, they had more than a dozen sandwiches.

Bree felt like crying when she realized this was the sort of thing one did when there had been a death in the family and you expected friends and family to gather.

"When the kidnapper calls back, will the call be recorded?" Elena asked.

"I think so. They've tapped into Eric's cell phone."

"Can they do that without the police… Oh, never mind. I should know by now not to ask questions. Project Justice does what it does, and the results speak for themselves."

Bree nodded. She didn't care whether it was legal or not. She just wanted someone to find MacKenzie safe and sound—and make the son of a bitch who'd taken her pay.

"How do you think MacKenzie is holding up?" Bree asked.

"She's stronger than people give her credit for," Elena said. "Stronger every day. When I first met her, she was afraid of everything—thunder, the dark, bad dreams, strangers. It's amazing the progress she's made." Tears filled Elena's eyes. "It's just so unfair. How can so many bad things happen to one man— one family?"

Bree folded Elena into a hug. "We're gonna get her back. I know it in my heart." Her heart also told her that she belonged here, with this family. With Eric. Anything that happened to them might as well happen to her.

God, she hoped her heart was right this time.

"You want a cookie, MacKenzie?"

MacKenzie stared hard at the man, but she didn't answer. Her daddy had told her not to talk to strangers, but he'd been especially determined that she not take candy or cookies or any other food from a stranger.

"Suit yourself." He took a bite out of the cookie himself, and MacKenzie's mouth watered. Her breakfast seemed a long time ago.

The bad man had tied her to a chair. They were in a house somewhere. It was cold and quiet—she didn't hear any cars or sirens or dogs barking. Out the windows all she could see were the bare trees of winter.

She wished she'd put on a warmer sweater before going outside. She wished she hadn't gone outside by herself at all.

"Where's my daddy?" she finally mustered the courage to ask.

"Don't worry. You'll see your daddy soon."

It sounded as if he was lying. She knew a lot about lying—her foster parents used to lie to her all the time about what happened to the clothes and toys her daddy gave her. Grown-ups got this certain tone in their voices, and a shifty look in their eyes, when they were saying something untrue just to shut you up.

"I want my daddy," she said. "And I'm gonna cry if you don't take me home *right now*."

He looked up at her, a little surprised by her demand. "You can cry all you want. No one but me will hear you."

MacKenzie knew a thing or two about temper tantrums. She'd been having them for as long as she

could remember, and sometimes they worked wonders getting her what she wanted. She opened her
mouth and let out an ear-piercing scream, followed
by a series of loud sobs. She couldn't fall down on
the floor for a proper tantrum, but she kicked the
legs of the chair and swayed back and forth so hard
she almost knocked the chair over.

Her eyes automatically filled with tears. By sobbing, she kind of fooled her eyes into crying for real.
It wasn't too hard, especially now, when she was
scared.

But all of her howling seemed to have little effect
on the bad man. He just rolled his eyes and walked
out of the room.

Oh, she hated it when that happened. She howled
all the louder, but the bad man didn't come back.

At least she didn't have to look at him. He was
scary, the way he didn't smile or frown or yell. It
was as if he didn't have any feelings.

Eventually she got tired of crying and the sobs
slowed down. She tried to think of what else she
could do.

Dr. Bree had said when she was scared, she should
take some kind of action. Like, if the dark scared
her, she should turn on a light. Or if she was scared
of getting a shot at the doctor's, she should think of
something nice, like kittens or puppies or ice cream.

Speaking of puppies, the bad man had put the
white puppy outside as soon as he got done tying
MacKenzie to the chair. It was whining at the kitchen

door, but like MacKenzie's tantrum, the dog's pitiful cries had no effect on the man. He didn't love that poor little puppy. It meant no more to him than she had meant to the Stovers.

She'd always wanted a puppy. If it were her puppy, she wouldn't make it stay outside. And she would name it Snowflake.

She thought again about Dr. Bree's advice. Besides comforting herself by saying over and over that her daddy would come for her soon, MacKenzie tried to think of what she could do to make herself less afraid. She wouldn't be quite so afraid if she weren't tied up. Being tied up was scary. Bad guys always tied up people on *Scooby-Doo* and then they had to be rescued. Maybe the puppy would rescue her. That idea made her laugh, a little bit.

She looked down at her hands. The man had tied up her hands with silver tape. Her feet, too, so she couldn't run. Then he'd told her to sit on the wooden chair, and he'd wrapped stretchy cords around her—a whole bunch of them. They were tight against her arms and it kind of hurt.

She'd seen Uncle Trav use this silver kind of tape before. He called it duck tape. She had no idea why. Sometimes, when he wanted to tear it, he used his teeth.

MacKenzie leaned down to see if she could reach her hands with her mouth, but no matter how hard she stretched her neck, she couldn't reach.

Then she got another idea. The cords around her

were tight, but they were stretchy. She wiggled her arms a little. If she used all her strength, she could move them up her body, under the cords, an inch at a time. The cords rubbed her skin raw but she didn't care. Maybe she could get loose! Then she would run away from the bad man. She would run all the way home to her daddy and Elena and Uncle Trav. Then they would put the bad man in prison.

## CHAPTER SEVENTEEN

NOON CAME AND went with no phone call, and the minutes crept by.

Joe and Jillian had joined them. After checking every house and car on the street that might have a good view of their home, the two had concluded no one was watching. So they'd begun the task of searching for trace evidence. In their car they carried a portable evidence kit with rubber gloves, tweezers, bags and bottles and boxes for storing evidence, fingerprint powder and brushes, swabs for collecting DNA samples, and luminol and alternate light sources for finding blood.

For the tenth time in as many minutes, Eric flicked the living room curtain back and peered into the backyard. Jillian was on her hands and knees combing the winter-brown grass with a flashlight. It looked as if Kinkaid was examining something on the gate, close to the ground.

Bree joined him at the window. "How long will it take?"

"I don't know. As long as it takes, I guess."

She took his hand and squeezed it. "You're doing

great. I don't know how you've stayed so strong. I'm about to fall apart and she's not even my daughter."

If anyone knew what he was feeling at this moment, it was Bree. She knew what it was like to lose a child. Even if the child had lived only a few hours, the mother-child bond had formed. He squeezed her hand. "It helps a lot, your being here. And all these other people—I can't imagine going through this alone, like you did."

"I wasn't alone. I had Kelly."

Suddenly Eric understood. He knew why she was so loyal to Kelly. It wasn't that she was still in love with him. She was just standing by the one person who had stood by her at the lowest point in her life. He'd gotten her through it, even if ultimately their relationship had petered out.

"You're amazing, Bree."

She smiled uncertainly. "Me? Why?"

"Your heart was broken. But you still have so much love and compassion to give other people."

"My heart broke. But it's healing. You know what they say about time."

"If anything happens to MacKenzie—" His voice broke. "I'm not sure I'd ever recover. I'm not sure I could ever be a functioning human being again."

"It does feel like that at first. But, hey, we're going to get MacKenzie back safe."

"Do you know what the statistics are? Most children kidnapped by strangers are dead within twenty minutes—"

"Don't think like that. She was taken by someone who's looking for a ransom, not by a sexual predator. It's a whole different animal."

"Then why hasn't he called?"

"Things are just taking longer than he thought they would. When Travis kidnapped Elena, he had to be very careful how he made contact. He had to make sure Elena was in a secure location. Then he had to drive far away before he could turn on his phone and make the phone call. And he wasn't even trying to hide his identity—just his location."

"How did you hear about all that?"

She shrugged. "Elena and I talk. Quite a romantic story, the way he won her over and rescued her from the bad guy."

"*Our* meeting was romantic. I ripped off my shirt five minutes after I met you."

She smiled at the memory.

"Bree, there's something I've been meaning to tell you." He really needed to get this off his chest. At least under these circumstances, she would have to stay and hear him out. She wasn't going to leave this house until MacKenzie had been brought home.

"What is it?"

"You know I'm the one who killed Kelly's case at Project Justice."

"I know. You're also the one who got it reinstated."

"I didn't tell you the worst of it. I lied—to you and to Daniel. When I said Kelly bragged about his crimes, it was a fat lie. He never said anything. I lied because I was a coward. I was afraid he would get out of prison and come after me. But I know now it was wrong to punish Kelly for something he might do in the future. It's pointless to go through life afraid of things that might happen. Life is full of dangers no matter what precautions you take. That's certainly been proved to my satisfaction."

Bree looked down and said nothing.

"I'm sorry I said such horrible, untrue things about your friend. He didn't deserve that, and neither did you."

"Thank you for telling me."

"You don't sound too surprised."

"I never believed Kelly would do that. Even when I almost confronted him about it at the prison—I was pretty sure he would deny admitting his guilt to anyone."

So she'd known all along he'd lied to her. Maybe that explained her ambivalence toward him, hot one minute, cool the next.

"Bree, I want you to know—I don't lie. I've seen firsthand what dishonesty can do to a relationship."

"Don't lawyers lie by definition? What's that old joke? 'How can you tell when a lawyer is lying?'"

"'His lips are moving,'" Eric finished for her. "I'm not like that. I regretted the lies I told that day almost from the moment they were out. I knew it was the wrong thing to do, but once I'd done it—"

"Kind of like Philomene."

"Yeah. I understand why she kept perpetrating

that lie, even though she knew she might have sent an innocent man to prison. Once you start, it's hard to stop."

"You were trying to protect your daughter."

"I should have come clean a long time ago. But I didn't want you to hate me."

"Oh, Eric, I could never hate you.... I... The feelings I have for you—"

Eric's phone chose that moment to ring.

His hand shook as he looked at the caller ID Blocked. "It's him."

"Answer it."

He did, but not before he took three seconds to prepare himself to speak with the monster who had his little girl—and to remember everything Daniel had coached him to say.

He pressed the connect button. "Eric Riggs."

"Miss me?"

Eric refused to let the man engage his temper. He was supposed to encourage the kidnapper to talk; minutes from now a language expert would be deciphering the accent, the word choices, the cadence—all things the voice-disguising program couldn't mask.

"I've done as you asked. Now, where's my daughter?"

"All in good time. Did you call the police?" He made a tutting noise with his tongue. "Keep in mind, I'll know if you're lying. If you tell me one lie, we're through."

"I didn't call the police," Eric said. "Do you think I'm crazy, that I'd risk my little girl's life? I'll follow your directions exactly. Just please, don't hurt her."

"She's perfectly fine, for now. The first thing I want you to do is go to your mailbox. In it you'll find a cell phone. I'll call you back on that phone in thirty seconds." He disconnected.

Kinkaid had rushed inside almost as soon as the phone rang, and he was listening to his own phone with a Bluetooth headset. Clearly he had heard the kidnapper's orders.

"He's forcing you to switch phones so it can't be traced or recorded," Kinkaid said. "Damn!"

Eric wasted no time heading to the front door. The mailbox was on the front porch.

"Wait!" Kinkaid called. "You're gonna get yourself picked off like a fish in a barrel if you don't think before you—"

"I don't give a shit." Eric ignored Kinkaid's advice. "This is my little girl we're talking about. When it's your little girl, you can call the shots." He'd contacted Project Justice because he needed help, but that didn't mean he intended to let them roll all over him.

He threw the door open and stepped out. No shots rang out. He reached into the mailbox. His hand closed over something small.

The phone, as promised.

He'd scarcely gotten it out before it buzzed. It was

an ancient flip phone—probably didn't even have a GPS tracker.

"I'm here," Eric said into the phone, stepping back inside.

"Is the good doctor with you?" the hateful voice asked.

The question was confirmation that the kidnapper couldn't see Eric's house, or he would know the answer to that question. "Yes, she is. What do you want? If it's money, I might be able to scrape together something."

There was a pause. "How much?"

Kinkaid gestured with his fingers.

Eric deciphered the gesticulations. "Maybe twenty thousand?"

The kidnapper said nothing.

"It's enough that you could make a new start somewhere."

"Not much of a start. But if that's what you have available, I guess I'll make do. How fast could you get it together?"

Eric didn't want to delay this thing. Every minute the monster had MacKenzie in his control was another minute of terror she had to endure. "Immediately."

"Excellent. Gather together the cash. Then you and the doctor get in your car and start driving. Get on I-45 and head north. You'll hear from me in about thirty minutes."

"Wait—why does Bree have to come?"

"If you have to worry about her safety, you won't try anything. Keep in mind, you deviate from my instructions one bit, and she'll be the first to go. I'll slaughter her right in front of you, and I'll make it last a long, long time. If you don't bring her with you, you'll never hear from me again."

He disconnected.

Eric felt sick to his stomach. "I don't have twenty thousand dollars."

"Don't worry," Jillian said. "We've got it covered. I'll go get it."

"You brought twenty thousand dollars with you?"

"Actually, one hundred thousand. It's in a specially designed package with a tracking device."

"You were prepared to risk one hundred thousand dollars?"

"Of course," said Kinkaid. "It's not like we won't get it back. And he's not likely to find the tracker unless he takes the wrappers off every single bundle. Chances are he'll flip through a few to make sure you didn't supplement with newspaper or something."

Jillian returned shortly with a small duffel bag, and the two investigators went to work taking out some of the cash bundles.

"I'm surprised that he settled for such a small amount," Kinkaid said. "You know what that tells us?"

"He's not really interested in money," Eric theorized. "He just wants us to think he is."

"Exactly."

"I don't want to take Bree with me," Eric said. "It's too dangerous." But even as he said this, he realized there was no other way. Even if they dressed up Jillian with a wig or something, the kidnapper would recognize her as a fake almost immediately. And much as Eric wanted to keep Bree safe, he didn't want to see Jillian or anyone else killed.

"Of course I'm going with you," Bree said. "I won't let you face him alone."

"And we'll be close by," Jillian assured them. "We'll plant another tracking device on your car. More of our team will be in cars farther back. We'll be in constant communication with you. Daniel even has a helicopter on standby."

"What about arming ourselves?" Eric asked.

Kinkaid shook his head. "I assume neither of you has firearms training."

Bree and Eric both shook their heads.

"If you end up face-to-face with this guy, the first thing he'll do is search you. And the last thing you want is to shoot him. He is very likely to have Mac-Kenzie stashed at a separate location. If he dies, you might never find her."

Eric let that weigh on him as hasty preparations were made. He wasn't sure he bought the logic. He could shoot the son of a bitch in the leg, then torture him into telling where he'd hidden MacKenzie.

"Eric," Bree said, "I know you're feeling a lot of things right now, but Joe is right. We should take his advice. Project Justice has dealt with this kind of thing before."

"Many times," Jillian added. "I owe my life to them."

Eric tamped down the fear and anger that threatened to swamp him. Bree was right. This guy was obviously no idiot. He'd thought this through enough to snatch MacKenzie and plant the cell phone without detection. He wasn't just going to walk up to Eric and let himself be shot.

"All right. No gun."

"We've got Kevlar vests for you to wear," Kinkaid said. "They're the newest technology, pretty lightweight. Put them on under your clothes, and if you wear jackets, they won't be easily detectable."

Eric did as requested. A horrible numbness had started creeping into his body, and he recognized it as some biological defense mechanism to stop him from thinking about what MacKenzie might be going through. He would go mad if he dwelled on that.

While he and Bree got dressed, Jillian had been on the phone. "Our psychologist listened to the kidnapper's voice. She offered some insights. He's probably well educated. Also a native Texan. He's intelligent and angry. She agrees that the ransom demand might just be a way to flush you out into the open where he can stage some kind of confrontation. If he tries to draw you to some secluded location, you can't go along. It seems as if Bree might be the target and this whole setup is a way to get to her. So when he calls, you'll have to stand up to him. Tell him you'll leave the ransom in a garbage can in some public place where it won't be easy for him to pick you off."

"Okay."

"Also, it might be a good idea to let Bree talk to him. If she's the target, he might not be as cool talking to her." Kinkaid handed Bree some kind of plug-in device. "Plug this into the phone's earphone jack. It will relay the conversation via shortwave radio signal so everyone can hear it."

Eric was beginning to feel a little like James Bond with all these tricks and gadgets. He was willing to bet the police would not have handled the situation like this. They probably wouldn't have trusted Eric and Bree, as civilians, to do what they were about to do. They'd have deemed it too risky.

It *was* risky. It was insane. But what choice did they have?

A few minutes later, with twenty-four thousand dollars in cash in hand and a tracking device on his car, Eric set out with Bree. They wouldn't be alone; Kinkaid and Jillian would keep them in sight, and other Project Justice people would be close by, ready to formulate a plan on the fly and get into position as they learned more about where the kidnapper would lead them.

Still, Eric felt exposed as they drove off, heading for the interstate.

The call came about fifteen minutes later. They had just gotten onto the freeway.

"Hello, this is Dr. Johnson speaking," Bree said in a businesslike way. He admired her bravery. She didn't have to do this. She could have stayed safe at his house. But she hadn't even considered staying behind.

"Let me speak with Riggs, please," the caller said, matching her polite tone.

"He's busy driving. I've got the phone on speaker. He can hear you."

He also had the silver encrypted cell phone in his pocket, connected to a Bluetooth earpiece so he could get prompts from the Project Justice team listening in.

"Fine, I'll talk to both of you, then. Drive twenty-three miles north of the city limits. At mile marker one-fifteen, take the exit for Boylston Road. Wait there until you hear from me."

"Don't hang up yet," Eric said quickly. "I'm not comfortable driving out into the country somewhere. I've got the money here but I want to leave it for you in a populated area. Otherwise what's to stop you from simply taking the money and killing me?"

"You'll follow my directions, or you won't hear from me again. Is that clear?"

"Tell him it's clear," the psychologist, whose name was Claudia, said into Eric's ear. "Sounds like he's not going to budge."

"No, you listen to me, asshole," Eric bellowed. "I'm done taking orders from you. You want the ransom money, you do as I say. Follow *my* orders and the police will never know you exist. Screw around with me, and every cop in the country will be hunting you down. If anything happens to me, I've left a detailed account of my dealings with you, which a close friend will turn over to the police. *Is that clear?*"

The kidnapper hung up.

"Um, that didn't go exactly according to plan," Kinkaid said into Eric's ear.

He yanked the earpiece off in frustration, hoping he hadn't hosed the whole operation. What if he'd just put his daughter at further risk? He hadn't forgotten the initial threat involving itty-bitty pieces.

BREE PICKED UP the silver phone and brought it to her ear. "What now?"

"Bree, do what you can to get him to stay with the plan. I can't even imagine what he's going through right now—"

"I'll do what I can— Oh, the phone is ringing again."

"You talk to the kidnapper. Turn off the speaker if you have to."

Eric had already grabbed the phone and answered. "I'm only going to say this once." Eric's voice was a low animal growl that sent a chill down Bree's spine. "Downtown Tuckerville. Garbage can on the corner in front of the café. You leave a note there telling me where I can find my daughter, I'll leave the money. Call me back as soon as the note is in place. Now let me talk to MacKenzie. And she better be alive and well or I call in every law enforcement agency in the state of—"

"You want proof your daughter is alive?" The kidnapper's odd tinny voice came over the cheap speaker. "Have a good listen."

A piercing child's scream filled the car. The look of horror that came over Eric's face was almost as frightening.

"Dear God." Eric barely breathed the words.

"She's alive, Eric," Bree said. "Focus on that."

Eric grabbed the phone out of Bree's hand. "I'm going to kill you. I'll shoot you in the head like a rabid dog."

At that moment Bree didn't doubt Eric would do just that if given the chance. She only hoped it wouldn't come to that. What a nightmare if Eric found himself charged with murder again.

"And then you'd never get the kid back," the kidnapper said, laughing. "I don't think so. I'm giving you one last chance to do this my way. Take the Boylston Road exit. Once I see your car, and I confirm you and the doc are alone, we'll proceed. And if by chance you have involved the police…let's just say I have ways of finding out, and it'll be game over." He hung up.

Bree could hear Kinkaid's voice coming out of the discarded Bluetooth earpiece. She picked it up and hooked it over her ear. "It's Bree," she said. "Can you repeat?"

"We're damn lucky the guy still wants to play. If he gets nervous, he's going to bolt. Please, do this my way."

"Okay. But honestly, I think Eric rattled him by standing up to him. He said if we didn't follow his directions to the letter, we'd never hear from him again, yet he called back. He wants to go through with this. And I don't think it's for some stinking twenty thousand dollars. Joe, this guy has to be Philomene's killer. He's luring us someplace so he can kill us. Which means we must be close to figuring out who he is."

"If he gets rid of us, he solves his problem," Eric said, having returned to his senses. Bree was amazed he could still drive the car after hearing his daughter shriek in fear or pain. "No one else is pushing to tie Philomene's death to the man who raped her six years ago or to a series of murders. But the weird thing is, I don't feel like we're close at all. We have theories, but not much in the way of hard facts."

"We must have done something to scare him," Bree said. "Otherwise why would he take such a big risk? Kidnapping a child, going through this elaborate setup—we must be close and not know it."

"It must be the DNA," Eric said. "The Hollings County case. None of the other murders yielded any usable trace evidence. But that one—maybe the killer believes it's only a matter of time before we match it up to him."

Bree felt a trace of hope. "Which means he must

be someone close to the investigation. Someone who knows we requested the evidence from that case."

"Someone in law enforcement," Eric said grimly. "Like we've been afraid of all along.

"Joe," Bree said, "can you focus in on the Tuckerville deputies and people in the D.A.'s office? Maybe one of DeVille's inner circle is involved, and he's been covering up for them. Good ol' boys and all."

"I'll get someone on it. Beth has been hard at work running more tests on that DNA. Depending on the quality of the sample, she might be able to isolate certain gene markers."

It was just a theory, Bree knew. But it felt right. Requesting the evidence from all of those murders was the one thing they'd done that a lot of people knew about.

"What about other Range Rover drivers in the area?" Bree asked.

"A pool of about thirty-four in a three-county area. If we start getting into Houston, it gets hairy. But we're checking out those closest to Tuckerville. So far no red flags."

Bree sighed. "Okay." One final thought occurred to her. She hated to even mention it, but she didn't want to leave any stone unturned. "What about the coroner, Dr. Gentry? He is a part of the sheriff's good-ol'-boy network, if only a grudging member. And he was with the sheriff right around the time Philomene went missing. We saw them having dinner together. He said he'd been fishing with Needles and the sheriff the night before."

"We already thought of that," Joe said. "It was relatively easy to check his DNA against the sample, since he's in the national database."

"Oh." And here she thought she was coming up with an original idea. It seemed those Project Justice people thought of everything. Truthfully, she was relieved she could rule out Ted, especially since they'd confided in him.

"There's the exit sign." Eric's voice was tight, all business. He veered the car off the highway and down the ramp, slowing to barely thirty miles per hour.

The kidnapper couldn't have chosen a much more desolate area, at least not in this part of the state. Boylston Road was a two-lane blacktop that appeared to lead nowhere. To their right was an overgrown pasture. At the end of the ramp, across the road, was one derelict gas station. Other than that, it was just a few scraggly mesquite trees and open prairie.

"He must be in that gas station." Eric eased his car to the shoulder. "There's nothing else around." He turned off the engine, unfastened his seat belt and opened the door.

"Wait!" Bree called, alarmed. "What are you doing?"

"I'm going in there."

Bree couldn't stop him, so she got out, too, hurrying to catch up with him as he headed across the road. "Eric, she won't be in there. He has to know there's a chance we're not doing this alone, that someone else will know where we are, where we've stopped. MacKenzie won't be someplace so obvious. And if the kidnapper is hiding in the gas station and you confront him, he might never tell you…"

Eric slowed down. "Damn it. You're right."

"I know it's hard for you to be cautious, but let's just wait for him to contact us."

A muscle in Eric's jaw ticked. "Yeah. Okay. Hell, for all we know, he's nowhere near here. He could pretend to see us stopped here, and how would we know he's lying?" Eric scanned the horizon. "If he really was here, watching, he'd have called by now."

As if on cue, the phone Bree was holding rang. Eric held out his hand, and she gave it to him, praying he would stay calm. It seemed to her that losing their cool would only play into the kidnapper's hands, making them more vulnerable.

But it wasn't her daughter in jeopardy.

Eric flipped the phone open. "We're here."

## CHAPTER EIGHTEEN

SO FAR, SO GOOD. Riggs and that interfering whore were playing right into his hands.

They had followed his directions, and they were alone. He'd watched them for a few minutes before calling. They didn't appear to be talking to anyone else on any other phone. Not that his observation was any guarantee.

"Go west on Boylston Road for seven-point-two miles. You'll see a dirt road off to your left. Park the car and head up that road on foot. I hope you brought your walking shoes."

"How far do we walk?" Riggs demanded.

"Until I tell you to stop."

"Let me talk to MacKenzie. I need proof she's okay or this little game is over."

"You want to hear her scream again?"

"Do you want to sign your own death warrant?" Riggs shot back. "Just let me talk to her."

The man thought about it, then sighed. "Okay. Tell her to for God's sake stop crying. I'm sick of listening to it." Maybe a small concession would entice Riggs to be more cooperative.

He stepped back inside the house from the deck overlooking the lake. It was a great location for his purposes, perfectly isolated. This time of year, no one was on the water or hiking the woods, not with the weather so cold.

The man stepped into the kitchen—and froze. "I changed my mind," he said abruptly. "Just drive where I told you to go." He hung up the throwaway phone and stared in disbelief at the empty chair, the colorful tangle of bungee cords lying on the floor.

MACKENZIE RAN WITH the wiggling puppy in her arms and a cell phone in her pocket. She couldn't believe she'd done it! She'd worked her hands up through the stretch cords and freed them, then bitten at the silver tape until she could rip it. Once her hands were free, she had leaned over and peeled the tape from her feet.

The stretchy cords had been trickier. They'd been hooked behind the back of the chair, where she couldn't reach. But then she'd figured out she could slide them around so the hooks were in front.

Once, the bad man had walked back into the kitchen. She had quickly folded her hands in her lap and bowed her head, sobbing, so he wouldn't look at her. He didn't like looking at her, didn't like hearing her cry.

When he walked back out, she'd unhooked the last of the stretchy cords and was free. She'd been so scared he would see her, and she'd stood there frozen for a few seconds, wondering what to do next.

That was when she'd noticed the phone he left on the kitchen counter.

Not the one he'd been talking on; a different one. She'd picked it up and studied it. It was just like Elena's phone.

She couldn't speed dial her daddy, of course. But in kindergarten the teachers had made all the kids learn their parents' phone numbers so they could call for help if they ever needed to. She'd put in the first two numbers; then she'd heard the bad man rustling around in the other room and decided she'd better run first, then call. She'd shoved the phone into her jacket pocket and tiptoed to the back door. The noise had been awful loud when she'd opened and closed it, even though she'd tried to be quiet, and she'd expected the bad man to come running into the kitchen and grab her.

But he hadn't. She was out the door. She was free.

Grabbing the puppy had been a last-minute decision. The poor thing—it had been crying at the door ever since they got to the house. The bad man had been so mean to the puppy, not even talking to it. Afraid that he might get mad and hurt the dog when he realized MacKenzie was gone, she had decided to take it with her. As soon as she got to a safe place, she would call her daddy.

But the puppy was heavier than she'd thought it would be, especially after she'd been running for a bit. It was slowing her down.

"MacKenzie!" the bad man called from the house. "Where'd you go? You want a cookie?"

Did he think she was stupid? She'd learned a lot about people who tried to get her to do stuff with promises of cookies and ice cream and candy when she'd lived with her foster family. One time she'd hidden in a closet from Mrs. Stover when it was bath time. Mrs. Stover had said if she would come out and take her bath, she could have a glass of chocolate milk. But what she'd gotten was a spanking.

She ran faster. She was in among some trees and bushes, and when she looked over her shoulder, she couldn't see anything of the house except the tall chimney. Maybe that meant the bad man couldn't see her, either.

But he could for sure run faster than she could, and if he came after her, he would catch her. So she kept running.

After another couple of minutes, she stopped and put the puppy on the ground. "Snowflake, you'll have to run to keep up with me."

The little white dog jumped up against her leg as if he wanted to play.

"Maybe later. C'mon." She took off running again, though the brush was getting thicker. Vines and thorny branches grabbed at her ankles. She just wanted to stop and sit down on the ground and cry until someone rescued her.

The bad man's voice rang out across the woods.

"MacKenzie? I talked to your daddy. He's coming to get you, but you have to come back to the house."

His voice was fainter than before. That was good. But she still couldn't stop. The puppy ran ahead of her, seeming to have no trouble with vines and thorns. Every so often he would stop and look back at her, whining, encouraging her to keep going.

"I'm coming," she said, climbing over a fallen tree. She would run all day and all night if she had to.

Then she saw something in front of her that brought her heart into her throat.

A fence.

A fence that went as far as she could see in both directions. It was tall and made of metal, and it had barbed wire on top.

She walked along the fence for a while, hoping she might find a gate. But there was no way she could get to the other side. Meanwhile, the bad man's voice was getting louder again.

MacKenzie had to do something or the bad man was going to see her. She looked left, then right, then all around. And then she looked up.

She had seen cats get away from dogs by climbing trees. Maybe she could do the same thing. She was a good tree climber. Her foster brother Wesley had shown her how to climb the tree in the Stovers' backyard, a big tree with lots of branches and funny pink flowers that looked like fireworks and smelled sweet. Up in that tree, she could be alone. No one except Wesley knew to look, and he never told.

MacKenzie had climbed the tree in her new back-yard, too. Aunt Elena had found her up on a high branch once, and she'd turned pale and told her to get down immediately. It was the only time she remembered Elena yelling at her.

But not every tree was a climbing tree. She had to find one with lots of branches low to the ground.

There was one! Half of it was dead with no leaves, but none of the trees had very many leaves to hide behind because it was winter. She would just have to hope the bad man didn't look up.

Clenching her teeth together, she started to climb—one branch, then another.

The puppy whined. If she could have brought it up with her she would have, but she needed both her hands.

Once she made the mistake of looking down and almost fell. She had never climbed up this high before. She sure hoped the bad man wasn't a tree climber.

When she felt she'd gone high enough, she straddled the branch she was on and clung to the trunk. Once she felt comfortable there, she let go with one of her hands and pulled the phone out of her jacket pocket.

It wasn't easy holding the phone with one hand and punching in the numbers at the same time. She almost dropped it. But finally she had all ten numbers entered correctly. Holding her breath, she hit the green-phone button and held the phone up to her ear.

ERIC AND BREE had been walking for twenty minutes down the rutted dirt road, which ran through a thick mixed forest of pines and deciduous trees. Maybe it was a logging road; Eric wasn't sure. But it seemed to go on forever. The clouds had burned off in the past few minutes, and dappled sun filtered down onto the ground. Between the mild exertion of walking and the rising temperature, it was almost comfortable to be outside. Under any other circumstances, this would be an idyllic walk through nature with the woman he loved.

He *did* love Bree. How could he not? Little by little, without even meaning to, he was sure, she'd chipped away at his armor, until the risk of loving again was preferable to the pain of losing her.

When this mess was over and he had MacKenzie back safe and sound, he would tell her. But not now, when everyone's emotions were heightened. She might not believe him. Or she might not react honestly for fear of hurting him when he was most vulnerable. For now, all he could do was to let her know how much he appreciated her staying by his side, putting herself in danger for his daughter's sake.

They definitely were in danger. It still wasn't clear what the kidnapper ultimately wanted from them. Yes, they had Project Justice backing them up. Kinkaid and Jillian were making their way through the woods, keeping a visual on them even as they stayed well out of sight. The unmarked helicopter was in the air not too far away and would do a casual flyover when it seemed they might be getting close to their quarry. But no one would make a move on the guy until they had confirmed Mac-Kenzie's whereabouts—or he started shooting.

Then all bets were off.

"We're not getting very good cell reception out here." Bree had taken control of the old phone while he'd been updating Kinkaid, and he'd let her keep it. Under the circumstances, she was calmer than he was. If he lost his cool again, the kidnapper might very well cut his losses and break off communication altogether, as he'd threatened.

Eric checked the reception on his phone. "Mine's okay. If he can't get through to that one, maybe he'll try this one."

"Or maybe he won't need to talk to us at all."

That was a cheerful thought. How easy would it be to gun them down without warning?

"Philomene's killer didn't use a gun," he reminded Bree. "He most likely hit her on the head. The other murder victims died by strangling."

"But getting rid of us would be a different kind of kill for him. One born of expediency—so he doesn't go to jail. So he can continue to prey on young women."

"He must know that if we disappear, Project Justice won't let this go. Daniel would take it very personally if one of his employees was murdered."

"We don't know what this guy is thinking," Bree said glumly. "I guess we'll find out."

Just then Eric's phone rang. He looked at the screen. "It's blocked." He answered it anyway. "Eric Riggs."

"Daddy?"

A jolt of pure joy shot up Eric's whole body. "MacKenzie! Baby, where are you?"

"In a tree. I ran away from the bad man."

Oh, my God. She'd escaped? His six-year-old daughter had escaped on her own from a serial killer and had the presence of mind to get to a phone and call him?

Both Eric and Bree had stopped cold in the middle of the road. Bree already had the silver phone out and was talking directly to Daniel, reporting the new development.

"Are you okay? Where are you?"

"In the woods. In a tree. Please, Daddy, come get me before the bad man does."

Bree had leaned close so she could hear MacKenzie's side of the conversation. "She called Eric on his regular cell phone," she reported to Daniel. "Is there any way to trace where it's coming from?"

Eric couldn't hear Daniel's reply, so he kept his full focus on his little girl. He could hear a dog barking in the background and MacKenzie trying to shush it.

"MacKenzie, honey, don't hang up the phone, okay?" Eric implored.

Her voice dropped to a whisper. "Daddy, I'm scared. What if the bad man finds me?"

"If he does, you just be brave. I'm trying to find

you, baby." His eyes filled with tears. He couldn't even imagine what she was feeling, but he was in awe of her right now. "Don't hang up. The phone is going to lead us to you."

"Okay, Daddy. I can see him now. He's getting close—" Her voice cut off abruptly.

"MacKenzie? MacKenzie!" He checked the screen. Call dropped.

"Bree, are you still there?" Daniel asked.

"Y-yes." She'd been momentarily distracted by the panic in Eric's voice, the devastation on his face. "The call was disconnected."

"We're trying to get a bead on it now. Wait, hold on." His voice was slightly muffled as he spoke with someone else. After a few moments, he came back. "I'm afraid it's not good news. MacKenzie is using a phone with a disabled GPS. But we can still figure out the general area where the call came from by triangulating which towers the signal went through."

She related the news to Eric.

He nodded tightly, still staring at his phone. "C'mon, ring, damn it." He looked at Bree. "She escaped. She got away from him. But she's out there somewhere alone and he's looking for her. She said she could see him, that he was getting closer."

"We'll find her."

"She got his phone. I can't believe— A month ago she was terrified of everything. If a branch scratched a window, she would cower under the covers and refuse to come out."

"Sounds like she's reclaiming her real self. Didn't you say she used to be fearless?"

Eric nodded.

"Bree?" It was Daniel again. She turned on the speaker so Eric could hear. "She's actually not far from you. But the location isn't precise. We'll get the chopper over there in a few minutes, but with all those trees it won't be easy to spot her from the air."

"Then we need a search party on the ground."

Orders were given. Kinkaid smoothly took over the operation, and Eric gave up any illusions he might have had about a peaceful end to this kidnapping.

Cooperation was out. Negotiations were out. Project Justice would go in and find MacKenzie—and take out her kidnapper if necessary.

How FAR COULD she have gone? The man cursed his damnable luck. He had assaulted and murdered nine women without a hitch, but a six-year-old brat had gotten the best of him. It didn't seem possible.

He should have just gotten rid of her as soon as he got to the house. But he'd delayed executing her in case Riggs required proof she was alive before following the man's orders. But now that decision had come back to bite him in the butt.

She *couldn't* have gotten far. Granted, she was a strong, robust little girl, as she'd proved when he'd first grabbed her. He would have the bruises to prove it for days. But she was still only three feet tall. His legs were a lot longer than hers. Maybe he couldn't negotiate the thick brush as he once could, but it blew his mind he couldn't find— Wait a minute. What was that?

The dog! She'd taken that damn puppy with her. It couldn't have gotten out on its own; he'd thrown it onto the back patio, which was fenced all the way around. He should have left it by the side of the road, except he was afraid it could be traced back to him. He'd taken it from a kid in front of the grocery store who was giving away a whole litter of mongrels. The kid might just remember the face of the man he'd given the white puppy to.

Besides, he wasn't heartless. He would take no pleasure in killing a little girl or a puppy. He had nothing against them. It was the grown women who deserved to die. The high-and-mighty Bree, who thought she was so far above him, just because he didn't have sculpted pecs and a six-pack of abs.

He whistled as he got closer to the dog. It looked up, then galloped to him with ears flapping and tongue lolling, too stupid to know he wasn't the puppy's friend. Christ, he hadn't even fed it. Dogs were just like that—everybody's best friend.

If the dog was here, the brat had to be close by, as well. He petted the puppy, then scooped it up. "MacKenzie? Look who I've got. It's your puppy! Tell you what, I'll give you this puppy to keep for your very own if you'll just come back to the house and wait there for your daddy. I talked to him—he's worried about you."

Nothing.

He scanned the woods. A little kid like that could hide herself just about anywhere and he wouldn't see her. She could stand behind a tree trunk or squat behind some brush or a stump.

Suddenly he got a better idea for how to get her to come out. He held the puppy in one hand and took his hunting knife from its holster. He held the tip of the knife to the dog's neck. The dog wiggled helplessly and whined.

"See, you stupid mutt?" he said softly. "Not everyone is your friend." Then more loudly he called, "MacKenzie? You come out from wherever you're hiding right now or I will slit this dog's throat. Do you know what that means? I'll stick a knife in it, and it'll die. I'll cut off its head."

He heard it then, the little gasp she couldn't muffle. She was close—very close. He swiveled his head slowly back and forth, listening for her breath or the rustle of leaves. Then, slowly, he looked up.

Bingo.

He dropped the dog and it ran away from him, pausing when it got twenty or so feet away to turn and look at him worriedly. But he didn't care about the dog anymore. He had the little girl treed.

"MacKenzie, honey, you come out of that tree right now."

"I can't," she said.

"Yes, you can. You just come down the same way you went up. If you come down right now, I won't punish you, and I won't hurt the puppy, okay? I want us to get along."

"I can't climb down. I'm stuck. I'm afraid I'll fall."

"I'll catch you if you fall. But I'm sure you won't." Christ, he didn't have time for this. Riggs and the bitch doctor were probably wondering what happened to him. While he didn't think they would do anything rash right away, if he left them to their own devices for long, no telling who they might contact.

"I can't move."

She was way the hell up there. How had such a little girl climbed so high?

"MacKenzie, if you don't come down right now, I'll leave you up there. You'll be there all night. It's gonna get cold. And you'll get pretty hungry."

She said nothing, but she whimpered.

Damn it. Sometimes he wished he didn't have such an aversion to guns. It would be easy to pick her off, watch her fall, the little troublemaker. Maybe he *would* enjoy snuffing her. But it was too damn hard to get your hands on a gun that couldn't be traced to you. Knives were so much simpler.

He could throw a rock, but she was too far up, and he'd never been good at throwing. Besides, he didn't see any rocks lying around. Just sticks and leaves.

There really was no choice. He was going to have to climb up and drag her down. Then he would strangle her and be done with it.

He wasn't much good at climbing. When other boys had been playing ball and running and climbing trees and throwing rocks outside, his asthma had confined him indoors. He'd eventually outgrown the asthma, but his athletic abilities had never caught up. Now even a casual game of softball was beyond him.

Climbing a tree, though—that he could manage. He just had to be careful. And this looked like an easy tree to climb, with plenty of hand- and footholds. With a resigned sigh, he started up. "I'm coming to get you, MacKenzie." He schooled the anger out of his voice. "I'll get you down safe and sound." She would be an idiot to trust him at this point, but kids were stupid. Anyway, she had no one else. He would be her hero.

Climbing was harder than he'd thought it would be. His muscles, unused to the strain, protested. Each time he hauled himself up a little higher, the pain increased and it was more of a struggle. He wouldn't be able to climb down holding the girl, that was for sure. But he didn't need to. He would knock her off that branch. If the fall didn't kill her, it surely would incapacitate her long enough that he could climb back down and finish the job.

*Almost there now.*

The branch she sat on was rotted out. The man didn't want to add his weight to it. But he felt around for another handhold and came up empty. Moving his foot up to a slightly higher position, he inched up so that his head was almost even with MacKenzie's knee.

"Can you climb onto my shoulders?"

"I can't let go," she said again. But even as she spoke, she climbed to her feet and seemed ready to ascend even higher. The brat was putting him on! She wasn't afraid to climb down. She had manipulated him into climbing up here after her.

Just as she would have gone higher, he grabbed on to her ankle. "Oh, no, you don't."

She shrieked and shook her leg, trying to dislodge him. "Let me go!" She kicked out and landed a glancing blow to his forehead. He nearly lost his balance. He let go of the girl's ankle and grabbed blindly for anything to keep him from falling. His fingers curled around the rotten branch. It cracked under the added weight. His feet slid off the slick branch he'd found to stand on. He was still holding on to another branch with his left hand, but his own weight was too much for his diminished grip and the branch ripped out of his hand. He, the branch and MacKenzie all plunged toward the ground in a dizzying free fall.

They both screamed.

He bounced off one branch, then another, like a pinball. Pain screamed through his body until he slammed into the leaf-strewn ground.

Then, nothing.

# *CHAPTER NINETEEN*

"THERE'S A SMALL lake just on the other side of these woods," Jillian said urgently. She navigated from the passenger seat while Kinkaid sped down country roads that weren't designed for triple-digit speeds. Eric and Bree leaned forward from the backseat, trying to get a better look at the satellite map on Jillian's tablet computer. Eric was going to have a concussion given the number of times he'd bashed his head as the car hit one bump after another.

Bree gasped. "Willowbrook Reservoir. Isn't that where Ted Gentry said they were fishing?"

"That's right." Eric pondered the implications.

"I see some houses around the lake," Jillian said into the phone. She was talking to Mitch back in Houston. "See what you can find out about who owns them. Our guy isn't going to just walk out in the middle of the woods. He would have a place to stash his hostage well out of sight."

A tense silence descended on the car as they waited for Mitch to scour online tax records. Eric found himself again holding hands with Bree. She shouldn't be here. He would feel better if she were safely tucked away in some hotel until this was all over. At the same time, he didn't know how he would get through this without her.

"Bingo," Mitch said, his voice on speaker. "We've got a winner. One of those homes is owned by Sheriff Bobby DeVille."

Eric let that sink in for all of half a second before his logical mind kicked in. "But the sheriff—I thought we ruled him out. His DNA doesn't match the Hollings County evidence."

"It's possible we were wrong to include that murder with the others," Kinkaid reasoned.

"Do we know where DeVille is right now?" Bree asked.

"I'm checking. Give me a minute."

The minute dragged by. Kinkaid swerved to avoid a mourning dove pecking at gravel in the middle of the road. "Damn stupid critter," he muttered.

"I'm back," Mitch said. "Conveniently, it's the sheriff's day off. The dispatcher says he's unreachable—imagine that."

"I'm gonna kill the son of a bitch," Eric said, grateful now that no one had provided him with a gun. He would have been all too tempted to use it.

The name of the housing development where Sheriff DeVille owned a weekend home was Lost Harbor—aptly named. The entrance was hard to find, the sign classy but inconspicuous. Kinkaid pulled his vehicle behind other cars that already lined the roadway near the entrance. Several men and women were strapping on bulletproof vests and helmets and checking weapons. They looked like a SWAT team, minus the official designation.

"Dear God," Bree said, staring at a wiry gray-haired woman in hot pink leggings and army boots. "Is that Celeste?"

"That's her, all right," Eric said. "Don't let appearances fool you. Apparently she's well trained and has the heart of a grizzly bear."

"She's certainly not going to sneak up on anyone."

Eric got out of the car and, without saying a word, headed toward the lake.

Joe stopped him before he'd gone very far. "I'm gonna want you and Bree to stay back until we check things out."

Eric started to object, but Bree, who had hurried to join the men, placed a hand on his arm. "Eric, we need to let them do what they do best. I'm sure it won't take long. Either the sheriff is there, in which case they'll take him by surprise and shut him down, or he's not there, and this has been a huge red herring."

"He has to be there. MacKenzie *has* to be there."

Bree took his hand and squeezed it. "We'll find her."

Kinkaid gave Eric a walkie-talkie so he and Bree could at least hear what was going on. As the team made their stealthy way into the housing development, they engaged in minimal chatter. They seemed calm, as though they did this every day. Eric had to hope they knew what they were doing.

Doubts assailed him. What if he'd made a terrible mistake in trusting Project Justice rather than the police? No, he had to trust them; most of them were ex-cops, ex-military. They'd all been trained well, probably better than anyone the local sheriff could scare up in such a short time. That was the main advantage of trusting his coworkers to handle this—they mobilized faster than a greased pig. Every minute that ticked away was another minute Mac-Kenzie spent scared and alone. Another minute that depraved animal could find her, catch her, hurt her.

His own phones, both of them, had remained ominously silent.

"On my signal," someone said on the walkie. "Three, two, one, go!"

Eric strained his ears as he heard a lot of commotion—doors being broken in, glass shattering, orders being shouted. But no high-pitched screams and nothing like a confrontation. Next he was hearing, "Clear."

"Clear."

"Clear."

Then, "Eric? You there?"

Eric pressed the talk button. "I'm here."

"We didn't find anyone. You can come on down the road now. Just drive my car. I left the keys in the ignition."

"Damn it. On our way." He climbed behind the steering wheel, and Bree joined him.

The sheriff's house—probably a weekend retreat—was easy to find, one of the first houses they saw along the bumpy little road that ran alongside a small man-made lake.

"Isn't that the sheriff's Range Rover?" Eric asked, alarmed. It was parked in the driveway.

"Sure looks like it. He's here somewhere."

"Maybe in one of these other houses." Just as he finished the sentence, Celeste opened his door and dragged him out of the car.

"Down, get down, both of you. We think he might be in the house next door. Jillian noticed a broken windowpane. We can see lights and a car in the garage." Celeste got them both out of the car and sitting on the pavement behind it. "You'll be safe enough right here in case bullets start to fly. Just a precaution. That probably won't happen."

Eric had left his walkie-talkie on the car's passenger seat, but the window was cracked and he could still hear the static and the quick bursts of urgently whispered conversation.

"Number Two in position."

"Number Three at the patio door."

"On my signal…"

The drill was repeated. Eric found himself squeezing Bree's hand, his heart in his throat for the second time in five minutes. But again, no shots fired, nothing to indicate the sheriff or MacKenzie had been found. Like before, the all-clear signal was given. Eric got to his feet and helped Bree up.

Kinkaid joined them. "They're not here, but they've definitely been here. We found where Mac-Kenzie was tied up. Either he released her or she escaped and ran."

"Go with the second theory," Eric said immediately. "She told me she'd escaped." He looked around. "She must have run into those woods right there. Probably thought it would be easier to hide there." They were close—he could feel it.

Kinkaid turned. "Listen up, everyone. We need to get organized and search these woods."

"There's not enough of us," Bree said.

"Ian is on his way here with Violet. She'll make quick work of finding anyone who set off on foot from this house, I guarantee it."

"When will Ian get here?"

Kinkaid checked his watch. "An hour. Come on. We can cover a lot of ground in an hour. We might find her before then."

Eric nodded and moved to join his coworkers where they gathered in the driveway, awaiting orders. They all looked at him. Some squeezed his shoulder or offered a sympathetic smile. Some spoke to him, a few brief words of comfort and encouragement.

He hadn't known these people for long, but he couldn't think of any group he would rather have on his side. They weren't just good at their jobs—they cared. They were personally invested in bringing MacKenzie home safely.

"I don't suppose I could convince you to stay here while we search," Kinkaid said.

"She's my daughter."

"The problem is, there's also a dangerous man out there."

"I know."

Kinkaid nodded. "This goes against everything I've ever been taught, but here." He handed Eric a pistol butt-first. "I refuse to send you out there with no defense at all. For emergencies only. That means defending yourself against a lethal threat. If you shoot someone who's unarmed or someone running away from you, you could find yourself back in prison."

"Understood."

Kinkaid gave him a fifteen-second lesson on how to use the weapon. It was pretty straightforward. Take off the safety, point and pull the trigger He stuck the gun in his jacket pocket, intending to forget it was there. But the extra weight would be a constant reminder.

"Are you sure about that?" Bree nodded toward Eric's pocket.

"You don't have to worry. Much as I'd like to, I'm not gonna go sideways and shoot this guy." Despite what he'd been thinking only a few minutes ago. "Not unless he tries to shoot me first." Or if lethal force was needed to stop him from hurting Mac-Kenzie. But that was what Kinkaid had meant.

By silent mutual agreement, Bree stuck close to Eric. Whether it was because she was afraid of confronting the killer by herself or because she wanted to make sure he kept the gun in his pocket, he didn't know, but he was glad of her company.

The patch of woods they were searching was triangular in shape. They started at one point, then fanned out in a line, getting farther and farther apart until gradually they couldn't see each other. They called MacKenzie's name over and over but heard nothing in response. The silence settled heavily around Eric's heart. He'd never been a religious person, but he prayed now.

Another few minutes passed with no one talking on the radio. No sign of MacKenzie or the kidnapper.

Suddenly Bree stopped and grabbed Eric's arm. "Look, what's that?"

Eric squinted in the direction she pointed. He saw something moving, something white. "MacKenzie!" *Please, let that be her.*

The thing moved closer and Eric's heart sank as he realized it wasn't MacKenzie at all, just a dog. The animal came right up to them, tail wagging, obviously wanting to make friends.

He'd heard a dog barking when MacKenzie had called; maybe it was *this* dog.

"MacKenzie loves animals," Eric said. "The kidnapper could have used a puppy to gain MacKenzie's trust. She tends to drop her defenses around puppies and kittens."

"If we're right, then we must be on the right track. She's got to be around here somewhere."

Eric used the walkie-talkie to tell the others about finding the dog.

"We'll head that way," Kinkaid said. "You two stay on your toes and be extra careful. I don't want anyone hurt at this late date."

As if Eric wouldn't be alert in this situation. But cautious? If he spotted MacKenzie—when he spotted MacKenzie—he might throw caution to the wind. He tried to keep that in mind as he continued to scan the woods left to right, left to right, for any sign of his daughter.

Finally he did see something. Movement. It was no animal this time; that was a human being coming toward them. An adult-size person. And he carried a large bundle in his arms.

Eric reached for Bree's hand just as she did the same.

"Is that...?" The question died on her lips. Yes, it was. Sheriff Bobby DeVille walked right toward them holding MacKenzie, who looked to be unconscious—or worse.

Eric suddenly understood the concept of "seeing red." Heat rose in his body from somewhere deep inside him, filling him with a burning rage that threatened to erupt into violence. His hand went to the gun in his pocket.

"Eric, no," Bree said under her breath. "I can see both of his hands, and he's not holding a weapon."

"Hey," the sheriff called as they got closer. "I've got a medical emergency here. Either of you have a cell phone?"

To hell with caution. Eric rushed forward, arms outstretched, ready to take the child from him by force if necessary. "What happened? What's wrong with her?"

"Oh, it's you." DeVille sounded surprised. "This is your girl? She looked familiar. I saw her just that one time at the café that night." He handed MacKenzie to her father without any prompting. "I think she's suffering from hypothermia. She's wet, and her skin is cold. We need to get her warmed up and get an ambulance right away— Oh, hell, Bree, you're the doctor here. I'm sure you know what to do. Did she get lost, wander away or something?"

Bree and Eric exchanged a confused look. Was the sheriff actually trying to pretend he'd just stumbled across MacKenzie, just now, by accident? What a load of crap!

Bree had somehow gotten the walkie-talkie in her hand and was speaking into it. "We got her. She's alive but unconscious. I don't know the extent of her injuries yet but she needs an ambulance. Life Flight if you have to."

Now that Eric had MacKenzie in his arms, he was loath to let go of her. But he couldn't just leave her kidnapper standing there, free to pull a weapon or run. He kissed MacKenzie on the cheek. Her skin was cold on his lips. Then he handed her to Bree, who immediately laid her out on the ground and started to examine her.

"Do you need me to support her head, keep her off the ground or something?" the sheriff asked anxiously. "I'm so sorry I couldn't call for help right away but I didn't bring my phone with me when I took off hiking. Stupid."

"Sorry, my ass." Eric hauled off and punched DeVille in the face, putting every ounce of anxiety he'd felt for the past few hours into the blow.

DeVille staggered back. "What the hell?"

Eric didn't stop there. DeVille was bigger than Eric by a good thirty pounds, but he didn't have rage on his side. Eric head-butted him, knocking him to the ground. While the sheriff was still stunned, Eric rolled him over onto his stomach and sat on him.

"You might as well give it up, DeVille. Everybody knows you're the one who took her. And it seems pretty obvious you killed Philomene, too, and probably a whole slew of other women."

"Have you gone crazy?" DeVille screamed once he found his voice again. "You just assaulted a cop. I'll have your license for this, and you'll do jail time, too."

"Just shut up. I have a gun, and if you start acting like a threat to me or Bree or MacKenzie, I won't hesitate to use it."

Bree ignored the testosterone-fest and focused on

her patient. She peeled off her jacket and laid it over MacKenzie's incredibly small, still form. "We need to get her warm. Give me your jacket, Eric."

He complied immediately, though he first removed the gun from his pocket and transferred it to the small of his back. He was grateful that the sheriff had decided not to fight him. He hoped to hell one of his coworkers had handcuffs—and where the hell were they, anyway? He twisted around to look behind him, relieved to see movement through the trees. The cavalry was on its way.

Celeste, spry as a deer making her way through brush and over logs, reached them first. "Got something you want me to take off your hands?" She reached into her pocket and pulled out a zip tie.

"All yours, Celeste."

The elderly woman cuffed DeVille and flipped him over. "Damn, Eric, what did you do to him?"

"Punched him out like he was in an Old West fist-fight," Bree said as she gathered MacKenzie into her arms again. "Is an ambulance on the way? There's only so much I can do without the proper equipment, but we really need to get her someplace warm."

Kinkaid joined them, followed shortly by the others.

One of the Project Justice guys had a reflecting space blanket with him. "Here, let's get her wrapped in this. Then I'll run her up to the house, turn on the heat and get her under some blankets."

"I'll take her," Eric said. He needed to hold her.

Maybe he could transfer some of his life force to her just from the sheer power of his love. She was so tiny, hardly weighed anything.

Bree walked ahead of him, clearing a path and holding back branches, helping him balance when he had to negotiate uneven ground. The puppy trotted along with them.

It didn't take them long to get back to the sheriff's house. They left the neighbor's house alone, since it was the more obvious crime scene.

Once they got her onto the sofa, Bree checked her over more thoroughly. Paramedics were en route, but they were miles away.

Out the window, Eric saw them put the sheriff in the backseat of an SUV. He was yammering away to Kinkaid, who didn't appear to be listening very hard.

Jillian joined Eric at the window. "Daniel is going to fire us all when he finds out how this went down. You were *not* supposed to be the ones to confront the kidnapper."

BREE SAT IN the corridor at the East Texas Health Systems Medical Center, nursing a cup of coffee and trying to hear what was going on inside the treatment room.

She'd been banished. The E.R. doctor in charge here had said she was too close to the situation and that she was interfering. She supposed she didn't blame the guy; she would do the same thing if some strange doctor showed up in her E.R. shouting orders.

It still rankled.

"Bree?"

Bree's head snapped up. "Oh, Ted. What are you doing here?"

"I came when I heard. I mean, I just feel terrible. Bobby DeVille? The guy is a friend. How could I have not known? How could I have not seen it? Surely I must have missed something, some small piece of evidence…."

"He fooled a lot of people. I guess some criminals are pretty good at compartmentalizing. And as far as not being able to find evidence, what better person to cover up his own crime than a cop? He would know exactly how his crime-scene investigators processed a scene and make sure there would be nothing for them to find."

Ted pulled his baseball cap lower on his forehead. "Yeah. How is the little girl doing?"

"MacKenzie is holding her own. Her vital signs are strong, and her body temperature has returned almost to normal. Everyone seems to think there's a good chance she'll make a full recovery. But she hasn't regained consciousness."

"And how about you? How are you holding up?"

"Feeling a bit like a criminal rather than a hero," she admitted. "The Hollings County sheriff took statements from all of the Project Justice people and me. He's not particularly happy with the fact we went 'all vigilante' on him, but he's not a stupid man. He recognized right away that if they'd done things his way, MacKenzie probably would not be alive right now. I think that's the only thing that stopped him from arresting the whole bunch of us. He could have filed charges if he'd wanted to. Trespassing, assault—Eric bruised up DeVille's face pretty good."

"Eric's a brave man. I tell you, *I* wouldn't go toe to toe with that man."

"You might if it was your daughter's life at stake." Bree sighed. "Ted, what do we do if he ducks the kidnapping charge? He might press for those assault charges against Eric himself. Unfortunately, we don't have a slam-dunk case against him. DeVille has repeatedly insisted he *rescued* MacKenzie. He says he came out to his vacation house for a couple of days of R & R, he went for a hike and he stumbled across MacKenzie lying on the ground near the creek that ran through the woods.

"Since the crime scene isn't in his house but the one next door, his story is plausible. Not to me, but we don't have any proof."

"Surely the police will find evidence at the crime scene that points to Bobby," Ted said. "His prints must be all over that house."

"Maybe, unless he wore gloves. Of course, once MacKenzie wakes up, she'll be able to identify the man who grabbed her. But she's only six years old. Will she be a credible witness?"

"Hey, any kid old enough to talk can be a good witness. She'll be fine." Ted patted Bree on the arm.

Bree struggled not to make it obvious that she

didn't like him touching her. It was a perfectly innocent gesture, but she hadn't forgotten his botched attempt at seduction when they were in med school.

The door to MacKenzie's room opened and Eric stepped outside, grinning.

"Good news?" Bree asked.

"She woke up, and she's talking. She's still groggy, but I think she'll be fine. They're taking her to X-ray right now. She might have a broken ankle."

"I told them to check out that ankle an hour ago," Bree said, exasperated. She didn't think it was broken, just sprained, but an X-ray would tell them for sure.

"Is there anything I can do?" Ted asked.

Bree had almost forgotten he was there.

"Oh, hi, Dr. Gentry," Eric said. The two men shook hands.

"I was just asking if there's anything I can do. Do you all have a car? I could give you a ride so you're not stranded."

"You know, that's a good idea," Eric said. "I need to stay here with MacKenzie—I'm not letting her out of my sight. But, Bree, you could go to my house, wash up, grab something to eat, get MacKenzie and me some clean clothes and drive my car back here. When they release her, she'll like having her own clothes and riding home in her own car. She's had to contend with a lot of new and strange things today."

"I would be happy to do that, if Ted doesn't mind."

"Not at all. I told you I wanted to help."

"Then I'll see you in a couple of hours." The hospital was only about an hour outside of Houston.

They hesitated for half a second, then Eric leaned in and kissed her, then pulled her into a hug so he could whisper in her ear. "Thank you for everything, Bree. I'm not sure I could have gotten through this without you. I love you."

*Really? Here, and now?* But she grinned. "I love you, too." The conclusion was inescapable. "Once we get MacKenzie home, we'll talk."

# CHAPTER TWENTY

"C'MON, SWEETHEART, TAKE another bite of Jell-O."

MacKenzie obediently opened her mouth, and Eric shoveled another spoonful inside.

"Are you feeling better?" Eric was worried. The doctor had said it was highly unlikely MacKenzie would suffer any lasting physical effects from her ordeal. But psychologically, Eric wasn't so sure. "Does your ankle hurt?" he asked when she remained silent.

MacKenzie shrugged. "It's okay."

"Do you want to talk about what happened?" He didn't want to push her if she wasn't ready, but he sensed something was weighing on her. She'd had a brief psychiatric evaluation; the doctor had felt strongly that MacKenzie hadn't been sexually abused while in the hands of the kidnapper. Her physical examination—most of which had occurred while she was blessedly unconscious—had borne out that opinion. She had a few bruises and the sprained ankle—that was it.

MacKenzie looked up at him, her face filled with indecision.

"Honey, you know you can tell me anything. I

promise I won't get angry. You are an amazing girl and I'm so proud of how brave you've been."

Her lower lip trembled. "It's my fault."

"What? What's your fault?"

"You told me not to talk to strangers. You told me not to pet a stranger's dog."

"Oh, honey, it's okay. I give you a million rules to follow and I know sometimes you can't remember all of them." Jeez, the last thing he wanted was for his daughter to feel guilty for her part. "I have rules to follow, too, and sometimes I don't remember all of them. Like when we finally found you, I got so excited I hit the man who kidnapped you. Hitting people is wrong, but for a moment I forgot."

She pondered that for a moment. "Like I got excited when I saw the puppy."

"That's exactly right. Everybody makes mistakes, but you have to be able to forgive yourself. It's part of being human. We all try our best, and sometimes we goof up. That doesn't mean it was your fault. The sheriff is a very bad man. He is the one who did something wrong, not you. You were brave and so smart! I still don't know how you managed to call me."

Soon enough MacKenzie was going to have to tell what happened to the Hollings County sheriff if they wanted to make kidnapping charges stick.

"He left his phone sitting on the counter, and I took it," she said, as if it were no big deal. "But then I dropped it."

Maybe that explained the abrupt end to their conversation.

Someone tapped softly on the door, and a uniformed woman stepped inside carrying a folder. "Hi, mind if I come in?" she asked, all friendly and smiling. "I'm Deputy Meeks with Hollings County. I wonder if MacKenzie is feeling well enough to talk to me."

"How about it, MacKenzie?" Eric asked. "Do you want to tell the deputy what happened so we can keep the bad man in jail?

MacKenzie nodded.

The deputy pulled a chair up close to the bed. She was probably in her late thirties, plump and maternal looking. The Hollings County sheriff had probably sent her because she would be less threatening than a man would be, and she seemed comfortable with children.

"Sounds like you've had a very busy day," the deputy began. "Can you tell me what happened? Start with this morning."

"Daddy had a flat tire. I went outside to play."

"I think someone deliberately flattened my tire," Eric interjected, "maybe to disrupt our morning routine and distract me."

"Okay." The deputy took some discreet notes in a pad on her lap. "Then what, MacKenzie?"

"Then I was playing, and I saw a white puppy." She looked at Eric. "Daddy, what happened to the puppy? Is he okay? The bad man was real mean to him."

"The puppy is fine," Eric answered, though he had no idea what had happened to it after he had taken MacKenzie up to the house. Hopefully, it hadn't just been left in the woods to fend for itself.

"Can I keep him?" she asked hopefully.

"We'll see." He didn't want to promise her *that* particular puppy, in case he couldn't locate it or it belonged to someone else. "You answer all of Deputy Meeks's questions, and we'll talk about getting you a pet. For real."

She grinned, and a light came back into her eyes that had been missing. Suddenly she became the most cooperative little witness ever. She told her story from beginning to end in a very coherent fashion—much better than most adults would have done. Eric bit his tongue to keep himself from interrupting. This was the first time he'd heard the story, and every revelation astounded him anew. She'd been tied up with bungee cords and duct tape, and she'd somehow managed to get loose. Though she must have been terrified, she managed to rescue the puppy, too, and escape with it, running through the woods.

And when she was about to be recaptured, she had climbed a tree. Then, when the man was about to pull her out of the tree, a branch had broken and they'd both fallen. That was how MacKenzie had sustained the sprained ankle. It was a miracle she hadn't been killed.

"When the man fell, was he hurt?" Meeks asked.

MacKenzie nodded. "He was just lying on the ground like he was asleep, and he had blood coming from his head."

Meeks and Eric exchanged a look. Eric didn't recall seeing any such injuries on Sheriff DeVille. But a cut could have been hidden under his hair, and he might have washed off the blood in the creek.

"So then what?" Meeks asked.

"I tried to run again but my foot hurt a lot. And there was a little river and I was real thirsty and I thought I would drink some water, but I slipped and fell in the water."

"I bet that was cold."

"It was real cold," MacKenzie agreed.

"Then what happened?"

MacKenzie screwed up her face and thought hard. "I don't know."

"You don't remember?"

"I think that's when I fell asleep."

"What's the next thing you remember?" Meeks prompted.

She shrugged. "I don't know."

"Okay. I just have one more question to ask, and then I'll let you get some rest. I'm going to show you pictures of six different men. I want you to look very carefully and tell me if any of them is the bad man.

"Now, it's okay if the bad man isn't in these photos. You don't have to pick any of them."

"Is this really necessary?" Eric asked. He was

afraid the sight of DeVille's face would upset Mac-Kenzie.

"Unfortunately, it is, and I'll tell you why in a minute." Meeks opened the folder and pulled out a color photocopy of six mug shots. All were of Caucasian men with brown hair who appeared in their early forties. The picture in the upper right corner, Number 3, was Bobby DeVille.

MacKenzie studied the six pictures seriously. She didn't pick out the sheriff right away, which made Eric nervous. Finally she pointed to Number 3, and Eric relaxed. But her next words brought him up short.

"I remember this man. He was at that place, remember, Daddy, when we drove a long way and I ate tomato soup? He talked to Dr. Bree."

"Yes, that's right," Eric said. He'd had no idea his six-year-old had such a phenomenal memory.

"And is he the man who put you in his car this morning?"

MacKenzie looked confused. "No," she said flatly. "He's not the bad man."

"MacKenzie, are you sure?" Meeks asked gently. Meanwhile Eric was about to come out of his skin.

MacKenzie nodded.

"Okay." The deputy took away the photo lineup and returned it to the folder. "Mr. Riggs, can I talk to you outside?"

Eric already knew most of what she was going to say, but it still felt like a bucket of ice water to the face. "We have a problem. Sheriff DeVille has a pretty damn good alibi. He bought gas just outside Tuckerville about fifteen minutes before the time you estimate MacKenzie was taken. He has a credit card receipt to back up his story, and the gas station attendant remembers him specifically."

"So unless he can be two places at once…"

"He couldn't have done it."

"Then he has an accomplice," Eric said immediately. "There's that car parked at the house next door to DeVille's—who does it belong to?"

"Stolen, I'm afraid. But as of now, we don't have enough to hold Sheriff DeVille. Plus, he doesn't have any injuries indicating he fell out of a tree. Nothing beyond what you gave him, anyway."

"This is a nightmare. He's still out there. And Bree—she's out there without any protection."

"Why don't you call her? Let her know she needs to be careful."

Eric was about to do just that when his phone rang—the silver one. He answered impatiently. "Riggs."

"Eric." It was Kinkaid. "I just wanted to check in—"

"We got the wrong man," Eric blurted out. "He has an alibi. Airtight. And MacKenzie says he's not the one. She knew exactly who he was, and she was positive he wasn't the man who kidnapped her."

"Ah, hell. You mean he was telling the truth about hiking through the woods and finding her?"

"I don't know. He might still be responsible. He might have an accomplice. But we're looking for a man with a cut on his head. He fell out of a tree."

"What?"

"Long story. I don't have time—I have to warn Bree."

"Okay. There's one more piece of information you should have. I wasn't even going to mention it, because I thought it was irrelevant. But Beth has been doing some more sophisticated analysis of the DNA from the Hollings County case. Turns out the perp in that case has the genetic marker for Huntington's disease."

"What does that mean, exactly?"

"If the perp is over thirty, there's a good chance he's starting to show symptoms."

"What are the symptoms?" Eric asked.

"Huntington's is a pretty nasty disease," Kinkaid said. "According to Beth, it attacks the central nervous system. Early symptoms might include a problem with balance, slurred speech and an overall lack of coordination."

Eric's mind whirred. "Holy shit. It's Dr. Gentry— the coroner. Bree thought he might have a drinking problem. I've seen him stumble a couple of times, and he definitely seemed a little bit off to me. Joe, she's with him right now. He offered to take her and pick up my car, but God knows where he's actually taken her. We have to get to her—now!"

"I'm on it. How long have they been on the road?"

Eric checked his phone for the time. "Fifteen minutes or so."

"Get Bree on the phone. Give her some kind of warning in case he hasn't shown his hand yet."

They ended the call, and Eric immediately speed-dialed Bree's cell. *Please, please, dear God, let her answer.*

"What's going on?" Deputy Meeks asked.

Eric quickly explained the situation to the deputy. She didn't question how he got his information, taking it at face value. "I'll get some people working on my end."

He got Bree's voice mail. Crap. "Bree, I don't have time to explain, but you're in danger. The sheriff wasn't the kidnapper—Gentry is. I suspect he's behind everything else that's happened, and he's going to go after you. Please call me as soon as you get this. I'm coming."

He returned to MacKenzie's room long enough to let her know he had to leave for a short while. He hated to leave her alone at a time like this, but he had to go after Bree. The more people hunting down the killer, the better.

But when he entered MacKenzie's room, she was asleep. After explaining to the nurse at the desk what was going on and securing her solemn promise that no unauthorized personnel would enter MacKenzie's room while he was gone, he went with Deputy Meeks. He would do whatever he could to bring Bree home alive and well.

BREE DIDN'T QUITE get to her phone in time, and the call went to voice mail. She checked the caller ID. "Oh, that was Eric. I need to call and find out what he wanted. Excuse me. I hope nothing's wrong with MacKenzie."

She looked up and realized they'd left the interstate. "Wait, where are we going?"

"Shortcut," Ted said easily. "I hate taking the freeways through downtown, don't you?"

At this time of the evening, she didn't think traffic would be much of an issue, but she didn't argue. The man was nice enough to give her a ride, so she wouldn't complain about what route he took. She couldn't imagine that this two-lane blacktop would be any faster than the freeway, but, oh, well.

She started to call Eric back when Ted abruptly knocked the phone out of her hand. It fell into the darkness near her feet.

"What the hell?"

"Sorry, Bree, I can't let you call Eric back."

"Why not?" Her heart hammered inside her chest so hard she thought it would beat its way out. Something was very, very wrong.

"I can't believe you didn't figure it out." He pulled off the blacktop onto an even smaller road, full of bumps and potholes. The car lurched along the suspension-challenging path.

"Stop the car. Let me out."

Ted chuckled. "Soon enough."

"Why are you doing this? What's going on? What is it I didn't figure out?"

"You've got the wrong man behind bars."

"Kelly?" she said, confused. "This isn't news to me."

"Yeah, Kelly's innocent, but that's not who I was talking about. I meant the sheriff. He really did have the bad luck to go hiking in the woods and stumble across MacKenzie. He got to her just minutes before I would have." He yanked off his baseball cap. "I got a nasty bump on my head falling out of that tree. Not sure how long I was unconscious." He laughed softly, shaking his head. Bree thought she had never heard a more evil sound. "Still can't believe a six-year-old got the best of me. Although she's not my usual type, I think I would have enjoyed doing away with her. She would have fought me. But no matter how clever she is, she's not stronger than me."

Ted was insane! Bree wasn't going to stay in this car one minute longer. She had no interest in finding out what his plans were for her. A car accident was more preferable. She reached over and grabbed the steering wheel, yanking it hard to the right.

"Hey!" Ted screamed as the car careened off the road and landed with a thud in a ditch. It landed at a forty-five-degree angle, nose-down.

Bree unfastened her seat belt and scrambled to get out of the car, but her door was blocked by something and would open only a few inches.

"You bitch! What the hell have you done?" Ted unfastened his own seat belt and made a grab for her.

She hit him with her purse, which was not such a small weapon. It packed a pretty good wallop.

He was stunned for about half a second and she hit him again, but he grabbed the purse and wrestled it out of her grip, shoving it behind him.

"It might be over for me. It's only a matter of time before they figure it all out. But you... I'm going to end it like it should have been ended a long time ago, the very first time I got wind of the fact that you didn't believe Kelly Ralston was guilty of rape."

He grabbed her by the arm, opened his door and started yanking, nearly dislocating her shoulder.

She fought like a wildcat, screaming and scratching. But the angle of the car was in his favor; he had gravity on his side. Eventually he separated her from the car, then nearly broke her arm as he bent it behind her while placing his other arm across her chest in a travesty of an embrace.

"I'm not going anywhere with you!"

His reply was to slam her up against the car hard enough that her head bounced against the metal roof, making her see stars. Twice more he repeated the action, and she didn't see or feel anything.

When next she became aware, she was upside-down, and it was dark.

It took her a few moments to realize she was being carried in a fireman's hold through the woods. She didn't cry out or let Ted know she was awake, hoping she could take him by surprise when he got to wherever he was taking her.

She could tell he was getting tired. With each step he grunted and groaned, and he breathed hard, his gait uneven, and twice he stumbled on the rough path he'd chosen to take through the woods. The longer he carried her, the weaker he would be, so she kept her body as limp as possible and let him keep going.

She'd better figure a way out of this, fast, or her hours, her minutes, were numbered.

Finally it seemed Ted couldn't go any farther; his breathing was so labored he sounded as if he might pass out any second. Abruptly he pushed her off his shoulder and she dropped onto the ground like a sack of wet sand.

She could outrun him! She lay in an inert pile, peering at him through barely open eyes, waiting for just the right moment. He held a flashlight, but it wasn't aimed at her. This might be her only chance. She leaped to her feet and started running, crashing through the woods in the general direction from which they'd come.

But, Jesus, it was pitch-black out here. She thwacked into tree trunks and branches, and her feet became hopelessly entangled in underbrush with each step. She'd made hardly any progress at all before he snagged her arm.

"Nice try, princess. But you can't get away from me. You're gonna die, and it *will* be painful."

"You'll never get away with it," she said as he dragged her along until he had her back where he wanted her. It appeared to be a small clearing; she could make out the remains of a campfire and some rudimentary seating made of logs and boards. "Eric knows I left with you. When I go missing—"

"Yeah, I know." He sounded only mildly regretful. "It was all winding down anyway. I've got Huntington's. I bet you didn't know that."

"Oh, God, Ted. I'm so sorry." In that moment she meant it. He might be a monster, but not even monsters deserved to die of that horrible, debilitating disease. She was so thrown off balance by his revelation that she didn't even fight as he wrapped something around her wrists.

"I'll plead guilty. They'll give me the death penalty. Providing I can make it through all those mandatory appeals in a couple of years, the execution will be more of a mercy killing."

"You killed all those women?" she asked, just to be sure. "And Philomene. You were the one who raped her."

"That's right."

She hoped this fact came to light, so Kelly could at last be freed. Then Bree's and Philomene's deaths would mean something. Although she wasn't committed to the whole dying idea. Eric and his Project Justice buddies would come looking for her. They could find Ted's car in the ditch—her cell phone ping would get them that far. Then they would have to follow the trail they'd taken on foot.

But how long would all that take?

"Why do you have to kill me?" she asked. "We were friends once."

"Friends? Is that what you call it? You know I wanted more." He wrenched her arms over her head and secured them to a branch.

She tried to kick him, but he was prepared for the move and easily sidestepped her puny efforts.

"We'll have none of that now."

"So, what, you asked me out and I said no. We were in med school. Nobody had time for a social life."

"Ah, that's not quite true. What was that guy's name? Barry somebody…"

How did Ted know about Barry? She thought they'd been discreet. "What about him?"

"Everybody knew you slept with him."

The bastard must have bragged about his conquest. "An ill-considered one-night stand. So what?"

"I'm not stupid, Bree. You rejected me because you found me repulsive. All the girls did. 'Undead Ted,' that's what they called me."

He was still hung up on grammar-school taunts?

"Even if that were true, which it isn't, lots of people get rejected. They don't become serial killers."

"Yeah, well, it takes a certain set of circumstances to produce a serial killer. I've researched the subject exhaustively. Do you want to hear what my mommy did to me?"

No, she did not. But the longer he kept talking, the longer she lived. "If you want to tell me, I'll listen," she said as sympathetically as possible.

"Oh, it's all very cliché. Locked in dark closets, forced to eat…well, things you won't see on the menu at any restaurant. She did worse than that, too. I have the scars to prove it. Do you know what it's like to be impotent by age fifteen? No, of course you don't."

"Impotent?"

"If you're wondering how a rapist can be impotent— let's just say there are lots of ways to violate a woman that don't involve having a stiffie."

Her stomach roiled as she recalled what Philomene had told her about the rape.

"She got worse around the holidays," Ted said. "I think she got depressed. But instead of taking antidepressants or swallowing a handful of uppers just to *feel* something, she found a different way to stimulate herself."

"That's why all the murders occurred around the holidays."

"Yup. Something about the smell of roast turkey flipped a switch in my brain. Exams and all the holiday stress—killing became my own personal Xanax. I paced myself—only one per year. I would spend weeks picking out just the right girl and planning how I would do it so I wouldn't leave any incriminating evidence behind."

"And if you did, being the person who examined the bodies was an extra insurance policy. No wonder there was so little evidence…." Except for that first murder. "Wait. In Hollings County. There was DNA, and it wasn't yours."

"Yeah, actually, it was. The DNA in the database with my name on it isn't mine. That was easy to finagle. I was asked to provide a sample, so I swabbed the nearest cadaver's cheek. A little sleight of hand, and bingo.

"But that was the one detail that might come back to haunt me."

"Because of the Huntington's."

"Exactly. You just kept pushing and pushing, zeroing in on that case the way no one else did. Once you got Project Justice involved…" He sighed. "They have practically unlimited resources."

"So you thought if you got rid of me, the pressure would be off and Eric would lose interest in the case? That's not really how it works. Once my life was threatened, every resource Project Justice has went toward finding the threat and eliminating it. And taking MacKenzie—how did you think that was going to work?"

"The plan was to pick you both off once you showed up, bury you all in the woods, dispose of your car. It could have worked."

"I still can't believe you would harm an innocent child." The slightest thread of sympathy she might have felt for him evaporated on the spot.

"Innocent, my ass. That child is in league with the devil. She nearly killed me. Got herself untied, stole my phone, climbed a tree, then kicked me in the head and made me fall." He wiped his face. "The cut on my head is bleeding again, thanks to you. And I've got the mother of all headaches."

Despite her bleak situation, Bree found herself

smiling. Good for MacKenzie. Bree had told her that if she was ever afraid, she should take action to make herself feel better, and damned if she hadn't taken that advice to heart.

"What about those tire tracks near Philomene's car?" Bree asked.

"Easy. We were all at Bobby's lake house that night—him and me and Sam Needles. When the other two were asleep, I took the Range Rover and drove back to Tuckerville. Philomene was so easy to manipulate. A call from a pay phone pretending to be one of her boyfriends, a rendezvous, a knife across her throat. Really wished I could have taken more time with her, but carrying her across that field to the cattle tank, tying her into that tarp—it all took time. I barely got back to the lake house before the others woke up and wanted to start back."

"Pretty clever, driving the sheriff's car. No one would take accusations against him seriously."

"It was almost the perfect crime. But, hey, I didn't have as long to prepare."

"What about the bomb? Was that your work?"

He shrugged modestly. "My parents owned a construction company. I worked summers there— learned a lot about explosives. The timing device and the trigger—that information is easily available on the internet."

Comforting thought. "The beige Acura—was that you?"

"Of course. The car belonged to my aunt, who

died recently. Added a stolen license plate, and I was in business."

She struggled for another line of questioning. He seemed to enjoy talking about himself. The longer he talked, the better chance she had of surviving.

"If I had agreed to go out with you," she finally asked, "would I have been one of your victims?"

"No, it didn't work like that. I always selected women who had no connection to me. In fact, I told myself that if things between you and me worked out, I wouldn't need to kill anyone. But they didn't." He shrugged. "So Mary Ann Pratt had to die."

Bree's stomach heaved. That name wasn't even familiar, yet Bree was partially responsible for her death.

"Oh, yeah, there were others you haven't found. Three in and around Waco, one for each year I was in med school there. One in Austin, where I did my premed. You'll be my tenth, in fact. It's a nice round number, don't you think?"

"I always wanted to be a ten."

"Once I go to work on you, you won't be making jokes. You'll be my most ambitious project yet. A true masterpiece."

She saw the knife in his hand then.

# *CHAPTER TWENTY-ONE*

BREE CALCULATED THE minutes since Eric's phone call. An hour, maybe? How close could they have gotten in that time? Had they found the car yet?

She was lucky Ted hadn't gagged her. Her voice would carry through these still woods. But she wouldn't scream yet. The second she did he would shut her up, so she would wait until she had the best chance of someone hearing her.

Ted brandished his knife, tossing it from hand to hand. It looked sharp. Despite the cold wind, Bree broke out in a sweat. "Now, then, where shall I start? Oh, wait, can't have you waking the neighbors, now, can we?" He put down the knife and pulled a bandanna from his pocket. "Duct tape would be better, but sadly, I didn't bring any with me."

This was her last chance. Bree took a deep breath, opened her mouth and screamed for all she was worth.

Ted hit her in the face, then quickly knotted the gag over her mouth. The bandanna tasted like stale sweat. "No more of that. Every time you try to call for help, you get a new cut. Now, if you cry out in pain—that's a different story. How will I tell the difference? Hmm, not sure I can. Oh, well.

"Now, then, I think I'll start with that beautiful neck. I'll just nick the carotid artery—enough that you'll bleed to death but not quickly. You'll slowly weaken, and I'll watch as you struggle to breathe. I'll hear the death rattle and see the light go out of your eyes. It's a beautiful moment to watch. Death is so much more interesting than life. It's why I chose pathology. Figuring out what caused the spark of life to leave a body, turning a vibrant human being into a lump of meat—it never ceases to fascinate me."

Bree watched in horror as the knife came closer to her neck, the shiny blade reflecting the firelight. He made his cut; she was surprised by how little it hurt. The blade was sharp, so one precise swipe did exactly what he said it would. She could feel warm blood trickling down her neck.

Not spurting, at least. At this rate it could take her hours to die.

He would probably finish her off, though, if he saw that capture was imminent. If he heard anyone coming through the woods or calling for her. There didn't seem to be any way out of this.

Poor Eric. He'd finally found the courage to risk loving again, and this was what happened. And MacKenzie. She defied all kinds of odds to escape a devious killer, only to have that killer take away someone else from her life.

*I love you both so much.* And they would never know how much.

"Where next? The face? Seems a shame to mar that beautiful creamy skin, but, oh, well." He took one menacing step forward, and Bree saw an opening. She used the only weapon she had—her head—and butted him. Their skulls cracked together as if they were bighorn sheep, and Bree saw stars again.

Ted roared with anger and raised the knife. Bree held her breath, waiting for the death blow.

But it never came. Ted went still, then wobbled slightly as he squeezed his eyes shut, then opened them again. "This damn headache," he muttered. "What did you do to me? How can I enjoy this when my head is pounding.… Oh. Venal bleed in the cerebellum." With that he collapsed.

Could it be? Had his head injury stopped him when nothing else could? He might be the only medical examiner in history to declare his own cause of death.

But it might be too late for her. She was slowly bleeding to death. There was nothing she could do except stand here and wait and hope someone at Project Justice could track through the woods at night.

"I'M GOING AFTER HER." Eric had heard what sounded like a scream five minutes ago. It might have been an owl, but his gut told him it was Bree. They'd been waiting by Ted's wrecked car for Ian and Violet the

Labrador to arrive, but Eric had stood around help-less for as long as he could.

"Can you track someone through the woods at night?" Kinkaid asked. "Can you even tell if they left the road, or where?"

Eric hated to admit it, but he couldn't. He didn't care. He had a flashlight, a phone and a general di-rection. "Call me if you find her before I do."

"You shouldn't go alone—"

"Save it." He took off down the road, contem-plating where he would climb over the chain-link fence that sectioned off this part of the forest as pri-vate property. But after a couple of minutes, he saw that he wouldn't have to do any climbing; there was a break where someone had used snips to trespass. The cuts looked old, but it was as good a starting point as any.

After squeezing through the gap, he called Kinkaid and let him know about the makeshift gate.

He found himself on a trail. Not much of one, maybe just a deer trail. When he was a kid, he and Travis used to go out into the woods and pretend they were Native Americans tracking deer. Not to hunt them, just to find them. He shined his flashlight onto the trail and a thrill went through him.

The leaves had been recently disturbed. He was on the right track.

He debated about whether to call out to Bree. But to do so would remove the element of surprise. He didn't want to risk Gentry panicking and killing Bree any faster than he planned to.

The coroner did plan to kill her, no doubt about that. He'd wanted her dead all along—wanted both of them dead. This kidnapping was the desperate act of a killer who felt the noose tightening around his neck—one final, defiant act, striking out at the person who had brought about his defeat.

The trail was tough going. In a land as flat as South Texas, hills were rare, but there certainly was one here if the burn in his thighs was any indication.

After about fifteen minutes of hiking, Eric stopped to catch his breath and smelled something in the air. Smoke. Just a hint, but undeniable. Either the woods were on fire, or he was nearing a campsite. He was counting on the latter.

A few minutes later, and the trail branched into a Y. Figuring the smoke had to be carried by the breeze, Eric chose the path that ran against the wind and kept going.

Would Gentry have brought his victim this far into the woods? Whether he dragged an uncooperative conscious hostage or carried an unconscious one, this would have been tough going. Was Eric on a fool's errand? What if they hadn't come this way at all? What if Gentry had called an accomplice, who had picked them up and driven them to some other location?

The possibilities were so endless and so terrifying that Eric pushed them out of his mind and moved on. He'd chosen this course of action, right or wrong. Kinkaid, Ian and Violet had another course. And if neither of them found Bree—

No. He wouldn't even consider the possibility.

BREE TESTED THE ropes around her wrists, but the bindings were too tight for her to slide out of them, and she couldn't reach the knots. She put her whole weight on the branch she was tied to, but it hardly gave at all and it certainly wasn't going to break.

But one thing she could do was slide the ropes along the branch. It wasn't easy. The rough bark abraded her wrists until she felt blood running down her arms. More bleeding meant she would die just that much faster. But she kept at it, shoving the ropes as far as she could toward the end of the branch until smaller branches feeding off the one she was tied to made further progress impossible.

Now, however, she could bend the branch.

She put all of her weight on it. The fire had burned down, so it didn't give off much light, but she could hear the wood cracking.

Unfortunately, green wood doesn't snap in two. The branch was severely bent at its midpoint, the end part touching the ground, but she was still trapped.

She tried twisting the end part, a maneuver that required her to swivel her whole body. The effort made her head swim, and she found herself breathing hard. By exerting herself, she made her heart beat faster, pumping blood out of her carotid artery that much more quickly.

But if she could free herself…she had to try.

It took five complete circles to twist the branch free of itself, but finally it came loose.

She slid her hands free, then slumped to the ground to rest. She removed the gag, wadded it up and pressed it to her neck. Maybe that would slow down the bleeding a little. Then she gathered her strength once again and screamed.

She screamed until her throat was raw and her energy spent.

What were her chances if she took off down that trail? How far had they come? Surely it was less than a mile. She couldn't get her wrist bindings loose, but she was able to untie her ankles. She forced herself to her feet, then staggered and dropped to one knee.

Her shirt was soaked with blood. The bandanna was soaked, too. She had done all she could do. She lay down in the carpet of leaves to await her fate.

"SHE'S HERE, JOE," Eric said into his phone. Amazing that they had cell service out here in the boonies. "I heard her screaming. It was no owl. And I'm getting closer."

"We're right behind you. Violet's got the scent."

"There's a fork in the trail—"

"We just passed it. We went right."

The smell of smoke was stronger now, and when Eric switched off his flashlight, he could see a dim glow in the distance. He tried not to think about what it meant that Bree's screams had stopped a couple of minutes earlier.

A little farther, and he could see a clearing up ahead and the embers of a campfire. He should have approached more stealthily; it would be stupid to come all this way only to blunder into Gentry and have the guy pull a gun and shoot him dead. But he was so close now.

He still had Kinkaid's gun in his pocket. He pulled it out, took off the safety, burst into the clearing— and almost fainted.

Two bodies. One covered in blood.

"Bree—" He was beside her in an instant. She wasn't dead. But her pulse was fast and weak. There was so much blood he couldn't even tell where it was coming from. He pulled his phone from his pocket again.

"I found her. She's alive—barely. Gentry is here, too. I think he's dead." Judging from the open eyes and the vacant stare, he was pretty sure.

"Life Flight is already on the way."

"Stay with me, Bree. Please don't leave me." He didn't know what he would do if she died.

"According to the GPS, there's a shorter, easier way out," Kinkaid said. "The chopper will land in a farmer's field less than a quarter mile due north."

Eric could hear his friends now. Violet bayed mournfully. They burst into the clearing. The dog galumphed to Bree and sniffed her furiously, then gave a little yip.

"Good girl," Ian cooed, offering his talented dog a treat.

The three men picked up Bree, forming a human stretcher, and set off.

ERIC YANKED THE for-sale sign out of the ground with MacKenzie's help while Bree took their picture. They'd closed on the house this morning, and it was officially theirs.

His old house, the one he'd shared with Tammy, had finally sold, so buying this one had been easy. It was nothing like his old house, but the plain little frame cottage with its big front porch and a yard full of pecan trees suited him.

Suited them.

They were a family now. He and Bree had tied the knot last week in a simple ceremony in Travis's backyard. The azaleas were just now coming into bloom, the most beautiful time of year in South Texas. They were going to plant a garden in the backyard, and Bree was going to learn how to can vegetables as her grandmother used to do.

His last day at Project Justice had been two weeks ago. The job was never intended to be permanent, and he was only too happy to give it up once the lawyer he'd been subbing for came back from maternity leave. Criminal law, life-and-death issues—it was more stress than he wanted to deal with.

Neither did he want to return to the high-pressure world of real-estate law. A little storefront office would suit his new small-town lifestyle just fine. He would help people with their divorces and landlord disputes and car accidents. He'd probably do his share of criminal defense, too, but not anything big.

Long workdays were a thing of the past. He would be home every evening to see his beautiful wife and daughter. They would drive down to the Galveston beach for weekends and go to potluck suppers at the church.

Bree would return to work soon, but she'd committed herself to day shifts only so she could be home with the family, too. Though she'd come perilously close to dying that night in the woods, once they'd gotten her to medical help, she'd held her own, then made a swift recovery. She would probably always have a small scar on her neck. It would be a reminder to them of how precious life is and to cherish every minute of it.

Kelly Ralston had been released from prison. He had thanked everyone involved in proving his innocence, but had declined any further help from Bree. In fact, he'd left the area, intending to start fresh somewhere where no one had ever heard of him.

Bree carried in a sack of groceries from the car. Most of their belongings had been delivered that morning, but they didn't have much. Most everything Bree had owned had been demolished in the explosion, so they were starting from scratch.

Eric liked that idea. Everything they owned, they would pick out together. No baggage.

"So what should our first meal in our new house be?" Bree asked.

"Something easy. Like chili dogs."

"Chili dogs!" MacKenzie agreed.

He hardly recognized her these days. Contrary to what he'd feared might happen, MacKenzie's ordeal hadn't scarred her or caused her to go deeper into herself. It had jolted her back to life. Taking her fate into her own hands and escaping from the kidnapper had empowered her in a way nothing else could have. She was more like the little girl he'd known before Tammy's death—happy, outgoing and a real chatterbox.

"Chili dogs it is."

"Before you do that," Eric said, "there's something in the backyard I need your help with, MacKenzie, you, too."

Jillian had made a special delivery a few minutes ago, sneaking around the side of the house so Mac-Kenzie wouldn't see. As soon as they opened the back door and stepped out onto the patio, a white streak sped toward them, yapping madly.

"It's Snowflake!" MacKenzie screamed in delight, dropping to her knees. The puppy went right to her, licking her face in a tongue frenzy. MacKenzie laughed, and Bree got it all on video with her phone.

Jillian had rescued the puppy at the sheriff's house when they found MacKenzie. She'd hauled it around in her car the rest of the day. Later she'd claimed she'd done it because the dog was "evidence." But really she'd just been worried about it.

All attempts to find out who owned it had failed, so Eric had volunteered to adopt it. MacKenzie had been asking about the puppy, wondering what had become of it and if it had a home. Now she wouldn't have to worry.

"You gonna feed him and brush him and bathe him?" Eric asked. "Teach him how to walk on a leash?"

MacKenzie wasn't listening. She was too busy rolling in the grass with her new companion.

Bree slipped her hand in his. "You realize we're going to be the ones doing all that, right?"

"I know. I don't care. It's worth it just for this moment."

He caught a glimpse of Bree's scar, now just a thin red line, and remembered to relish this moment—the sights, the sounds, the smells, the feel of his wife standing next to him. He thought about all the wonderful moments to come, and he sighed as his muscles relaxed.

Just when he thought life couldn't get any better, it did.

\* \* \* \* \*

# LARGER-PRINT BOOKS!

HARLEQUIN *Presents*

PASSION GUARANTEED SEDUCTION

## GET 2 FREE LARGER-PRINT NOVELS PLUS 2 FREE GIFTS!

**YES!** Please send me 2 FREE LARGER-PRINT Harlequin Presents® novels and my 2 FREE gifts (gifts are worth about $10). After receiving them, if I don't wish to receive any more books, I can return the shipping statement marked "cancel." If I don't cancel, I will receive 6 brand-new novels every month and be billed just $5.05 per book in the U.S. or $5.49 per book in Canada. That's a saving of at least 16% off the cover price! It's quite a bargain! Shipping and handling is just 50¢ per book in the U.S. and 75¢ per book in Canada.* I understand that accepting the 2 free books and gifts places me under no obligation to buy anything. I can always return a shipment and cancel at any time. Even if I never buy another book, the two free books and gifts are mine to keep forever.

176/376 HDN F43N

| Name | (PLEASE PRINT) | |
| --- | --- | --- |
| Address | | Apt. # |
| City | State/Prov. | Zip/Postal Code |

Signature (If under 18, a parent or guardian must sign)

### Mail to the Harlequin® Reader Service:
**IN U.S.A.:** P.O. Box 1867, Buffalo, NY 14240-1867
**IN CANADA:** P.O. Box 609, Fort Erie, Ontario L2A 5X3

**Are you a subscriber to Harlequin Presents books and want to receive the larger-print edition?**
**Call 1-800-873-8635 today or visit us at www.ReaderService.com.**

\* Terms and prices subject to change without notice. Prices do not include applicable taxes. Sales tax applicable in N.Y. Canadian residents will be charged applicable taxes. Offer not valid in Quebec. This offer is limited to one order per household. Not valid for current subscribers to Harlequin Presents Larger-Print books. All orders subject to credit approval. Credit or debit balances in a customer's account(s) may be offset by any other outstanding balance owed by or to the customer. Please allow 4 to 6 weeks for delivery. Offer available while quantities last.

**Your Privacy**—The Harlequin® Reader Service is committed to protecting your privacy. Our Privacy Policy is available online at www.ReaderService.com or upon request from the Harlequin Reader Service.

We make a portion of our mailing list available to reputable third parties that offer products we believe may interest you. If you prefer that we not exchange your name with third parties, or if you wish to clarify or modify your communication preferences, please visit us at www.ReaderService.com/consumerschoice or write to us at Harlequin Reader Service Preference Service, P.O. Box 9062, Buffalo, NY 14269. Include your complete name and address.

HPLP13R

# *ReaderService*.com

## Manage your account online!

- Review your order history
- Manage your payments
- Update your address

---

**We've designed
the Harlequin® Reader Service
website just for you.**

---

## Enjoy all the features!

- Reader excerpts from any series
- Respond to mailings and
  special monthly offers
- Discover new series available to you
- Browse the Bonus Bucks catalog
- Share your feedback

*Visit us at:*
## ReaderService.com

RS13